MY, WHAT SOFT KISSES YOU HAVE

"I need to get back, now. Grandma will be worried."

"Go ahead." Wolf turned his back on her and wandered upstream, his steps slow and long.

Molly turned toward the forest, glimpsed into the darkness. She would never be able to find her way back to the footpath without Wolf's guidance.

"Won't you walk me back?"

"I don't think so." He didn't even turn to look at her as he denied her request.

"But you said...you said you wouldn't let me get lost."

Wolf spun around, and at last there was a grin on his face. A wide smile that did nothing to make Molly feel better. "It doesn't matter what I said. I break all the rules, remember?"

"I can't find my way back, not alone."

"I'll take you back, for a price."

Molly didn't back away, didn't even flinch. "What price do you ask?"

"A kiss," Wolf said, already leaning toward her.

LINDA JONES

Big Bad Wolf

LOVE SPELL ◆ NEW YORK CITY

LOVE SPELL®

February 1997

Published by

Dorchester Publishing Co., Inc.
276 Fifth Avenue
New York, NY 10001

The name "Love Spell" and its logo are trademarks of Dorchester
Publishing Co., Inc.

Printed in the United States of America.

This is for David, my number one son and a true lamb in wolf's clothing.

Chapter One

Kingsport, Maine, 1893

"Stay on the road."

Molly nodded obediently as she took the basket from her mother.

"Goodness only knows what waits in those woods. You could get lost very easily."

Molly smiled. Her mother worked so hard and worried so much. The shortcut Molly usually took to Grandma's house saved time, and there was really no reason to worry her mother unnecessarily.

Believing that Molly was an obedient daughter, Mary Kincaid smiled as she straightened the hood of Molly's red velvet cape. "I'm sorry to ask you to do this day after day, but your grandmother is stubborn. If only she would stay with us until she's completely well . . ."

"I don't mind," Molly said. Then she kissed her mother on the cheek. "The walk is good for me, and the weather's been quite pleasant, lately."

She couldn't tell her mother that she loved walking alone through the woods, watching the changes from spring to summer. It was the one part of the day she wasn't rushing from one place to another delivering the bread her mother baked, or hurrying to finish the mending they took in, or washing someone else's clothes.

They'd managed fine since her father's death three years earlier. The Kincaid women worked hard.

The shortcut through the woods was Molly's gift to herself: A peaceful interlude in a hectic day, a bit of beauty to enjoy.

She followed the road until it turned and she could no longer be seen from the house, and a short distance down the way passed the narrow and rarely used road that led south to Vanora Point. Then she ducked into the sheltering shade of the trees, venturing away from the road and going deeper into the woods.

There was a path of sorts, a narrow meandering trail that would take Molly to her grandmother's house. The light that fell here shot through the white pines in widely spaced bands that touched the forest floor, fingers of light tinged with blue as they reached for the ground.

Molly slowed her pace as she stepped deeper into the forest. She hated to lie to her mother, but it seemed such an innocent lie. The time saved was spent with her grandmother, a woman who was as stubborn and willful and loving as her only son, Molly's father, had been.

The red velvet cape Molly wore had been a gift from Grandma Kincaid. It was the only extravagance evident in her wardrobe. Her clothing was serviceable, plain, and sturdy, and consisted entirely of neutral shades of brown and gray and the occasional white blouse. Her mother insisted that with the bright red Kincaid hair curling down her back, Molly needed no more color. Grandma disagreed, and so she'd spent a portion of her savings on the red velvet. Molly so loved the bright cape that she wore it year round.

Molly's mother and her grandmother disagreed often. That was the reason the elder Mrs. Kincaid refused to move to town, Molly suspected. Not because she so loved the house she'd shared with her late husband, Molly's grandfather, who had been gone for more than ten years, not because she wanted to express her independence. She just didn't want to live with her daughter-in-law. Perhaps she even wanted to hurt Mary Kincaid a little, or to make her life more difficult than it already was.

Molly kept her eyes on the path before her as she entered a heavily wooded and dark region of the forest. This was like another world, far apart from her everyday life in Kingsport. Molly had always been convinced that there was magic in the forest of some sort. Some days she was certain it was good magic, other days she felt an ominous chill. However, she was not afraid of unknown magic or of getting lost—not as long as she stayed on her narrow footpath.

"What's in the basket?"

Molly spun around at the intrusion of the distinct, low voice.

"Who's there?" She was surrounded by tall, thick trees, and she could see nothing else. Her heart beat fast as she searched for a man to go with the voice. "Who's there?" she repeated.

She heard the interloper a moment before she saw him. His footsteps were loud in the silent forest as he came near and stepped between two tall white pines. He was dressed in simple hunting gear—a checked shirt and heavy trousers, a thick waistcoat and stout boots—and there was a rifle cradled easily in his arms. He was dark haired and tall, but what struck Molly most strongly was the wicked grin on his face.

"What's in the basket?" As he spoke he stopped and leaned against one of the sturdy pines.

Molly looked down at the basket she clasped with both hands. Running wasn't an option she considered for long. The man she faced was long limbed and strong, wide in the shoulders and a full head taller than she was, and wasn't hampered as she was by a heavy skirt and red cape. "Bread and wine, some cheese and fish. That's all."

She lifted her eyes to the man again, undaunted even though she knew everyone in Kingsport and this man was a complete stranger to her.

"Really?" His interest seemed casual, and there was no threat in his stance. "All I have is some hard bread and a bit of pork."

Molly took a single step forward, in order to get a better look at the shaded face of the stranger who, oddly enough, intrigued her. Her curiosity made her bold. "I would happily share, but this is for my grandmother, and she's been ill."

He had a face that looked as if it had been sculpted with a knife, rather than molded with loving hands. There was a harshness in the sharp features that was not relieved by his humorless smile, and was only intensified by the keen gleam in his green eyes. Eyes a dark green that seemed to belong here in the forest.

"Too bad," he growled.

"My name is Molly Kincaid," she offered, hoping he would introduce himself if she did so first. He had the look of a traveler, a wanderer, with his knapsack and rifle, and she sensed he was a man more animal than human in spite of his sturdy clothing and well-cared-for weapon.

"What are you doing in the woods, Red?" he asked. "Are you lost? I'll be happy to help you find your way out, for a price."

She didn't ask what price he would demand, but instead stepped closer. Just one more single step. "I'm not lost. There's a narrow path from the road to my grandmother's house. The road is shaped like an L, and the path is fairly straight, and so it's shorter. As long as I stay on the path, I won't get lost."

"I see," he breathed in a low voice. He was no wanderer, Molly decided. For one thing, his black hair had recently been neatly trimmed. It didn't hang over his collar, but was as sharp and precise as the lines of his harsh face.

Molly's curiosity won out over her good manners. "I don't believe we've ever met before, and I know everyone from Kingsport."

He grinned again, showing Molly straight, white teeth that for some reason she couldn't explain made her shudder. "I have a house south of the village."

"There's nothing south of Kingsport but Vanora Point and the Trevelyan house," Molly challenged.

The grin didn't fade. "That's right."

Suddenly Molly knew who the stranger was. Oh, the stories she'd heard, the whispered tales . . .

"You're Wolf Trevelyan," she whispered.

"That's right." The wicked smile died slowly, and the green eyes darkened. Hardened, perhaps.

Molly knew she should run, should take her chances even though Wolf Trevelyan was stronger and undoubtedly faster, and if he decided to give chase he would surely catch her. He didn't have the look of a man who would chase her through the woods—in spite of the stories she'd heard, in spite of the fact that the way he looked at her chilled her to the bone.

But goodness, if her mother knew . . . her mother could never know. "How do you do, Mr. Trevelyan," Molly said with a brief curtsey.

Her response surprised him, evidently. There was a flash of puzzlement on his face, but it came and went quickly. "Quite well, Red," he answered dryly. "And you?"

"Very well."

Big Bad Wolf

The grin came back, a little less dark, a little less menacing. "I left New York City to escape the niceties of society, and here we are having a proper conversation in the middle of the forest. You surprise me, Red. Haven't you heard about me? Didn't your mother warn you?"

How embarrassing. She had tried to pretend that she didn't know about his reputation, but she wouldn't actually lie about it. "Well, yes, I have heard some rather shocking stories, and my mother did warn me about you."

"Then why are you still here?"

It was a very good question. One she should be asking herself. "I don't know. Perhaps I don't believe everything I hear, Mr. Trevelyan."

"Call me Wolf."

Molly smiled. The name suited him, in an odd way. He looked like a predator, and she had no doubt but that he could be quite dangerous. But not to her. That easy confidence was instinctive, inexplicable.

"I must be going, Wolf." Molly backed away, two short steps. "My grandmother will be waiting."

"For her bread and wine and fish," he said in a low voice.

"And cheese," Molly added.

He watched her so strangely, with a momentary light in his forest green eyes.

"Stay on the path," he warned.

"I will."

He turned from her, and Molly spun around to continue on her way. The chance meeting with

15

Wolf Trevelyan left her feeling oddly exhilarated.

"Red."

She spun around when he called her. Already he was disappearing into the shadows of the tall trees that seemed to swallow him up.

"Do you come this way every day?" he called.

"Yes," she answered, raising her voice so he would be sure to hear. "Will I see you here again?"

There was a pause before he answered, and all Molly could hear was the sound of Wolf Trevelyan moving away from her rapidly. "Probably not." His answer echoed, hollow and faint, and Molly's smile disappeared.

Grandma Kincaid's cottage faced the road that led to Kingsport and backed up to the dense woods. The path Molly followed was one her grandmother had forged herself years earlier, as impatient with the wasted time on the road as Molly was.

Today, Molly practically ran as she neared the cottage. She had no time to waste conversing with men in the forest, no matter how interesting they might be. Of course, she had no time for a social life at all . . . between her mother and her grandmother. They needed her, and they left no time for courting. That was why Molly found herself unmarried as she approached the age of twenty-four.

While she'd never been fiercely sought after like the truly beautiful girls in town, there had been several Kingsport bachelors to express an interest in her, usually older men looking for a wife to care for their homes and even their children. The widower Pyle had been quite persistent for several months, and Mr. Dodson had expressed an interest at one time, even though he was old enough to be her father.

Molly wasn't attracted in even the mildest way to any of the men who expressed an interest in her. She'd used her mother's need as an excuse to avoid these men for the past three years. Before that, it had been her father's illness.

She wanted to be married, one day, but not to just anyone. Certainly not to a man who was only looking for a housekeeper and a cook.

"Sorry I'm late," she called as she threw open the back door.

Grandma was sitting in her favorite chair, a book in her lap and a warm shawl around her thin shoulders. "You're not late, Molly." She closed her book and lifted her inquisitive eyes. "Good heavens, you're as red as that cape. Are you all right? Has something happened?"

It would be so easy to assure her grandmother that this day was like any other, that nothing out of the ordinary had happened, but Grandma Kincaid saw everything, and Molly couldn't lie to her beloved grandmother. "Well, I did meet someone in the woods today. A man. He was hunting, I think."

"You think?"

"He had a rifle and, I think, an India rubber knapsack that might have held ammunition, and he had bread and pork."

"How do you know he had bread and pork?"

"He told me so."

17

Linda Jones

Grandma Kincaid was not as cautious as Molly's mother, but she looked awfully concerned. "You should take the road home, Molly. All my years on that path, and I never met a single soul, let alone a stranger."

Molly placed the basket on Grandma's table and began to lay out the food she had brought. "Well, he's not exactly a stranger."

The moment of silence was so heavy and uncomfortable it made Molly itch.

"Molly?" Her grandmother asked as she stood slowly, gripping her polished cane and leaning forward. "Who was this man?"

Molly faced her grandmother with an innocent smile, hands clasped before her demurely, eyes wide. "Wolf Trevelyan," she said softly.

"Saints preserve us," Grandma whispered, rolling her eyes heavenward and placing a hand over her heart. "Did he hurt you? Did he touch you?"

"No," Molly said indignantly. "He was quite polite. Very much the gentleman."

"Have you not heard the stories? I know your mother tries to keep unpleasantness from you, but—"

"I've heard," Molly assured her grandmother as the old woman reached the table and placed a trembling hand on Molly's arm. "But they're just stories, Grandma. Tales, gossip, scandalous babble."

"They're true." Grandma maintained a tight grip on Molly's arm as she took her seat at the table. "I knew Jeanne, and her mother, and her grandmother. It's been seven years since that terrible

18

night. You were young when it happened, I realize, and your father didn't want you exposed to such unpleasantness. Jeanne's family left Kingsport, not long after she died, so it would be easy to forget what happened. Poor Jeanne. We can't allow the truth to die with her."

"No one knows the truth," Molly said defensively.

"Why does a woman kill herself on her wedding night?" Grandma whispered. "When Jeanne went over that cliff, she was still wearing her nightdress, as if she ran straight from her bedchamber and over the cliff. There are some that say Wolf Trevelyan didn't drive his bride to her death, but that he threw her off the cliff himself. We'll never know exactly how Jeanne died, but we do know Wolf Trevelyan is to blame."

Molly knew better than to argue with her grandmother. "He must have been very young. I always expected that he would be older, but he can't be much more than thirty."

"He was twenty-four when it happened, five years older than Jeanne. Yes, that's young, but that doesn't make him less evil."

Molly wanted to assure her grandmother that Wolf was not evil. She would have known, would have sensed it, but she'd felt no danger from the man who had confronted her so boldly in the forest. "Eat," Molly said. "We shouldn't have such conversations if they're going to upset you."

"I'm not upset."

Molly knew that wasn't true. Her grandmother's voice gave her away, with its weak tremble.

Linda Jones

"Molly, dear?" A thin hand reached out, and bony fingers wrapped around Molly's wrist. "You musn't take the path through the woods again. Your mother was right, and I was wrong to encourage you to disobey her on this matter. If anything happened to you, goodness, I would never forgive myself." Grandma turned piercing eyes upward. "You must promise me."

Molly hesitated. She had spent only a few minutes in the company of Wolf Trevelyan, but it was undoubtedly the most exciting few minutes of her life. Still, she couldn't make a promise to her grandmother and then immediately and deliberately break it.

"I promise you," she said carefully, "that I will not put myself in danger. Goodness," she added quickly. "What would you do without me? You'd be forced to move to town and live with mother, and you'd both be miserable, and the neighbors would complain about all the noise—the yelling and the sounds of pots and pans flying about the house."

Her grandmother eyed her suspiciously. "You promise?"

"I promise," Molly said solemnly. She wouldn't be putting herself in danger simply by walking through the woods. Wolf had told her he probably wouldn't see her again, and even if he did . . . even if he did . . . he wouldn't hurt her. She knew that as surely as she knew that her own grandmother would never do her any harm.

"Now eat up," she encouraged. Grandma Kincaid was getting much too thin. "I baked this bread myself, just last night. It's not as good as Mother's, of course, but I think it will do."

Grandma tasted the bread carefully, and Molly knew that no matter how good or bad it was, the response would be positive.

Wolf took his time making his way back to the house through the woods that separated his family home from Kingsport. He'd had no success hunting, but all he'd wanted was to be alone, to lose himself in the quiet of the forest for a time.

New York City was becoming more and more tedious, but it seemed he was able to return to his home in Maine less often as the years passed. Business required an increasing amount of time and dedication, and his social life was almost as demanding.

In New York the scandal of his marriage and disastrous wedding night seven years earlier had faded. It had not died completely, however, and in some cases the tales gave him a mysterious edge that some women—those silly whimpering females he detested—found attractive. Lately an increasing number of brave or desperate matrons had been thrusting their naive daughters upon him.

On occasion, he found it to his advantage to see that the rumors circulated again, whispered in drawing rooms and at balls, in smoky libraries and gambling halls. He then, often, made a point of pursuing a daughter or niece or sister of the shocked party. It was great entertainment that rarely lasted long enough to satisfy him.

There was no need to perpetuate the rumor in Kingsport. He hadn't been able to walk the streets of that small village in seven years without being scorned. Women cowered and crossed the street, afraid and unable to hide it. Men glared, an open threat in their eyes. When he found himself in his family home, a home he maintained even though he was the last of the Trevelyans, he stayed there or in the surrounding forest. There was no reason for him to venture into the village and watch the reaction he caused.

He had become accustomed to their scorn, had even come to expect and appreciate it. Big, bad Wolf Trevelyan, who either killed his bride, tossing her from the cliff because she couldn't satisfy him on his wedding night, or drove her to suicide, sending her screaming from their bedchamber preferring death to life as his wife.

Had he tried to defend himself, long ago? It seems he had, briefly and to no avail. It had not taken him long to understand his options. He could forever apologize for that night, or he could accept his reputation and even glory in it.

Wolf had never been one to apologize easily.

He'd been surprised to see the girl in red walking so carefully on the narrow footpath through the woods. Molly Kincaid would be impossible to miss, in any circumstance, but that red cloak had teased him, flashes of color amongst the brown and green, glimpses of swirling red velvet that had become more and more enticing as he'd neared her.

It had started as a game, he supposed. He'd intended to scare her a little, to see how long it took before she realized who he was, how long she would speak with him before she ran screaming down her narrow path. Already he was bored with the big house, with the sea at his back door. And yet, he wasn't ready to return to New York.

But Molly hadn't been scared. Not when she'd first seen him, and not when he'd told her who he was.

She looked all innocent, with those wide gray eyes and those untamed red curls that had escaped from her velvet hood, but Wolf knew that a true innocent would have run from him as if from the devil himself.

Molly Kincaid had been more curious than frightened, more inquisitive than innocent. What were her vices? Wolf knew that everyone had them. A weakness for drink or for gambling. Perhaps vanity, or a lust for money and the things that could be bought with it. Maybe even lust of another, more pleasurable sort.

Wolf was well acquainted with each and every one of these vices. It might be interesting to discover just what vice he shared with Molly Kincaid, what depravity would appeal to this young woman.

It might be entertaining to expose such shortcomings. To do a bit of investigating and see what came up. Wolf had become convinced, over the years, that no one was as pure and guileless as Molly appeared to be.

Wolf stepped from the woods and onto the road that led to the Trevelyan house. Already he could see the rooftops, and a portion of the third floor with its stone gables and stained glass windows. Wolf's grandfather, the Trevelyan who had built this house, had undoubtedly longed in his childhood to live in a castle, because that was what his mansion appeared to be, at first glance.

All the Trevelyan house needed to complete the picture was a moat and drawbridge, and a fair maiden imprisoned on the third floor.

Wolf could not yet see the cliff, but it was there, behind the mansion, as much a part of his home as any room within. And the sea crashed against that cliff, far below the house, an eternal reminder of the night that had changed his life forever.

As Molly stepped from the footpath and back onto the road to Kingsport, her thoughts were unfailingly of Wolf Trevelyan.

Her mother had always tried to protect her, too much, Molly sometimes thought, and that protection included an attempt at preventing scandalous gossip that would be unsuited for a young girl from reaching Molly's ears.

Molly was not as sheltered as her mother liked to believe. While she was certainly innocent, she was not ignorant. Her limited social life was no more than occasional afternoons in the company of other young women close to her age, in particular Stella Warwick and Hannah Meredith. Stella had been married two years, and had a child, a little boy. Hannah was a beautiful girl and a terrible gossip, who couldn't keep a secret if her life depended on it.

Big Bad Wolf

They'd both mentioned Wolf Trevelyan at one time or another, though neither of them had actually met him. His notorious reputation extended well beyond the scandal of his wife's death.

Molly didn't pay much attention to gossip, but she tried to remember what they'd said. He was supposedly a womanizer, a man who thought nothing of seducing young innocents and then abandoning them without a second thought. Of course, neither of them actually knew a woman who had been misused by the notorious Wolf Trevelyan.

They'd both said he was horribly ugly, but Molly knew that wasn't true. While there was a harshness about him, he was far from ugly. His eyes were lovely, and his sharp features were strong. Masculine. Perhaps Wolf was not beautiful, but he was definitely handsome.

Hannah and Stella had painted the unknown Wolf Trevelyan as a cruel monster. So, for that matter, had Grandma Kincaid. They'd painted a picture of a man who should have had horns growing from that lovely head of black hair, a man who had no soul. Molly didn't believe it.

She didn't believe it, even though he'd grinned at her so wickedly, and he'd offered to assist her—for a price. Even though he'd called her *Red*, with such an intimate and familiar ring in his low voice that just the memory made her shiver.

"I'm home," Molly called as she threw open the door to the little house she shared with her mother.

There were three rooms to their comfortable

25

house. A large main room, a single bedroom, and a kitchen. The furnishings were plain and colorless, but always clean, and the rugs that covered the floor were worn, but did manage to keep bare feet from the cold floor in the wintertime. All in all, it was a simple and comfortable home.

Molly found her mother still in the kitchen, tired as she labored over the loaves of bread that were in several stages of the process: some cooling, some rising, some baking and filling the small house with that incomparable aroma.

"You must have run home, you're so flushed," her mother observed in a tired voice.

"I did," Molly confessed. "There's laundry to be done, and I wanted to get started as soon as possible."

Molly was relieved when her mother didn't take note of the cheer in her voice. She was never excited about doing the laundry.

Molly hung her red cloak on a peg not far from the front door, and she set about helping her mother in the kitchen. Before she realized it, she was humming almost merrily, and her mother did, just once, look at her askance.

Chapter Two

Molly did feel a twinge of guilt as she turned off the road and into the woods. But there was more excitement within her than guilt, more anticipation than trepidation.

Once again she'd allowed her mother to believe that she'd stick to the road, never intending for a moment to take the chance that Wolf Trevelyan walked the forest while she stayed on the road.

She felt a little sorry for him, though he didn't look like the sort of man who was normally pitied. Everyone believed the worst of him, some even hated him. Molly had never before doubted the truth of the scandal that tainted Wolf, but having met him, having looked into his face, she continued to wonder.

He'd said he probably wouldn't see her today,

Linda Jones

but in her heart she didn't believe it. What a terrible disappointment it would be if he didn't appear somewhere along the path to her grandma's house.

Molly smiled. Her life had become so predictable, so dull, that a chance meeting with a stranger was the most exciting event she could remember. If she'd been given to more feminine pursuits, if she had energy at the end of her long day for visiting with Stella and Hannah more often or even courting with one of the local men who'd pursued her, perhaps she wouldn't be so easily entertained.

Turning a corner, lost in her own thoughts, she saw him. Today, Wolf Trevelyan waited blatantly on the path, and to pass him Molly would have to leave the path and wind her way through the pine trees. The path was not so narrow, Wolf Trevelyan just seemed to fill it nicely, with his wide shoulders and long legs. His feet were placed far apart, as if he actually were trying to block her progress.

"Good afternoon, Red."

"Good afternoon." Molly stopped when she was still several feet from him. Wolf was dressed as he had been the day before, though the checked shirt was a different color if she remembered correctly. He cradled his rifle as lovingly as a mother would a child, and that same knapsack was slung over one shoulder.

He gave her a wicked smile. "What's in the basket?"

"The same as yesterday. Bread, wine, cheese and fish." Molly reached into the basket and withdrew a small loaf of bread. "I did bring extra today, in case you're hungry and have nothing but hard bread and pork." She offered him the loaf. "I made it myself."

He didn't take the bread, but settled his rifle against the trunk of a tree, and swung his knapsack forward. "That's very nice, Red. And it just so happens that I came prepared myself."

He withdrew a thin blanket, and spread it at his feet—there in the middle of the footpath, and then he pulled from his knapsack a bottle and two small glasses. These he held carefully as he lowered himself to sit on the far edge of the blanket.

Molly didn't move, and when Wolf was settled comfortably he lifted that harsh face to her. "Have a seat, and bring your bread with you, if you'd like."

With just a touch of uncertainty, Molly closed the short distance that separated her from Wolf Trevelyan, and she lowered herself to the edge of the blanket, tucking her feet beneath her skirt and pushing the hood of her cloak back.

"I really shouldn't," she protested meekly. "Grandma will be worried if I'm late." The beating of her heart betrayed her ruffled nerves, and she hoped Wolf Trevelyan couldn't tell that she was anxious. Given his reputation, he might take her apprehension for fear, and that wasn't true.

She placed the loaf of bread between them, a barrier of sorts, the simple loaf marking the center of the blanket and separating his territory from hers.

Wolf was apparently unconcerned about

Grandma's state of mind. "Have a drink," he said, opening his bottle and filling one of the small glasses nearly to the rim.

"What is it?" she asked as she took the glass he offered across the space that separated them.

"Brandy." He poured his own glass, and drank it down quickly. Wolf was refilling his glass before Molly had even lifted hers to her lips.

She smelled it first, lifting the full glass cautiously to her nose. Of course, she occasionally had a glass of wine with supper, but she'd never had anything so strong as Wolf's brandy.

"Drink up," Wolf encouraged, and Molly lifted the glass to her mouth, barely touching her lips to the liquid before she lowered it again.

"I shouldn't," she said. Molly sat the brandy aside, on a relatively flat portion of the blanket. "Are you hungry?" She tore a piece of the bread and offered it to him as he downed his second glass. "I hope you like sweet bread. There's cinnamon and raisins in this loaf."

"And you made it yourself," he said dryly as he took the piece she offered. His fingers brushed hers, and Molly snapped her hand back into her lap. "You drink my brandy, and I'll eat your bread."

Molly retrieved her glass, and reluctantly lifted it to her lips. She swallowed a little bit, and her eyes immediately watered. The brandy burned her throat, and without hesitating she handed the glass to Wolf.

"I can't drink this." She thought for a moment that he was going to refuse to take the glass from

30

her, and she would surely insult him if she tossed what remained in the glass into the woods. Besides, it would likely kill a tree if it soaked into the ground and into the roots.

"Why not?"

He reached out, but instead of taking the glass from her he wrapped his fingers around hers. His hand was so large it dwarfed hers, and his fingers were long and strong. She could see just a touch of her own pale skin peeking through those dark fingers.

His hand was warm, and soft, and steady, and his touch made her heart beat so fast she was afraid he would hear it. His green eyes glinted so dark and hard that she lowered her gaze to his strong jaw. A muscle there jumped. Was that a tic? Even that was too distracting, and Molly lowered her gaze again to his throat.

Wolf's throat was not like hers at all, but was dark and rippled with muscle and sinew. A vein throbbed, and she watched the steady beat of his heart. Unlike her own, it seemed quite normal and unaffected.

She was staring at a button on his waistcoat when he finally took the glass from her, dragging his fingers lightly across the back of her hand.

"I have to be going." Her voice was too soft, but it was all she could manage.

"So soon?"

His voice was light, and Molly chastised herself for being so foolish. It had been innocent, such a simple touch. He had held his hand over hers for a few seconds, no more, and here she was acting as if he'd tried to kiss her. Instinctively, she licked her lips.

"I haven't even tasted your bread yet." He took the piece Molly had torn off for him, and ripped off a small corner. He was looking right at her when he popped it into his mouth and washed it down with the remains of her brandy. "Pretty good, Red."

She got the strange feeling, watching him finish off the small bite, that he'd rather be finishing her off, one tiny taste at a time. It was the eyes, she decided, those intense green eyes that watched, unflinching, unblinking, as if he were trying to stare her down, or paralyze her under his powerful gaze. She was the deer, and he was the wolf, and she didn't have a chance. . . .

"You have . . ." Molly fluttered her fingers at her own cheek. "A crumb."

He swiped at his cheek with those long fingers, but it was the wrong cheek.

"No, over here." She was still pointing to her own cheek, and Wolf missed again. Right cheek this time, but much too high. "Down a little."

Wolf dropped his hands and narrowed his eyes. "Why don't you get it for me?"

Molly didn't hesitate, but rocked up on her knees and leaned forward. Not too far forward, but close enough so that she could reach his face without straining.

It was a tiny crumb, white against his dark face. Her fingers brushed skin that was just a little rough with the stubble that grew there. Surely he had shaved that morning, and already she could feel the tiny coarse hairs on his cheek.

His skin was warm, and rough, and just that brief graze of her fingers was enough to set her heart to pounding again.

"There," she said as she resumed her seat. "All taken care of."

He looked at her as if he knew something she didn't. Something important. Something that would change her life. All in all, she hadn't spent half an hour in his company, and yet she felt this time was somehow momentous.

He looked at her as if he wanted to eat her up, as if he were truly everything her mother had warned her about, everything Hannah and Stella accused him of being, and yet Molly trusted Wolf Trevelyan. That trust went against everything she knew of him, and even against her own common sense.

"You're blushing," he accused.

"I am not." She defended herself needlessly. Of course she was blushing. She could feel the telling heat in her cheeks.

"If you say so," he said.

"You shouldn't make fun of me. It's not polite."

Wolf raised his eyebrows as she chastised him, as if he couldn't believe that she would dare to speak to him so boldly. His surprise made him look more vulnerable, more human, and Molly smiled brightly.

"Don't looked so shocked," she said, relaxing. "Does no one tell you when you're being rude?"

"No one," he revealed in a low voice.

"Perhaps if they did, your manners would be

much improved." She didn't mean to sound so prim.

"My manners?" he repeated softly.

"Yes."

He seemed to contemplate her suggestion, and whatever surprise he had felt faded away. She could see it, the control that stole over his face and clouded his eyes. "I do many things well, Red, but I'm not known for my good manners."

"What a revelation," Molly said with a widening grin.

She didn't fall into his trap and ask just exactly what it was he was known for, what he did well. Wolf's stare hinted that they both knew perfectly well what he was implying.

It was not much more than a twitch, a tightening of his muscles that told Molly that Wolf was about to move forward, to come toward her, and she wasn't ready for him to touch her again, not even a simple brush of his hand on hers.

"I really do have to be going." This time Molly stood, gathering her basket from the corner of Wolf's blanket.

Wolf didn't rise, and so Molly rounded a pair of trees before she found herself on the footpath again. She glanced over her shoulder, and found that he still hadn't moved. His back was rigid.

"Red?" he called, and she stopped, spinning to face him.

Wolf glanced over his shoulder. "Thanks for the bread. Stay on the path."

"You're welcome, and I will." She allowed herself a smile. "And thank you for the brandy. I'm sorry I didn't like it very much."

He grumbled. Was it "So am I"? Molly couldn't be sure.

His back was to her again. "Wolf?"

At the sound of his name his back stiffened, and he turned to her.

"Will you be here tomorrow?" Molly knew she shouldn't sound so hopeful, but she couldn't help it.

"I'll be here," he growled. "Stay on the path," he reminded her again. "We can't have you getting lost, now can we?"

Molly spun around, and her smile widened when her back was to Wolf Trevelyan. She'd spent much too much time with him today, but then Grandma would think she'd taken the road, and so perhaps she wouldn't worry.

She ran, just in case.

He wouldn't be able to corrupt her with drink, that was certain. Her entire face had reacted when she'd placed the brandy to her lips, eyes watering, mouth puckering.

She had reacted when he'd touched her, a response much stronger and more pleasant that any brandy might bring on. The touch had been so inconsequential, such an innocuous brush of his fingers over hers, but Molly had held her breath and stared at him with the brightest, clearest questioning eyes he'd ever seen. A few minutes later, when she'd brushed the crumb from his face she'd turned several interesting shades of pink and red.

He heard her even before he saw the swirl of red between the trees. She was . . . good God she was humming something softly as she hurried back to Kingsport. The basket, now empty, swung easily in her hand, and the red velvet hood was pushed back, so he had a clear view of those magnificent red curls.

Her hair was not auburn, not strawberry-blonde, but red. Thick red curls that were soft, never kinky, teased him, falling past her cheek and over her breasts. He could imagine too vividly that if he removed the cloak he would see those magnificent curls falling to her waist, soft, heavy curls he could bury his hands and his face in.

He held his breath as she passed. It wouldn't do for Molly to know that he watched her, even now. That he had waited for her to come this way again. Why did he find himself fascinated with a country girl like Molly Kincaid? She was different from the other women he knew, that was the truth, but it was more than that.

She knew what he was, and still she was not afraid.

On the path, Molly stopped to admire a beautiful aster. She bent at the waist, and a handful of curls tumbled forward, hiding her face from him.

Molly looked, to all the world, like a naive angel, all goodness and light, Wolf's opposite in every way. But he had seen a kinship in her, a spark in her eyes that told him she was not all she appeared to be.

He knew what her downfall would be, how he would, eventually, corrupt Molly Kincaid.

She had held her breath when he touched her hand, and she didn't even seem to realize it. Her fingers on his face had trembled, just a little, and there was craving in her touch and in her eyes. Maybe she didn't know yet that she wanted him, maybe she didn't know yet exactly what it was she wanted, but it was true.

Hell, he wanted her hard enough for both of them, and it made no sense at all.

It made no more sense than the fact that he felt compelled to watch her, to wait until she'd visited her grandmother and was on her way home. He could not explain, even to himself, why he was driven to follow Molly carefully through the woods, her red cloak always in view, until she stepped onto the road to Kingsport.

He would have followed her there as well, tracking her to her home, watching her stroll through the streets of Kingsport with that innocent smile on her face, if he didn't know he'd be seen and recognized.

Wolf Trevelyan still wasn't welcome in Kingsport, and never would be. Jeanne had been one of their own, a daughter of the town, and he was nothing more than the arrogant son of a rich man, and he was responsible for her death.

That would never change.

Wolf turned toward home, and already he was planning for the next encounter.

"What is wrong with you?"

Molly snapped her head up to stare at her mother. "Nothing."

"Then why have you just sewn Mr. Hanson's sleeves together?"

Molly glanced down at the mending in her lap, and saw that she had indeed sewn one sleeve to the other. "I'm just tired, I guess. It's been a long day."

Mary Kincaid nodded her head sympathetically, and Molly knew her mother had had a long day, as well. She hadn't had the respite of a moment in the company of a handsome and intriguing man.

"Will you ever remarry?"

Mary was shocked by the question, and her eyes widened. "Why do you ask such a question?"

Molly shrugged her shoulders. "You're young enough to have another husband."

"I loved your father."

Molly placed the mending in her lap and abandoned it for a moment. "Did you love him when you married, or did love come later?"

Mary still glowed when she talked about her late husband. "I adored him, before he even knew I existed. Yes, I loved him very much."

"How did you know?"

Mary's glow gave way to suspicion, which was evident in her narrowed eyes and thinned, stern lips. "Molly, is there something you're not telling me?"

Molly forced her eyes to open wide and to remain on her mother. "Of course not. But I am . . . well, surely I'll marry someday, and I want to know what to expect."

"What will I do without you, when that time

comes?" Mary sighed, and her pretty features softened as she relaxed. "Is that why you want me to marry again, so you'll be free to marry?"

"I didn't say I wanted you to marry, I only asked if you thought you might."

Mary Kincaid was still an attractive woman, with just a touch of gray in her dark hair, and a minimum of wrinkles on her pretty face. "I don't know. I've never given the possibility much thought."

"Mr. Hanson was giving you the eye Sunday after church."

"Wondering why his shirts had not been mended yet," Mary snapped. "Nothing more. Now, let's get back to work."

Molly removed the stitches that joined Mr. Hanson's sleeves at the cuff. "You haven't yet answered the other part of my question."

"What other part?" Mary asked absently.

Molly sighed. Must she be blunt with her mother? She didn't want to arouse suspicion, but who else was she to ask? "How will I know when I fall in love?"

Mary didn't take her eyes off of her own mending. "You'll just know," she said in a low, wise voice.

It wasn't a very satisfying answer. Molly frowned at the shirt in her lap, and tapped the needle lightly against sturdy cotton.

"When the time comes," she said softly, "do you feel any different? I mean, inside?"

Mary dropped her mending and lifted her head. "Molly Elmira Kincaid, has one of these Kingsport boys been putting ideas in your head?"

"No ma'am," Molly answered quickly and assuredly. She didn't like to lie to her mother, and she was thankful that Wolf was not a boy or from Kingsport. She was also quite certain that the intriguing ideas in her head were her own and not planted there by anyone else. "I'm just curious."

"Curiosity is not good for a young lady. It will get you into trouble every time." Mary's voice was stern, and Molly knew the conversation was over.

By the light of the fire, Molly removed the errant stitches from Mr. Hanson's shirt, and began again. This time, she kept her thoughts to herself.

Those thoughts were exclusively about Wolf Trevelyan. She could see his face in her mind, with very little effort. Harsh and handsome features, deep green eyes, hair as black as a raven's wing falling, just a little disobediently, over his forehead. She remembered the touch of his hand, and his face beneath his fingers. The roughness and the warmth of his skin.

Just thinking about him made her feel warm all over, and made her heart beat fast, as it had that afternoon when he'd stared at her so audaciously. She'd never been truly courted, and she'd certainly never had exhilarating and intense dreams about a man before, so she wasn't sure what to make of her reaction. At the moment she was only sure that there was not another man on the face of the earth like Wolf Trevelyan.

Molly looked down to find that she had stitched Mr. Hanson's shirt to her skirt, and she set about trying to undo the damage without drawing her mother's attention.

Perhaps Grandma Kincaid could tell her what love felt like.

Wolf stared at the fire that blazed before him, an unnecessary source of heat on a mild night. In the solitude of his bedchamber, sitting in his favorite chair, he enjoyed, for the last time that day, a fat cigar and a snifter of his best brandy.

His days began and ended in much the same way.

He'd never needed more than a few hours sleep a night, but usually by this hour he was either asleep or well on his way.

What he really needed right now was a sparring partner and a few rounds in a boxing ring.

Fighting had been, for the past five years, his way of venting frustration in a world that no longer allowed a man to express his anger in a physical way. Riding a horse through the park had never seemed sport to him, and he had no patience whatsoever with lawn tennis, but a match in the gymnasium at his gentlemen's club always put him right.

It was Molly Kincaid, that slip of a girl, who had him in such a knot. She'd worked her way into his mind, and it seemed that since he'd met her she was always there.

Wolf thrust his legs forward and took a long draw on the cigar. Women were usually so predictable, but not Molly. Had he become so accustomed to the spoiled society women of New York that he'd forgotten what a real woman was like, or was Molly as original and perplexing as she appeared to be?

He turned his gaze to the wide and tall bed. He always slept alone when he was at Vanora Point, so why did the big bed suddenly seem so damned empty?

It wasn't a sparring match he needed, it was Molly Kincaid. In that bed. Naked. His for the taking.

In spite of his sleeplessness and obsession, Wolf smiled. Molly was just a woman, and he was caught up in the dreariness of Vanora Point. She wasn't even, he had to admit, the most beautiful woman he'd ever seen. She was too wide-eyed, and when she wasn't blushing her face was too pale, and she was rather short. . . .

Wolf continued his list of her shortcomings well into the morning, but the bed continued to look too vast and lonely to crawl into alone.

Chapter Three

Wolf shook out the blanket before placing it over the path in roughly the same spot he had the day before. There was no sign of Molly yet, but it wouldn't be long now.

He couldn't remember the last time he'd anxiously awaited the arrival of a woman, and the awareness that he was looking forward to seeing Molly made him smile. It was the game, he reasoned, and not the woman.

Wolf knew women. He knew what they wanted, and what they despised in a man. Even before that night, before he was labeled a heartless murderer, he'd had a reputation for ruthlessness. A face that was harsh, even at twenty-four, and the distance he was able to place between himself and every-

43

one, even a woman he was bedding, had built that reputation.

Still, there were women who were drawn to darker men who had no interest or inclination in being tamed, and Wolf had always been able to manipulate those particular females. He didn't have the kind of good looks that women liked, but he could turn on the devilish charm when he needed to.

Wolf smiled grimly at the realization that he continued to divide his life into before and after that night, but he refused to dwell on the fact.

There were women out there who got a sick kick out of flirting with a dangerous man, and Wolf wouldn't deny a single one of them the thrill of a real scare.

It never lasted, the fascination that brought those women to him, but he'd learned to make the best of it.

His money didn't hurt. Wolf was well aware that there wasn't a woman alive who wouldn't forgive a man an awful lot if his fortune was healthy enough.

Wolf didn't consider himself cynical. He thought of his approach to the supposed fairer sex as realistic.

Today he was well prepared for his meeting with Molly. There was a deck of playing cards in one pocket, and a diamond and sapphire bracelet in another. He was determined to expose all of Molly Kincaid's weaknesses.

By the time she was in sight, her red cape dancing almost merrily down the path, Wolf was in place on his side of the blanket, the cards spread before him in a familiar game of solitaire.

"Hello." There was a tentative undertone to Molly's greeting, and Wolf smiled as he lifted his head.

"Do you play?" He gathered the cards swiftly, scooping them into one hand.

"No." Molly lowered herself to the far end of the blanket, placing her basket on the path behind her.

Wolf shuffled the cards briskly, never taking his eyes from Molly's face. Such wide eyes, she had, clear and so easy to read. Such pale, fragile skin, a complement to her bright hair.

Wolf smacked the deck of cards against the center of the blanket. "Take a card," he said as he drew his hand back. "Top card, one from the middle, it doesn't matter."

Molly hesitated, but she finally reached forward cautiously, as though she expected he might reach out and capture her wrist. She took the top card, as he had expected she would, and placed the ace face up beside the deck.

Smoothly, Wolf flipped over the next card. A measly four. "You win," he said as he scooped up the cards and shuffled again.

"I do?"

"One more time?" Wolf placed the cards between them.

"I suppose." Her voice was wary as she reached forward and again took the top card. A red queen.

Wolf turned over the next card. An eight.

"You're lucky. Some people have it, and some don't."

"Some people have what?"

"Luck." Wolf scooped up the cards and shuffled with a skill that had been years in the making. Molly watched the cards fly through his hands, obviously fascinated. It certainly didn't take much to impress her. Her gaze was riveted on the quick motions of his hands and the cards that flew through his fingers.

"How about we make it a little more interesting this time," he offered, and Molly lifted her eyes from the deck and his hands to his face.

"How would we do that?"

"A little bet."

He was making her uncomfortable. She wrinkled her nose, so softly she probably didn't even realize she'd done it, and squinted those wide gray eyes. "I don't have anything to bet, and besides it's not appropriate."

"Not appropriate?" Wolf repeated. "Why not?"

"It's gambling, and gambling is a sin."

"So are you refusing because you don't have anything to bet, or because gambling's a sin?"

Molly didn't seem to know the answer herself. She hesitated, and squirmed a bit there on her far edge of the blanket. Her red cape was tossed casually over her shoulders, revealing for him a very nice shape that tested the patience he was practicing. There was nothing enticing about the plain blouse she wore, or the heavy brown skirt that covered her legs, but her waist was so tiny he was certain he could span it with his hands, and the swell of her breasts was generous.

"Both, I suppose," she finally answered tentatively.

Wolf placed the cards in the center of the short space that separated him from Molly Kincaid, and slipped the bracelet from his pocket. A thin band of light, a hint of the sunlight that found its way to the forest floor, sparkled on the diamonds and sapphires as he tossed the bracelet to the blanket, where it landed with a musical jingle beside the deck of cards.

"If you draw the high card, it's yours."

Molly leaned forward to get a better look, but she didn't touch the bracelet. She kept her hands folded in her lap. "It's beautiful," she whispered.

All women loved beautiful things. Most especially beautiful expensive things that sparkled in the sunlight. Or the candlelight. Molly would be no different.

"Draw the high card, and it's yours."

She lifted her face to him, wide eyes staring at him boldly. "I told you, I have nothing to . . ."

"If I draw the high card," he interrupted. "I get a kiss."

He expected her to at least express surprise, but there was none on her face. He saw nothing there but utter calmness as she considered his suggestion, and he realized that Molly wasn't surprised at all.

This time, instead of taking the top card, Molly spread the deck across the blanket, fanning the cards slowly with her delicate fingers. Those fingers fluttered uncertainly over the deck, fingertips lightly brushing each and every card. Finally, she took a card from the middle, turning it over slowly. An eight.

He had planned to lose again, to see if she would take the jewels she'd won. The top card, the one that should have been hers, was a ten. The second card, the card he would have drawn, was another four. Wolf ran his fingers over the back of the deck. He'd been well prepared to lose, certain that the kiss he craved would come soon enough, in any case.

"What the hell," he muttered, taking his chances and picking a card at random from the middle of the deck, turning over a deuce.

"Oh." Molly's response was nothing more than a whispered breath accompanied by wide eyes.

"I said you were lucky, and it seems I was right." Wolf slipped a finger under the bracelet and tossed it to her. The light touched the stones again before they landed in Molly's lap.

Molly stared down at the bracelet, and finally lifted it carefully with both hands, as if it were a fragile flower that could be crushed in careless fingers. "I've never seen anything like this."

He wasn't surprised that this was a weakness Molly shared with others of her sex. He'd seen women who had everything a lady could ask for capitulate for something as rare and brilliant as the bracelet she'd won, and Molly, from what he'd seen, didn't have much. She'd certainly never held anything like her winnings.

She cradled it in her hands for a moment, and then she placed it carefully beside the spread cards. "But I can't keep it."

"It's yours, you won it," Wolf insisted.

Rid of the bracelet, Molly smiled. "And if it were mine, what would I do with it? Wear it to church on Sunday? I don't think it's appropriate, especially since it would be ill-gotten if I were to keep it."

"Ill-gotten goods are to be savored."

Molly smiled brightly, as if he'd been jesting with her. "Is that how you came by such a treasure? Did you win it in a card game?"

"It was my mother's."

Molly's smile faded, and she tipped her head to one side quizzically, sending those red curls falling softly over her shoulder. "That's another reason I cannot accept it. It's a family heirloom. What would your mother think if she knew you would gamble away something so precious?"

"I'm the last of the Trevelyans," Wolf muttered, wondering how this conversation got so turned about. "There is no family. Take it." He tossed the bracelet to Molly again, angry that she hadn't reacted as he'd been certain she would, and she stood quickly so that it fell to the blanket, landing with a thud there where she'd been sitting.

"I have to be going now," she said quickly, picking up her basket and moving past him. Today she didn't leave the path, but stepped across the blanket and over his legs.

"Red," he called, standing quickly as she moved down the path.

She stopped, and turned to watch him warily.

"Sorry I snapped at you," he said, not looking at her.

"That's all right."

"I wanted you to have it, that's all."

He knew she harbored no hard feelings when she smiled at him. "You're very sweet."

Wolf lifted his eyebrows. "Sweet?" No one had called him sweet in . . . no one had ever called him *sweet*.

Molly turned away and was stepping quickly down the path. Her hood was down, and so that enticing hair danced behind her. She didn't ask if he would be here again the next day. Perhaps she knew he couldn't resist.

Why had she refused the bracelet? And if she were going to refuse, why play the game at all? It occurred to him, belatedly, that perhaps she had wanted to lose.

"Stay on the path, Red," he whispered as she rounded a corner and disappeared into the woods.

"Did you love Grandpa?" Molly asked, trying to keep her question and her face as innocent as possible.

Grandma had finished her meal, though in Molly's mind she hadn't eaten nearly enough. "Of course I did. He was a good man."

It was as unsatisfactory an answer as her mother's vague 'you'll just know.'

"But how did you know?"

Grandma left the table, gathered her woolen shawl and cane, and made herself comfortable by the fireplace. In many ways, Molly was closer to her grandmother than to her own mother. Mary Kincaid had always been overly protective, since Molly was her only child, and so many times Molly had turned to her grandmother for advice instead of facing her mother. Grandma Kincaid was a sensible woman who never hesitated to speak her mind, and besides, sometimes Molly found it was easier to be forthright with the older woman than with her mother.

"It didn't come all of a sudden," Grandma said softly as she rocked rhythmically in her favorite chair.

"It didn't?"

"The marriage was arranged by our families. I barely knew Michael when we married." Grandma stared past the parted lace curtains, to the forest beyond.

"So you didn't love him when you married?"

Grandma was silent for a long moment, and Molly was reluctant to interrupt her thoughts. "I respected him greatly, and I knew he would make a good companion, but no. I didn't love him then. That came later."

Molly sat on the floor at her grandmother's feet. "But when it came, how did you know it was real true love?"

Grandma turned suspicious eyes to Molly. Eyes that, it seemed, saw everything. "You are certainly inquisitive today. Why all the questions about love?"

"I'll want to marry someday," Molly said defensively. "I should understand these things. Shouldn't I?"

Linda Jones

Grandma smiled. "You should. Unfortunately, there are no easy answers to your questions. Love is different for everyone. It comes slowly and with a lightning bolt. Strong and soft. And then, there are some poor souls who never find love at all."

"That's very sad," Molly said, and she shivered. What if she never found true love? Had Wolf Trevelyan ever found love?

As if her grandmother had read her mind, she answered one of Molly's doubts. "But you don't have to worry about that," she assured. "You have so much love within you that it shines from your eyes. And no man who is the object of a love like that can turn away from it or restrain himself from returning it." Her soft smile died. "Your mother and I have not been fair with you, child. We've depended on you too much in the past, when you should have been searching for a life of your own."

"You need me." Molly placed a hand on her grandmother's knee. "And difficult as you are," she teased, "I love you both."

Molly felt thin, fragile fingers in her hair. "Perhaps it's time we began a conscientious search for a husband for you, child. You're so beautiful, it shouldn't be a chore."

It sounded so unromantic and businesslike. A search. A chore. "I guess I thought I'd just . . . just stumble upon the right man, when the time came. Look at him and know, at that very moment, that he was the right man for me."

"Only in fairy tales, Molly," Grandma whispered. "Only in fairy tales."

Big Bad Wolf

Molly stayed longer than she should, and when she left her grandmother's house she practically ran down the footpath. There was bread to be delivered, and mending to do. Perhaps today she'd make better progress than she had the evening before, when she'd wasted hours on Mr. Hanson's shirts.

But she was certain to be as distracted tonight as she'd been since she'd met Wolf. It had been foolish to play his game, but she'd so wanted to lose that last hand.

How did a girl go about getting a man to kiss her? That was one question she couldn't ask her mother or her grandmother, but she desperately needed to know. It would be much too forward simply to ask Wolf to kiss her. Heavens, what would he think of her?

If Wolf kissed her, perhaps she would know if what she was feeling for him was really love.

She was almost to the road when she heard something. A rustle, deep in the woods, that shouldn't have been there. Instead of running, Molly stopped and faced the dark shadows of the forest and the direction of the sound. She could see nothing but trees and shadows and a few blooming asters close to the ground.

Placing the empty basket on the ground, Molly stepped off of the pathway. With a hand against a white pine, she leaned forward, straining to hear the sound again, but there was nothing.

"Wolf?" she whispered.

For the span of a heartbeat, Molly knew he was out there somewhere. Watching her. She would give anything for another five minutes, even for another glimpse of him before she had to return to Kingsport. It was an amazingly strong impulse that forced her, momentarily, from the path. What explanation could there be for her fascination? Was Wolf Trevelyan her one true love?

Wolf always told her to stay on the path, and the truth of it was her sense of direction was so poor she'd surely get lost if she didn't.

So she scooped her basket up and ran from the unidentified sound. It might have been a wild animal, one of the beasts Wolf had been hunting. It might have been her imagination.

It might have been Wolf.

"Will that be all, Mr. Trevelyan?"

Larkin's quiet question startled Wolf, so much so that he nearly jumped from his chair.

His supper was untouched, but his wine glass had been refilled several times. Wolf lifted his hand, and the still full plate was taken away. Once again, he was alone in a dining hall that was meant for a large family.

The table was monstrously long, the chairs that lined it monstrously empty.

Of course, he had come here to be alone, to escape the crowds and the bustle of the city.

The bracelet Molly had refused was sitting before him, sparkling in the candlelight, teasing him mercilessly.

She'd wanted it. Damn it, he was certain Molly had wanted that bracelet with all her heart. Her eyes had lit up, and she'd handled it almost reverently. She found it beautiful and still she spurned it. Ill-gotten, she'd said—and quite seriously.

There had been a moment, as he'd watched Molly head for home, when he'd stepped on a twig and she'd heard the resulting soft snap. She'd actually left the path before hesitating and turning back.

A few more steps into the forest, and she would have seen him. He didn't think she would have been surprised. Hadn't it been his name she'd whispered when she left the path?

Molly couldn't be had through strong drink, and she couldn't be bought with sparkling jewels. She seemed to be as innocent as she had first appeared to be.

So why wasn't she afraid? Why didn't she run from him?

Perhaps all she wanted was exactly what he needed more and more each day. Wolf refilled his glass again and watched the play of candlelight through the red wine. By now all the servants had retired to their third floor rooms, all but Larkin, who would stay awake and alert until Wolf decided to retire for the evening, and who would be awake and alert when Wolf rose in the morning.

Wolf had often wondered if the old man ever slept, ever caught a cold, ever lost his temper. Perhaps while Wolf was in New York the staff of the house at Vanora Point slept late and drank wine from the house stock and carried on illicit affairs on the third floor.

That thought made Wolf smile. Larkin and the

cook—what was her name? The stable boy and the girl who was supposedly an upstairs maid, but fluttered around and squealed endlessly whenever Wolf was home. All he had to do was look in her direction and she fell apart.

This place was a colossal bore, but if Molly would consent to be his mistress, he might spend much more time on the family estate.

Wolf toasted the empty room. "To Molly Kincaid." The words echoed off the high ceiling. "May she be as delicious as she appears to be."

Molly's basket was filled with loaves of bread, but her mind wasn't on the delivery route. Mrs. McCann waved as Molly passed, stepping from the mercantile and smiling brightly, but it was a moment before Molly remembered her manners and waved back. The smile was not a problem. She had the silliest grin plastered on her face, and she wasn't exactly sure why.

It had to be Wolf. He was on her mind all the time, and Molly found herself contemplating such notions as love and kisses and irregularly pounding hearts.

If she didn't tell someone she was going to bust. Hannah and Stella were her very best friends, but Hannah had never kept a secret for more than ten minutes.

Molly made a delivery to Mr. Hanson's house, and she smiled and gave all the right answers when he inquired after her mother. Orville Hanson was not very tall, but then neither was Mary Kincaid. He had a slightly rounded belly, but his face was rather handsome, in the way an older man's face might be.

It was soft, though, she noted as she nodded and listened to his endless questions about her mother's health and well-being. And his eyes, while kind, were rather soft. Not unfocused, exactly, but not sharp and exciting like Wolf's dark green eyes.

When she left Mr. Hanson's house, Molly found herself diverging from her usual path and heading toward Stella's house. Stella's husband was a fisherman, like many of the local men, and he was usually gone until late afternoon or early evening.

Generally Molly didn't have time to stop and visit, but today was different.

Stella greeted her enthusiastically, as she always did, but Molly couldn't help but notice how two years of marriage had changed her friend. Stella's pale brown hair was piled haphazardly on top of her head, and her apron was stained from what had already been a long day.

Wallace, Stella's husband, was a gruff but good and hard-working man. That was all most of the local girls wanted and expected in a husband, but Molly suspected there was more.

"Come in," Stella whispered, opening the door wide for Molly to enter her little house. Stella's house was much like the one Molly shared with her mother. A main room, a small separate kitchen, a single bedroom. The baby slept in the main room, just as Molly always had.

"I'm so glad you're here," Stella whispered. "I never see you anymore."

Molly felt guilty for taking the time to visit her

friend only when she needed someone to talk to.

Stella led Molly to the kitchen, grasping her hand and pulling her along with a smile, and Molly deposited her basket on the table. She still had three deliveries to make, so she couldn't stay long.

"I have to tell you," Molly began, but she was interrupted by a loud wail from the baby's bed.

Stella's face fell, and big tears welled up in her eyes. "I can't believe it. He just went to sleep a few minutes ago."

Molly couldn't believe her friend was getting so upset, and just because the baby was waking up too soon. Little Wally was a cute boy, just now a year old and the picture of his father, with pale hair and a round face.

"Let me get him for you," Molly offered, and she went to fetch Wally from his bed. The little cutie stopped crying the very moment she picked him up.

When she returned to the kitchen, Stella was seated at the table with her head in her hands. "What am I going to do?" She lifted her head, and Molly was certain she had never seen such despair. "He never sleeps any more, not in the day time, and now I'm going to have another one."

Stella's wail was as pleading as Wally's had been.

"Another baby?" Molly asked, taking a seat and bouncing Wally on her knee. "That's wonder—" Stella's loud sniffle stopped Molly's congratulations.

She couldn't possibly ask Stella about Wolf. Not

now. Molly listened to Stella's woes, and nodded her head when her friend complained about getting no sleep and being sick in the morning, and never finishing her work.

There was nothing Molly could do but tell Stella to take a nap while she finished her deliveries with Wally on her hip.

He was a good baby, and listened attentively as Molly extoled the virtues of a man everyone else seemed to hate. He even listened attentively to her lengthy discourse on love and her fledgling theories about exactly how it is to be found.

Wally didn't seem at all bored at her prolonged description of Wolf's green eyes, nor was he shocked when Molly revealed that she had actually hoped to lose that last hand, when there'd been a kiss at stake. As if he understood completely, Wally clasped a fat hand over his mouth and laughed brightly.

The fact that Molly made faces at the baby as she opened her heart to him might have had something to do with his delight.

By the time Molly finished her deliveries and returned to Stella's house, her exhausted friend was sound asleep in the cool bedroom.

Molly cleaned Wally up, and gave him a cracker, and set about trying to straighten Stella's kitchen, quietly, of course. She started a pot of stew, which was no trouble since Stella had all the fixings ready, and she even mended a shirt that had been thrown across the back of a kitchen chair.

Wally was good company, and a wonderful listener even after Molly lowered her voice to a whisper, and by the time Stella woke from her nap Molly had satisfied her need to tell someone about Wolf.

Chapter Four

She had known Wolf would be waiting, but as always he surprised her. Today he carried no rifle, no knapsack, and there was no blanket spread across the path.

Wolf leaned against a white pine, his stance casual as he blatantly watched the path for her. In one hand he held a small and rather ragged bouquet of wildflowers, blue and yellow and white.

His face was partially in shadow, but she could see that his mouth was grim and his eyes were hard. She felt as if everything inside her tightened, a physical reaction that was akin to fear but different. Lighter. Somehow the sight of Wolf exhilarated her.

"Since you refused your ill-gotten winnings yesterday, I thought you might like these instead." No greeting, no insolent "Hello, Red." Just the oddly reluctant offering of wildflowers.

"They're beautiful," she said as she took the bouquet from Wolf, being careful not to touch his hand. "Where did you find them? I don't think I've ever seen these growing in the forest."

He didn't answer immediately, but stared down at her diligently.

"They grow far from the path, near a stream."

"Oh." Molly bent her head to smell the wildflowers, and to escape Wolf's piercing gaze for a moment. Today there was nothing between them. No loaf of bread, no deck of cards. She missed the safety of a clear division of some sort.

"And you always stay on the path, don't you, Red?"

Molly lifted her face from the wildflowers and looked up at Wolf. There was no humor in the harsh set of his lips, no brightness in the hard eyes he glared at her with. He looked, at that moment, as predatory as the residents of Kingsport had always accused.

"Yes," she whispered softly.

"Afraid you'll get lost if you wander too far?"

"Yes."

Standing so close, Wolf seemed taller than she remembered, wider in the shoulders. She should have been intimidated by his strength, but she wasn't. If she felt intimidated at all, it was by the inexplicable power he had over her.

"I won't let you get lost." His voice was low, a gravelly murmur. He lifted his hand slowly.

"Come with me, if you want to see the stream and the wildflowers."

Molly hesitated, but Wolf's hand didn't drop. He held it there, palm upward, and waited for her to refuse his offer or else lay her hand in his.

If she turned her back on him now, she'd never get another chance. Never. There was no guarantee that Wolf would be here tomorrow, or the next day, or ever again. Hesitantly, she placed the heavy basket at the edge of the path, and then she touched her hand to his. Her hand looked so small compared to his, so pale, so fragile. Still, there was no helpless feeling welling up inside her.

"I don't have much time," she said softly. "Grandma will be waiting."

Wolf closed his warm, strong fingers over her hand, and she could swear he almost smiled. "Sometimes you have to live dangerously, Red."

He led her away from the path, through the white pines and around the blooming asters. Their course was a winding one, and led them deeper into the woods than Molly had ever dreamt of venturing. Infrequent fingers of sunlight shot to the forest floor, dotting their unmarked path with warmth and radiance.

Wolf held her hand tightly, and there was such a wonderful comfort in the simple touch of his hand and those long brown fingers. Warmth and strength flowed through her, all from the feel of Wolf's hand around hers. He walked before her cautiously, taking shorter steps to accommodate her pace. On occasion he had to stoop down to avoid a low limb, and he always looked over his shoulder once he was past, to make certain she watched her step.

With wildflowers in one fist and Wolf's hand in another, Molly followed without a second thought. Their path twisted and turned so many times during the short trip that she was totally disoriented. She couldn't possibly point in the direction of the footpath she walked every day, much less find her way back, but she was not alarmed.

Wolf wouldn't let her get lost.

Without a word, Wolf led her from the thick shadows of the forest and into a small clearing.

A stream did indeed cut through the middle of the clearing, and flowers—wild yellow lilies and blue flags—covered the grassy earth. A break in the cover of the tall trees allowed more sunlight to break through, and it sparkled on the rushing water and warmed the ground.

"It's wonderful." Molly smiled and lifted her face to Wolf's. "Like a little bit of paradise hidden here in the middle of the forest."

Wolf didn't return her smile, and he didn't release her hand. "Worth breaking the rules for?"

"Yes."

She slipped her hand from his and walked to the edge of the stream. The rushing water that sparkled in the sunlight was shallow and narrow. Wolf could probably traverse it in a single leap.

"I never knew . . ." She bent to pick a few of the wild yellow lilies, intending to give them to her grandma, but she stopped when she'd picked only two. How would she explain finding the flowers?

She couldn't. And she would never be able to find them again without Wolf's guidance.

Molly added the two newly picked flowers to her bouquet. She would leave the flowers on the footpath, somewhere, and collect them as she returned home. Even when they were dried and no longer bright, she would look at them and remember this afternoon. The bouquet and Wolf would have to remain her secret. It was rather sad to realize that this was a joy she could not share with anyone.

"So tell me," Wolf growled. "Are flowers plucked from the ground when you've stolen away from your path ill-gotten?"

Molly turned as she stood. Wolf stood there at the edge of the forest, hiding in the shadows, as if he didn't belong in the sunlight.

"I don't know. Perhaps."

"As ill-gotten as the winnings from a simple card game?"

"Definitely not."

Wolf had not smiled once today. Even now, his expression was austere. "So, you have rules that you can't even explain. Some can be broken, and some cannot."

"I never break the rules."

"You're here," he whispered harshly. "You left the path, left your grandmother waiting, and you let me bring you here."

"I wanted to see—" Molly began.

"So you break the rules when it suits you," Wolf interrupted, stepping into the sunlight. The bright light was not kind to him. It revealed the harsh planes of his face, the brutal cut of his features. "You might as well have no rules at all."

"Is that how you live? No rules?"

"Yes." Another step and he would have been upon her, but Wolf stopped abruptly.

"I can't live that way," she revealed.

She expected Wolf to argue with her, but he didn't. He just stared at her coldly, and at that moment she was certain he knew everything she felt and thought. An errant strand of black hair had fallen over his forehead, a crescent shaped sable tress above those mesmerizing eyes that was much safer to stare at than his eyes or his lips or even his broad chest.

"I need to get back, now. Grandma will be worried."

"Go ahead." Wolf turned his back on her and wandered upstream, his steps slow and long.

Molly turned toward the forest, glimpsed into the darkness. She would never be able to find her way back to the footpath without Wolf's guidance.

"Won't you walk me back?"

"I don't think so." He didn't even turn to look at her as he denied her request.

"But you said . . . you said you wouldn't let me get lost."

Wolf spun around, and at last there was a grin on his face. A wide smile that did nothing to make Molly feel better. "It doesn't matter what I said. I break all the rules, remember?"

"I can't find my way back, not alone."

In a few long strides, Wolf was standing before her. For the first time since their meeting in the forest, Molly felt threatened. She didn't believe that he would hurt her, but he did hold some power over her, and at the moment he knew it. She saw the knowledge in his glittering green eyes and wicked grin.

"I'll take you back, for a price."

Molly didn't back away, didn't even flinch. "What price do you ask?"

"A kiss," Wolf said, already leaning toward her.

It was a price she was more than willing to pay, and Molly lifted her face to meet the mouth that descended slowly toward hers.

Wolf's lips were soft and warm, and molded to hers instantly. Molly closed her eyes and drank it in, savored the heady sensation that washed over her as Wolf moved his mouth against hers.

Wolf's hands were at her back, and Molly allowed her bouquet to fall to the ground as she wrapped her arms around his waist. To keep from falling, she told herself. To keep her suddenly weak knees from buckling beneath her.

He parted her lips with his tongue, moaned against her, into her with a shared breath, and Molly was lost. Completely, totally, magnificently lost.

His tongue brushed lightly against hers, and the most unexpected bursts of pleasure shot through her. Her breath caught in her throat with a muffled cry that Wolf responded to by deepening the kiss.

When Wolf took his mouth from her, Molly protested softly. She wasn't ready for the kiss to end. It was too soon. But Wolf didn't release her. He lowered his lips to her neck, forcing her head to fall back gently. This was as bright and unexpected a sensation as the kiss, his gently moving mouth against her skin. Slowly, he trailed his mouth up to her ear, where she felt a little nip.

"Wolf?" she whispered breathlessly. "Did you just bite me?"

"Yes." His voice rumbled against her throat.

"Oh."

Wolf's mouth returned to hers, and it seemed so natural to meld her lips to his, to rock forward so that her body was against his.

"You know what I want, don't you, Red?" Wolf whispered, his mouth still touching hers.

"No," she breathed. It was a lie, and she recognized it as the breath left her lips. "Yes," she amended quickly, dropping her arms and backing away a single step. Wolf didn't try to hold her, but let his hands fall from her back. "I can't."

Wolf gave her a smile, a grin no doubt meant to soothe her fears. But there was nothing soothing about that grin. Nothing reassuring about the white teeth he had nipped her with, or the wicked curve of his mouth.

"Of course you can." His voice rumbled. "Life's a lot more fun when you forget the rules." He captured her hand and pulled her back into his arms. "Say it Red. To hell with the rules. All the real fun is off the path."

"I can't."

Wolf tried to change her mind with a kiss that made the ground beneath her feet tilt and her head spin. Molly held on, gripped his shirt with both hands and clung to him.

"I can't," she whispered again when he slipped his mouth from hers and to her throat. "Wolf, don't . . ."

With that plea he lifted his face from her throat and met her gaze. "I want you, Red."

Molly took a deep breath. She couldn't tell him that she wanted him, too, that she wanted something she could never have. A man like Wolf would never understand that to her there were more important considerations than what she wanted from the moment. She didn't think she could make him understand, but perhaps she should try.

"I don't have much," she said, reaching up to smooth back that errant strand of black hair that brushed his forehead.

Wolf held her, but lightly, and he narrowed his eyes.

"No dowry, no family land but the parcel my mother's little house sits upon."

"I don't care—."

"Hush." Molly laid two fingers over his lips. She wondered if her own lips were swollen and red as his were. "Listen, for a moment."

He took her wrist, kissed the palm of her hand, but said nothing.

"One day I want to marry, and all I have to offer my husband is my virtue. I've never even kissed a man until today . . ."

"I'll give you a dowry," Wolf offered huskily. "I'll buy you an estate of your own . . ."

"No." Molly pulled away, indignant at his vile suggestion. "You can't buy me."

Linda Jones

He glared at her through narrowed eyes, and the lips that had been so soft and warm moments ago looked hard and unforgiving. "I suppose that would qualify as ill-gotten goods."

"Of course." Molly turned her back to Wolf, and faced the forest. She couldn't look into his face and be certain that he didn't see with those piercing eyes how she was tempted, not by his offer of a dowry or an estate, but by the memory of that kiss. "Will you take me back now? I paid your price."

He grumbled angrily at her back. What if he refused to take her back to the path? It might take her hours to wind through the woods until she found the road or the footpath. Her basket was sitting there at the edge of the path, where she'd left it without a second thought to follow Wolf, and Grandma was waiting.

"Follow me," Wolf grumbled as he passed her, his long strides carrying him from the sunlight and into the woods. Molly had to run to keep up with him, for this time he didn't hold her hand or move at a leisurely pace.

She held her cloak off the ground and ran to keep up with Wolf until she was breathless. He didn't look back, not as he knocked low branches aside, not even as he made sharp turns that threatened to take him from her sight.

The kiss she had wanted so badly had come at a price. She should have known that Wolf would not be satisfied with something so simple and beautiful as a kiss. She should have known what he wanted when he'd offered his hand to her and invited her to leave the path. He wanted more. And Wolf Trevelyan was undoubtedly a man accustomed to getting what he wanted.

Soon they were back on the path, there where she'd left the basket. She was breathless, but Wolf seemed unaffected by the vigorous walk through the forest.

Molly leaned against the trunk of a tall tree, the basket at her feet. She had to catch her breath before she could continue. Surely Wolf would disappear without another word, angry and sullen, disappointed. He didn't seem like a man who was accustomed to disappointment, but rather one who got what he wanted. Always.

She never should have followed him into the forest, she never should have left the path. She was unaccustomed to the feelings that continued to well up inside her. Longing. Emptiness. Disappointment. Frustration. The sense of something important left unfinished.

Wolf Trevelyan would have no patience with disappointment and frustration, and she expected him to disappear into the woods without so much as a word.

But he planted himself in front of her, his body close to hers. Strong fingers gripped her chin, and he lifted her face so that she was forced to look into his eyes. He kissed her again, a soft kiss that made her insides whirl.

"We're not finished, Red," he whispered as he brushed his lips across hers.

Molly ducked down and escaped quickly, grabbing the basket and setting off on the path. She didn't tell Wolf, couldn't tell him, that it *was* finished.

She had wondered what it would feel like to be kissed, and now she knew. Her curiosity had led her from the path in more ways than one, but it could go no further.

Wolf Trevelyan would never marry a girl like her. He had money and social standing and could have any rich, beautiful woman he wanted. New York City was full of socialites who would make a suitable wife for a man in his position.

And no matter how much she wanted it, she wouldn't give herself to any man but her husband. Her virtue was all she had to offer.

Despite her resolve not to, she glanced over her shoulder to see that Wolf remained on the path, watching her. Legs spread and arms crossed over his chest, he looked as formidable from a distance as he did up close.

Grandma had been right all along. Wolf Trevelyan was a dangerous man.

That red cape danced down the path, and Wolf didn't take his eyes off of Molly once, not even when she glanced over her shoulder as if she were afraid he was giving chase.

He wanted to. Surely she knew that.

Now she was afraid of him. Not for rumors of the past, but because he'd awakened something in her she didn't understand.

Passion. It was in her kiss, in her eyes, an intriguing mix with the innocence that was always there.

No woman had ever spoken to him of virtue before. Of course, the women he knew were unlikely to be acquainted with morality, and he doubted any of them remembered what it was like to be a virgin.

Molly Kincaid wasn't his type, damn her, so why did he want her so hard it hurt?

Wolf stood in the center of the path long after Molly had disappeared, until he could no longer see even a hint of her red cloak through the trees.

There was nothing like this forest in New York. A park, no matter how vast, couldn't be compared to the real thing. There was beauty and peace here, something he rarely sensed anywhere else.

Perhaps because he didn't allow himself the luxury of peace, and what beauty he recognized was man-made, such as: the bracelet Molly had refused, fine architecture or art, a woman whose beauty was enhanced by an expensive gown and hours in front of a mirror.

In trying to explain away his obsession, Wolf associated Molly with this forest. She was real. Everything about her was natural—her beauty, her honesty, her innocence.

Escape. When he returned to Vanora Point that feeling of flight was always there. When he felt he could no longer stand the structure of his life, when he found himself in the gym four or five times a week, this was the sanctuary he sought.

Molly had made herself a part of this sanctuary, against his will, against her will.

Wolf stepped off the path, headed away from Molly and for the road to Vanora Point. He forced his way past low branches and stepped on and over low growing bushes, crushing leaves and flowers as he went, heedless of the beauty he had admired moments before.

Molly snuggled deep under the covers, hiding her face. Her mother had easily accepted her explanation of a headache for her sullen mood, and they'd both gone to bed early.

If only she'd listened to her mother and stayed on the road, then she never would have met Wolf, and she wouldn't be lying here, wide awake and feeling absolutely tortured. This was her punishment for not obeying her mother's strict order.

And punishment it was.

Why had she bothered to wonder if she loved this man she barely knew? It made no difference. She could love him as no woman had ever loved a man, and it would change nothing.

He was Wolf Trevelyan. Rich. Powerful. Well educated. Even if he didn't have a sensational reputation, this would be forbidden.

The most Molly could hope for was a fisherman like Stella's Wallace, or perhaps a merchant. Men like Wolf Trevelyan just didn't marry women like Molly Kincaid.

The heavy blanket didn't keep her warm enough, even though the night was mild.

Tonight there would be more dreams of Wolf, and they would most certainly be more intense than ever, after the kiss and the way he'd held her. She wasn't sure if she looked forward to the night ahead or dreaded it.

Big Bad Wolf

Molly squeezed her eyes tightly shut. Somehow, she had to get some sleep. Dreams or no dreams, she couldn't lie awake all night and envision what she couldn't have.

It didn't come easily, but eventually Molly drifted off to sleep. Her last conscious thought was—I should have stayed on the road.

Chapter Five

Wolf stood at the tall window as the sun set, his back to the study that had been his father's and was now his. The mahogany desk, the wall of books, the burgundy leather. Wolf didn't have to turn to study the room. It was ingrained in his mind.

Nothing in this house had changed in more than twenty years, since his mother's death. A portrait of Vanora Trevelyan hung in the parlor that had been her favorite room. When he remembered her, it was in that room with its pastel colors and opened windows. She had spent so much time in the parlor, declaring the rest of the house too dark for her tastes.

Wolf was ten when his father called him into this study to tell him that his mother was dead.

Just like that. There was no softening of the blow, no words of comfort. It wasn't that Penn Trevelyan hadn't cared for his wife. He'd loved her dearly, and in the years after her death he never even considered marrying again. He just wasn't what you would call a loving man, a man who would think to make a mother's death easier for her only child.

Wolf had known that his mother was sick. He was instructed not to bother her when she was not feeling well, which was often. During those days or weeks he had to tiptoe through the house, or else face his father's anger.

He expected that her illness would pass, as it always did, even though her spells in bed were becoming longer and longer. When she was well, the house would again be a lively place, filled with her laughter and a mother's love.

But she didn't get better, and Wolf was left with a father who knew nothing about raising a child. Penn Trevelyan mourned his wife, and left his only son's care to a succession of governesses.

All Wolf remembered of his father during those childhood years was his unbending intolerance. You met Penn Trevelyan's expectations or you suffered the consequences. That intolerance included everyone, even a child and the governesses who were dismissed regularly, usually just as Wolf was beginning to like them.

It didn't take Wolf long to decide that perhaps if he didn't like them, his father would allow them to stay for more than a month or two. He became as difficult a child, he imagined, as his father was dictatorial. The governesses continued to come and go on a regular basis. This nightmare continued until Wolf was old enough to go away to school.

Those years away had been somewhat more tolerable, but by the time Wolf returned home, his father was dying. An assurance of death didn't soften the old man one bit, but only made him more determined to see his empire established. That meant Wolf's marriage to Jeanne Rutledge, a quick heir to assure the continuation of the Trevelyan name and to assure that Wolf settled down to his responsibilities.

The disaster of his son's wedding night had pushed Penn Trevelyan over the edge, and less than three months later he passed away in his sleep.

Wolf was left with the flourishing shipping business, to which he had added in the last five years lumber, a saw mill, even a steel mill he'd recently acquired. It was all organized so well, managed so efficiently, that Wolf often found himself in times like these, with nothing pressing keeping him in New York.

And he returned here, subjecting himself to a sort of penance. He should have sold the big house years ago, and established a permanent residence in New York City. There was nothing to keep him here, and still he occasionally felt the undeniable call to return.

"Sir?"

Wolf turned to find Larkin standing just inside the doorway.

"Cook asked me to inform you that dinner will be on the table in half an hour."

Wolf nodded, and Larkin retreated into the hallway, face remaining forward, chin tilted up. Wolf had never seen the butler's back, that he could remember.

"Larkin," Wolf stopped the butler with a lifted hand. "You are acquainted with many of the residents of Kingsport, are you not?"

"Yes, sir," Larkin said as he stepped back into the study.

"Do you know a family by the name of Kincaid?"

If Larkin were surprised to be asked this question, or any question at all, he didn't show it. "There's a Mary Kincaid, sir, and her mother-in-law, Nelda Kincaid, who lives just outside town. They're both widowed."

The omission of Molly was significant, in Wolf's mind. Was Larkin trying to protect another young Kingsport maid from Wolf Trevelyan?

"How do they make their way?"

Larkin's face revealed nothing, not a spark of interest, but he hesitated before answering. "Mary Kincaid bakes bread. We've bought some from her on occasion. She also takes in laundry from a number of the unmarried fishermen, and does a bit of seamstress work as well."

"Sounds like a lot of work just to get by," Wolf muttered.

"I believe it is, sir," Larkin observed coldly. "Will there be anything else, sir?"

Wolf considered letting the man off easily, dismissing him and ending it here, but not for long.

"What about the girl?" Wolf asked sharply. "Molly Kincaid?"

Again Larkin was stone-like. Emotionless. "I do not know her personally, sir. She seems a nice young lady."

There was just a touch of censure in Larkin's voice. Everyone knew that 'nice young ladies' were not for Wolf Trevelyan.

"Does she have a suitor, Larkin?" Wolf persisted. "A nice young man?"

Larkin's eyes were dead. "I don't believe so, sir. She spends all of her time helping her mother."

"How noble," Wolf muttered under his breath.

"Yes, sir," Larkin replied. "Will there be anything else, sir?"

What did the old man expect? That Wolf would demand that he bring the virgin forth for sacrifice?

Wolf had no illusions about his place in this household. The servants in his own house liked him no better than the people of Kingsport. They tolerated his occasional presence because it was infrequent, and because he paid them exceptionally well. Everyone had a price.

At the moment, Wolf could believe that Larkin more than disliked his employer. Perhaps detest was a better description. No wonder the old man never showed Wolf his back.

"No," Wolf snapped. "There's nothing else. I expect you'll keep this conversation to yourself, Larkin."

"Yes, sir."

Larkin backed out of the room, and Wolf didn't

turn back to the window until the old man was gone and the door was closed.

He'd do well not to show the butler *his* back.

The sun warmed her, but Molly missed the cool comfort of the woods. She missed the tall trees, the sense of passing through a special place.

But she couldn't chance meeting Wolf again, and she knew he would be waiting. Waiting with another kiss, and with a request she would find harder and harder to refuse if he persisted.

She'd dreamed of him last night, after tossing and turning on her narrow bed for so long. She'd dreamed of the kiss and the passion in his eyes and had awakened wanting something she couldn't name. Something to ease the ache in her heart.

Wolf Trevelyan never stayed at Vanora Point for very long. A few days, a week or so, and then he was gone again. From everything she'd heard he didn't visit his family home more than two or three times a year.

Which meant that he would soon be gone. Back to New York City and out of her life. She couldn't allow what she felt for Wolf to be anything more than it was. A passing fancy, a fascination.

There would be no more shortcuts through the woods until he'd returned to New York.

Grandma was waiting, and Molly gave her a wide smile. She looked better every day. The cold spring had passed, and the longer, warmer days seemed to agree with the older woman. Today there was even a spot of color in Grandma's cheeks.

"You're awfully quiet today," Grandma said as she finished her meal. "Are you ill?"

"No, of course not." Molly tried to give her grandmother a reassuring smile, but judging by the frown she received in return, she failed miserably.

"You were quiet yesterday, too," Grandma observed. "Too quiet. No more questions about love and marriage?"

"No. That was just a . . . a passing fancy."

Grandma nodded, but Molly didn't think for a moment that her explanation was believed. "A passing fancy," Grandma repeated wisely. "And just what was this passing fancy's name?"

Molly sat on the hearth near her grandmother's rocking chair, and hugged her knees to her chest. It was a poor substitute for Wolf's warm body, but it would have to do. "Do you remember when I told you, a few days ago, that I met Wolf Trevelyan in the woods?"

"Saints preserve us," Grandma muttered.

Molly cut her eyes up to watch her grandmother's disapproving face. "That's what you said when I told you the first time. I didn't want to worry you, but I've been taking the shortcut against your advice, and every day he's been there."

"Did he hurt you, child?" Grandma whispered.

"No. He was very nice." Wolf was many things, but nice was not one of them. There just wasn't another word to describe the man, without alarming Grandma. "It's just that I think I'm falling in love with him, and I know nothing can ever come of it."

Grandma sighed deeply. "You must stay away from him."

"Today I walked the road." Molly rested her chin on her knees.

"Good," Grandma said energetically.

"And I will stay on the road until he leaves again." The certainty in her voice was for her sake, as well as Grandma's.

"Good."

"I can't . . ." Molly sighed. "I can't love him, can I?" She knew this fascination with Wolf was hopeless, but saying so aloud hurt.

"No, child, I'm afraid you can't."

Grandma sounded as if she understood, as if she felt sorrow for Molly rather than anger.

They tried to talk of normal, everyday happenings in Kingsport. Molly always kept her grandmother apprised of the latest gossip. She'd already shared the news about Stella's baby, and was sharing her theory that perhaps Mr. Hanson was sweet on Mary Kincaid when the knock came, hard and insistent at the front door.

Molly jumped up to answer, and Grandma was right behind her as she threw open the door.

She'd never seen Wolf looking so savage. His eyes were narrowed, and his mouth was hard, and his hands were balled fists. He seemed to tower over her, even though she knew he hadn't grown taller in the day that had passed since he'd kissed her.

Before either of them could speak, Grandma

rushed past Molly and raised her cane. She smacked Wolf once, twice, three times across the chest, driving him back and away from the door.

"Stay away from my granddaughter, you beast."

Wolf raised his hands to ward off the blows that continued, as Grandma followed him into the yard, flailing her cane in his direction, occasionally striking a solid swat. Finally, he tired of the unending attack, and reached out to take the cane in one hand.

Grandma maintained her grip on the handle, while Wolf clutched the end and turned his eyes to Molly.

"This is your sickly grandmother?"

"I'm not sickly, you animal." Grandma tried to wrest the cane from Wolf's grasp, but her struggle was futile and short-lived.

"I can see that," Wolf said through clenched teeth. "Listen, I only want to talk to Molly—"

"No," Grandma interrupted.

"Just for a few minutes . . ."

"Over my dead body."

Molly stepped away from the doorway. "It's all right, Grandma. This won't take long."

Somehow she would have to be strong and tell Wolf that she couldn't see him again, ever. That she couldn't give him what he wanted.

Wolf cautiously released Grandma's cane, watching for another assault that didn't come. He didn't say anything until the old woman was in the house and the front door was closed.

"If I'd known you weren't taking the footpath today, I would have gotten here before you and locked the old witch in the pantry," he grumbled.

She would have smiled, if there hadn't been a touch of truth in his voice. "Wolf, I can't—"

"Hear me out," he insisted, planting himself before her with his arms crossed over his chest. "I have a proposition for you."

Molly felt the blood drain from her face. He was going to try to buy her again, try to make her his mistress for a short while. "Don't," she whispered.

He ignored her plea. "I know your mother relies on you, and I'm not a complete brute, in spite of what your grandmother seems to think. Here's what I'm willing to offer you. A life-long yearly stipend for your mother. Irrevocable and substantial enough so that she'll never have to bake a loaf of bread if she doesn't want to, and she'll certainly not be doing laundry."

"Wolf . . ."

He continued to ignore her. "For your *lovely* grandmother, a paid, live-in companion, if we can find one who'll take the job. She'll have everything she wants and needs for the rest of her days, including the best medical care."

It was the most horrible kind of blackmail. He promised nothing to her, but to provide for the two people in the world she loved the most.

"I'm not . . . Do you think I have no . . . How could you do this to me?"

He raised his eyebrows in an annoyingly superior way. "It's a perfectly agreeable arrangement for everyone, Red."

"Not to me."

Wolf looked as if he couldn't believe she would

refuse him. He was trying to hold his irritation in check, but Molly could see it in his eyes and in the unnatural tenseness in his stance. "It's not as though you'll be bothered with me on a permanent basis. I'm at Vanora Point, two, maybe three times a year. Most of the time you'll have the place to yourself."

"I'll not be a kept woman," Molly insisted. "I thought I made that clear—"

"You made it clear I haven't yet offered your price."

"Wolf, don't . . ."

"It's just business, Red," he said with a smile. "Why don't we finish with this game, and you can tell me exactly what it will take."

"For me to be your . . . ?"

"Mistress," he finished the sentence she couldn't, with a cold and calculating gleam in his eyes.

She couldn't even say it, much less agree to his proposal. "Go away, Wolf," she said softly.

"Afraid?" he challenged. "If it makes you feel any better, I've kept a number of mistresses over the years. Not at Vanora Point, of course, but you'll be happy to know they're all alive and well. Even those I parted with on less than friendly terms."

"I'm not afraid," Molly whispered.

"No," he conceded. "You never were, were you?"

Molly shook her head slightly. It was true, she had never been afraid of Wolf. In fact, the more time she spent with him the more she knew the stories had to be false. That didn't mean she would consent to be his mistress.

Wolf stopped pacing, planted his feet in Grandma's front yard, and stared at her intently. She remembered the dream she'd had last night, the demanding kiss, the love she'd tried to deny.

"What do you want, Red?" he asked in a low voice.

Should she tell him? He would laugh at her if she confided that all she'd ever dreamed of was a husband who would love her. Children, and lots of them. She was an only child, and she'd missed having brothers and sisters. There was nothing in her dreams about living in a big house and waiting for the man she loved to pay her a visit.

"I want you to go away," she said softly. "Go back to New York, where you belong."

"I don't belong there anymore than I belong here, Red. Scandal doesn't stop at the state line, and I've broken far too many of your precious rules in my lifetime."

"Then why don't you tell the truth about what happened that night." It was a bold and uncalled for suggestion, and Molly immediately wished she could take the challenge back. It had not been her intention to hurt him, but before her eyes the savage and hardened Wolf Trevelyan paled.

"What if the truth is even worse than the rumor?" he suggested, recovering quickly. "What if I told you everything you'd heard was true?"

"I wouldn't believe you."

She'd managed to shock him, or at least to surprise him. Did no one ever speak to him of that night? Was it a dark, unspoken blight in his life?

Linda Jones

"There's nothing I can say to change your mind?" He ignored her soft assertion, her insistence that she didn't believe the rumors. "I promise you, Red, you wouldn't regret it."

"I would."

She waited for Wolf to try again to convince her. If he came toward her, if he touched her, it would be hard to say no. Another kiss and she might actually consider . . .

Wolf began to pace, in the shadow of Grandma's trees. He ran his long fingers through normally neat strands of hair, and while his attention was on the ground Molly almost smiled. It was true that there was nothing beautiful about Wolf Trevelyan, but there was something elegant about his harsh features and the way he moved his large body, with a grace that shouldn't come naturally to such a large man.

To see him disconcerted was like watching a fish out of water. Had no one ever said no to Wolf before? Had he come here actually expecting her to agree to his outrageous suggestion?

"There must be something you want," he said, stopping suddenly and turning to face her. "You want your own house? Is that it? You don't have to live at Vanora Point if you don't want to. I'll buy you a house in town, and you can stay at Vanora Point only when I'm there."

"Just what I've always dreamed of," Molly said softly. "To be the town whore."

Her choice of words shocked him, and he raised those black eyebrows rakishly.

"What?" she continued. "Would you really think

of me any differently? And what would I do when you were finished with me, Wolf? I suppose there would be another man in town who would eventually take your place, and when he tired of me there would be another, and another—."

"It wouldn't be like that," he protested.

"It won't be. I won't allow it."

At last he threw his hands into the air and walked away from her, taking the path that wound into the woods. Before he'd disappeared completely, Grandma opened the door.

"I was keeping an eye on him the whole time," she spat. "If he'd taken a step toward you I would have been here to defend you in a flash." Grandma waved her cane before her.

Molly led her grandmother back into the house, wondering what she could possibly say to explain away Wolf's visit. She got the old woman seated, and knelt at her feet.

"Grandma," Molly placed a hand at her grandmother's knee. "You worry entirely too much. I think you were much too rough with poor Wolf."

"Poor Wolf," Grandma scoffed. "Ha. I hope you put him in his place."

"I did. He won't be back."

"Good." Grandma nodded her head with satisfaction. "You're much too sweet to be exposed to a man the likes of Wolf Trevelyan."

Molly didn't agree, not entirely. Beneath his cynicism, there was a tender man. Beneath his chill, there beat a real heart. She'd felt it, for a moment. She'd seen it, in the pulse at his throat.

Beneath his brutal appearance there was

89

beauty. She saw it in his eyes, in his rare, true smiles.

But she didn't think he saw that beauty in himself. He probably hadn't noted it for a very long time.

And she would never get the chance to show him that beauty. What he asked of her was too much. More than she was willing to give, even to Wolf.

"Molly!"

Molly had been so lost in her own thoughts she hadn't even seen or heard her friends approaching, until Hannah shouted her name to gain her attention.

Stella carried Wally on her hip, and she looked much better. Fresher, smiling, her hair braided and her apron clean. Hannah was, as always, beautiful. Her blond hair was straight and soft, and she usually wore it hanging unrestrained down her back. Half the eligible men in town were courting or attempting to court Hannah, but no one had stolen her heart yet, and Hannah had declared she would settle for nothing less.

"Come to my house for cake and tea," Stella insisted. Wally reached out his fat, short arms to Molly and she gathered him as he all but jumped from Stella's arms to her own. "I feel so much better, and I want to thank you for everything you did."

"I didn't do anything," Molly said, making a face at the baby.

"Guess what I heard," Hannah said with a conspiratorial lilt in her voice.

They walked toward Stella's house, Molly sandwiched between her friends. She didn't have much time to spare, but perhaps a half hour or so wouldn't hurt.

Stella rolled her eyes. "What have you heard now?"

Hannah was unperturbed by Stella's lack of enthusiasm. "Wolf Trevelyan is at Vanora Point," she revealed with great pleasure.

Molly held onto Wally just a bit tighter, and made another face. "Well, it is his house, after all," she said defensively. "He has every right to be there."

Stella clucked. "You're entirely too polite. The man should have been hanged seven years ago. He shouldn't have any rights at all."

"I hear," Hannah whispered, "that there are mummified bodies kept on the third floor. That he brings women here from New York, murders them and hides their bodies in that creepy house."

Molly laughed, shocking both her friends. Wally decided to laugh with her.

"That's ridiculous. Surely you don't believe such a preposterous story." A quick glance at her friends told Molly that they did believe such nonsense.

"I saw him, once," Stella said as they reached her house and she swung open the door. "Right after it happened."

They all knew what *it* was, and they had all heard about the one time Stella caught a glimpse of Wolf Trevelyan.

"He came to town, riding the biggest black horse I have ever seen." Stella's voice always took on a hint of mystery when she told this story. Molly hadn't heard it in a while, and she wanted to hear the details again, now that she had a face to put with the man.

"I thought he was the devil," Stella whispered.

"Ridiculous," Molly whispered as they walked into the kitchen, unable to remain silent. "You were, what, fourteen years old?"

"Fifteen," she corrected.

"It's not fair," Hannah complained. "Molly and I didn't get even a glimpse."

Stella laid out three mismatched tea cups, and put on water to boil. "They threw stones, you know," Stella continued.

Molly had forgotten this part. It had been years since Stella had told the story, and she had forgotten about the stones. Her heart broke a little, for Wolf.

"How cruel."

Hannah and Stella stared at her as if she'd lost her mind.

"Well, it is." She bounced Wally on her knee, unable to sit completely still.

"He's the one who's cruel," Stella said defensively. "As he passed, he looked at me. Directly into my eyes like he was putting a spell on me or something. I swear, I shivered to my toes, and I almost fainted. I couldn't sleep for a week."

"Last time you told this story you said you had trouble getting to sleep that night," Molly said.

Hannah and Stella stared at her, and Molly

Big Bad Wolf

knew she should have kept her mouth shut.

Now that Stella had begun her story, Molly remembered. The gigantic black horse, the stare, the stones. "You threw a stone at him, didn't you?"

Stella nodded, not at all ashamed. "After he passed. Hit him squarely in the back."

Molly bounced Wally ferociously on her knee, and decided it was safer to look at the baby than at her friends.

She could never confide to them that she had fallen in love with Wolf Trevelyan. That he was no monster, but a passionate if, perhaps, impatient man.

Hannah stood to help Stella prepare their tea, and Molly placed her cheek against the top of Wally's head. "You'll keep our secret, won't you?" she whispered softly.

Wally answered her by throwing his chubby arms around her neck and squealing into her ear.

She took that as a yes.

Chapter Six

Wolf paced, his eyes on the floor, his brandy forgotten. This was a wrinkle he hadn't expected.

She'd said no.

Frail women had never taken to him easily, but Molly was no delicate flower. She was a woman who faced him without hesitation, who kissed him with passion. She did want him, and he knew it with every fiber of his being.

She wanted more. The revelation stopped him, and he lifted his head to find that Larkin watched him silently from the open door of the study.

"What do *you* want?" he snapped.

Larkin didn't flinch, didn't even blink. "Will you be dining this evening?"

How long had it been since Larkin had first informed him that the evening meal was served? An hour? Two? Wolf didn't remember and didn't care.

"No."

"Very good, sir," Larkin said, backing away from the door.

Wolf refilled his brandy glass, and resumed pacing. He couldn't stand still, had no appetite, and all because a simple country girl denied him.

It made no sense at all to allow an insignificant refusal to eat at him like this. Women had refused him before, and he'd turned away from them without a second thought. For every woman who rejected him because he was Wolf Trevelyan, or because they disapproved of his life-style, or because he wasn't pretty enough, there were three more willing to take her place.

New York was filled with willing women. "Larkin!" Wolf bellowed, and in seconds the butler appeared. Wolf emptied his glass, downing the brandy in one swallow. "Pack my bags," he said as he set the empty glass on his desk. "I'll be leaving tomorrow morning."

"Very good, sir." Larkin bowed crisply.

Wolf felt somewhat better, once the decision was made. His apparent obsession with Molly Kincaid was due entirely, he was certain, to boredom. He was tired of drinking alone, of playing solitaire. Bored with Vanora Point. Maybe it was time to sell this cursed place.

Calming himself, Wolf sat at his desk and took a deck of cards from the top drawer. He often thought that if circumstances had been different, he could have made a good living as a gambler.

He shuffled the deck absently, allowing the cards to fly through his fingers with a deftness that came from years of practice, and then, rather than spread the familiar game of solitaire, he fanned the cards across the desk, face down.

Molly had good luck, just as he normally did. When she'd fanned the cards across the blanket and ruined his third stacked hand, she'd beaten him fairly. He wished, too late, that he'd taken the top card and claimed his prize. A single kiss. The stray thought angered him. Why was she still on his mind?

Unable to wipe Molly from his thoughts completely, Wolf dragged his fingers across the cards, as she had that day. His fingertips barely brushed the edge of each card, and without enthusiasm he reached down and flipped over a card from the center of the deck.

The queen of hearts. The red queen. Molly Kincaid.

This was ridiculous. He still wanted her, and Wolf Trevelyan got what he wanted. Always. All he had to do was raise the ante. What would it take to sweep Molly off her sensible feet? What did she want?

When Larkin appeared again, Wolf was still staring at the red queen.

"Your bags are packed, sir. I laid out a suit of traveling clothes, the gray, and—"

"I changed my mind," Wolf said, "I won't be leaving tomorrow after all."

Larkin took a deep breath and exhaled slowly. "Very good, sir."

Big Bad Wolf

They'd barely begun the morning's baking when the knock came, surprising Molly and her mother. No one called this early.

Molly wiped her hands on her apron as she went to answer the insistent knock. It sounded as if someone were kicking at the door.

The boy who stood there was a stranger to her, and he juggled several packages in his hands. He had, indeed, been kicking at the door.

"Are you Molly Kincaid?" he asked as a small package toppled from the top. Molly caught it before it hit the floor.

"Yes. What is all this?"

"Mr. Trevelyan asked me to deliver these to you, with his best wishes, miss." He peeked over the top of the packages, and Molly realized that even though he was tall, he was just a boy.

"Take them back," Molly said, placing the small package she had caught back on top of the pile of plainly wrapped boxes. "And tell Mr. Trevelyan that I don't want or need his gifts."

Through an opening in the pile of boxes, Molly saw the boy's face turn red. "I can't do that, miss. He'll . . . he'll kill me if I fail him in this, I know he will."

"Don't be ridiculous," she murmured as she began to close the door.

"But, but," the boy placed his foot in the doorway so Molly couldn't shut him out. "Don't you even want to know what's in these boxes? I mean, aren't you just a little bit curious?"

Her curiosity had already gotten her into a predicament.

"No." Molly shoved his foot out of the way with her own, and closed the door. She hadn't even turned around when she heard the packages hitting the ground. One, and then another, and then the lot of them.

She smiled, pleased with herself, until she found herself face to face with her mother.

"What was that about?"

"Nothing," Molly said lightly, stepping quickly around her mother. "Some young man was trying to make a delivery, but he had the wrong house."

"Did I hear him mention the name Trevelyan?" Funny, how Mary Kincaid's voice lowered to a whisper when she spoke Wolf's family name.

"Yes, I believe so," Molly said as if she couldn't quite remember. "Shall we get back to work?"

Even though her mother knew nothing of Molly's meetings with Wolf, just the mention of his name sent her into a tirade. "That man shouldn't be allowed to walk free, after what he did."

"You really don't know what happened." Molly tried to keep her voice light, casual. It wouldn't do for her to defend Wolf to her mother. Hannah and Stella might let it pass, but not Mary Kincaid. "It might have been a tragic accident, for all we know."

"What was Jeanne Rutledge doing on the cliff in the middle of the night, and in her nightdress?" Mary hissed. "It was no accident that took her to that cliff and over the edge, and the only reason it was ruled a misadventure was because Penn Trevelyan bought and paid for the investigators who ruled on Jeanne's death. He protected his only child with his money. That's not justice, that's the worst kind of injustice."

"I still say it had to be, that it could have been, an accident," Molly continued as she kneaded a mound of bread dough on the square kitchen table. Even when Wolf had glared at her as if he'd wanted to eat her alive, she hadn't been afraid. She couldn't believe he had violence like that in his heart. "No one actually saw what happened."

Mary snorted, very unattractively. "It was no accident," she insisted. "What happened at that house was a terrible tragedy. Wolf Trevelyan might have gotten away with murder, but the people of Kingsport will never forget Jeanne and what happened to her. That *man* doesn't dare to show his face here."

"It's no wonder he never comes to town," Molly mused absently.

"We don't want his kind here," Mary insisted. "And we've made it very clear to that man." When she lifted her face, her stern expression faded. "You've a kind heart, Molly, but I'm afraid that there are those in this world who would take advantage of such kindness. You should have no sympathy in your heart for Wolf Trevelyan."

It wasn't sympathy that made her heart pound, she was quite certain.

The gifts continued to come, for two more days, and Molly continued to send them back, unopened. Apparently Wolf had not killed the boy who continued to fail in his attempts, though he seemed more and more certain every day that when he returned to Vanora Point with the gifts, that would surely happen.

Molly was able to meet and get rid of the delivery boy without arousing her mother's suspicions, looking for him early in the morning and meeting him outside the small house she shared with her mother, but if Wolf persisted, Mary Kincaid was bound to learn the truth.

The sun was warm, so warm that Molly had left the house without her red cape. She needed it in the shade of the forest, but not here on the road where the sun shone fully. If only Wolf Trevelyan would return to New York where he belonged so she could return to her daily routine! She missed the cool forest, the sense of magic, but she also realized she'd never again walk the footpath to Grandma's house without thinking of Wolf.

She had the road to herself today, and walked down the middle of it swinging her basket. Even Grandma didn't know about the gifts Wolf tried to buy her with. If she did, she'd likely make her way to Vanora Point and lash out at Wolf with her cane again.

The picture in her mind caused a smile to creep across her face. He was supposedly such a bad man, such an ogre, but he had taken Grandma's abuse without so much as a cross word.

Well, he had, in a way, threatened to lock Grandma in the pantry, but she was sure it was an empty threat. And he had called the dear old woman a witch, but she was sure he didn't mean it.

She heard the horse approaching from behind, and moved to the side of the road without looking back. This was a frequently used route, leading inland, but this was the first time all day she'd had to share the road. Soon she'd be at Grandma's house. She'd passed the more infrequently used road that led to Vanora Point and the Trevelyan house with no more than a quick and barely interested glimpse, and she'd covered quite a bit of distance since then.

Molly waited for the horse to pass, but instead the sound of hoofbeats in the dirt slowed and then stopped all together, and behind her booted feet thudded against the road.

She knew what she would see, even before she glanced over her shoulder.

Wolf was almost upon her, and he led a tall black stallion by the reins. "By God," he said without preamble. "You are a stubborn woman."

"Me?" Molly didn't slow her step. She didn't have time to spend conversing with Wolf when she was walking the longer route to her grandmother's house. "It seems to me that you're the stubborn one. Don't you ever give up?"

"No," he growled. "I don't."

Wolf walked beside her, and she couldn't take steps long enough or fast enough to leave him behind. "Poor Willie, he thinks you're going to kill him."

"Who's Willie?"

Molly glanced at Wolf. He scowled, but she answered him with a smile. "The young man who tries to deliver the packages you so persistently send."

"The stable boy," Wolf clarified.

"I asked him, that second morning, what his name was. It's much easier to argue with someone if you know what his name is, Wolf."

He sighed, muttered something under his breath that could have been a curse, and kicked up pebbles and dirt. "I have a proposition for you, Red."

"I thought I made it clear—"

"Just listen for a minute," he snapped, reaching out to capture her wrist and bring their progress to a halt.

Molly looked up into Wolf's face. His earlier anger was gone, replaced by a cold apathy.

"One of our short conversations has made me reconsider my current status. When you refused my mother's bracelet, in part because it was a family heirloom, I told you I was the last of the Trevelyans." The sun touched his black hair and a portion of his face, but his eyes were in shadow, and Molly could see no hint of his emotions there. "I suppose I haven't thought about that much in the past, but I do have an obligation to carry on the family name."

"Wolf, please." Molly tried to pull her hand from his grasp, but he wouldn't let go.

"I have what's considered a small but growing fortune. An estate, a flourishing and expanding business. Surely I need someone to leave it all to when I'm gone."

Molly tugged gently, trying to free herself, but Wolf held tight. She looked at his chest, because she couldn't bear to look into those cold eyes right now.

"I'm asking you to marry me, Red," he snapped. "Isn't that what you want?"

Molly stopped struggling. "Marriage? You're teasing me, Wolf, and it's not fair." She knew a man of Wolf's status would never marry someone like her.

"I'm perfectly serious."

When he was this close her heart beat furiously, and it was difficult to think clearly.

"Think of it as a business arrangement," he continued. "I'll provide for your mother and your grandmother, just as I offered, and you'll give me heirs."

She made herself look at his face, and she searched for a hint of emotion. There was none.

"Why me?"

His grip tightened slightly, and a look of pure impatience crossed his face. Had he expected that she would accept his offer without question, that she would fall at his feet in gratitude? If that were true, he didn't know her at all.

"There are several valid reasons, actually. You have a good nature, and I have no wish to be saddled with a demanding woman."

"That would be unfortunate," Molly said dryly.

"Yes." Wolf narrowed his eyes. "There are other advantages as well, of course. When I'm in New York to take care of business, the society mamas who have been trying of late to foist their little girls on me will have no more reason to harass me."

"I see."

"You can stay at Vanora Point with the children when they come, and I will continue as I have for the past seven years, dividing my time between Maine and New York."

Molly took a deep breath. "You have this all thought out, but it seems any number of women would suit your stated purpose." What did she want? A declaration of love? She knew that wouldn't happen, but there had to be something more than this.

Wolf dropped her wrist at last, and backed up a single step. He stared at her so hard she trembled, and she remembered the demanding kiss by the stream deep in the forest, the dreams of Wolf that had come to her for the past several nights. And she knew that no matter how she tried to deny it, she did love him.

"I have a sudden hankering for redheaded children," Wolf rumbled reluctantly.

Finally, Molly was able to smile. Wolf would never admit it, but he did like her, a little, and he did want her, or at least he had that day in the forest when he'd kissed her.

"Well?" he prodded impatiently. "Do you have an answer for me? I don't have time to play games, Red. I have to be back in New York in ten days."

"That's not much time . . ." Her smile died.

"Yes or no." Wolf demanded an answer.

"It sounds like a negotiation."

"Marriage is business," Wolf snapped. "It always has been."

Molly studied him silently for a long moment, wondering if there was love in his heart to be found. If it were there, it was buried deep, under years of hate and distrust.

If anyone could find it, she could.

"Yes or no." Wolf's teeth were clenched tight.

"Yes," Molly whispered.

She expected that he would move forward and kiss her, but he stood his ground. "I'll make the arrangements. We can be married at Vanora Point."

"I'll need time to have a dress made," Molly insisted. "I know exactly what I want, and Mr. McCann has everything I'll need at his store."

"Have him send me the bill," Wolf insisted. "Get whatever you want."

"I have a little money saved. I can buy my own—"

"Have Mr. McCann send me the bill, Red. Don't be difficult."

Molly smiled. "I forgot. You don't like demanding women."

"Three days," Wolf snapped, ignoring her jibe. "We'll be married at the house."

"Three days! That's not enough time!"

"It'll have to be. Invite whomever you wish, but please advise your frail and sickly grandmother to leave her weapons at home."

"I'll see what I can do," Molly promised, keeping her voice calm.

When the deal was made, Wolf was finished

Linda Jones

with her. He turned to his horse, dismissing Molly easily, and mounted without so much as a glance at her before heading back the way he'd come. So distant, so nonchalant. Molly stood and watched him ride away.

Married to Wolf Trevelyan! It didn't really matter that he was indifferent about their plans, that he rode away without a smile or a wave or a kind word. There *was* love in his heart. She knew it.

"Turn around," she whispered to herself. "Just once."

He presented a stiff back to her, and still she waited. He *did* care. If he was only interested in preserving the Trevelyan name, he could have married any of a number of more suitable women.

"Turn around," she breathed.

Just as she was about to give up on him, Wolf glanced sullenly over his shoulder.

Molly turned from him with a smile on her face. Goodness! Married to Wolf Trevelyan!

The remainder of the walk to Grandma's house flew by, as Molly's head was filled with images of her life with Wolf. Of their wedding, and the red-headed children he had a sudden hankering for.

But when she saw Grandma's house, her smile died. She was the only one who was going to be happy about this wedding.

Grandma was happy to see her, as always, and even greeted Molly with more energy that she'd been displaying lately. It was only fitting that Grandma Kincaid be the first to know.

"I have something to tell you," Molly said as she emptied the contents of the basket onto the table.

"Something very important."

When the basket was empty and sitting at her feet, Molly turned to her grandmother. "I'm getting married."

Grandma's eyes lit up, sparkled merrily. "And it's about time, child. Who's the lucky young man?"

Molly took a deep breath, preparing herself for the assault that was, no doubt, to come. "Wolf Trevelyan."

Grandma's eyes grew wide and her mouth dropped open. "Not him. Saints preserve us, tell me you're not marrying Wolf Trevelyan."

"I love him," Molly said softly.

"That's terrible." Grandma emphasized her opinion with the rap of her cane against the floor.

"I think it's wonderful."

Grandma gripped her hand tightly. "But he doesn't love you. He can't. I tell you, Molly, a man like that is incapable of love."

Was it true? Wolf had never spoken of love, but that didn't mean he would never feel the emotion.

"Well then, he needs someone to love him more than most, wouldn't you say?" Molly decided not to tell Grandma just yet about the stipend or the live-in companion. She would think that Molly was only marrying Wolf to see her family taken care of, and that wasn't the case. Not at all. "You told me, in case you don't remember, that you didn't love Grandpa when you married him, that the love came later."

"That was different," Grandma grumbled. "And don't be turning my own words back on me."

"Won't you wish us happiness?"

Grandma sighed, and the fingers that gripped Molly's hand loosened greatly. "You deserve the best of everything. Of course I wish you happiness, but you must think this over carefully. Won't you reconsider?"

"No," Molly answered with certainty. "This is what I want."

It was much more than that. It was everything she had always wanted, and more.

She would love Wolf, and give him redheaded children, and one day . . . one day he would return that love.

Wolf stared at the papers before him, figures he should be studying, but he couldn't make his mind focus on the numbers. All around him, the house was alive. There was an incredible amount of activity in the kitchen, and Larkin had been bustling in and out all day.

Wolf had managed to throw the household into turmoil, with his simple and unemotional revelation. Even the staid Larkin had appeared to be surprised when Wolf made the announcement.

Surprised because he was getting married, or because Wolf Trevelyan had found a woman who would have him, he didn't know.

Since his marriage proposal and Molly's acceptance, Wolf had remained surprisingly calm. The disorder in the normally quiet house was not at all disturbing, and he hadn't been plagued by a single doubt.

He had nothing to lose in this arrangement.

He wanted Molly, and soon he would have her. When he was tired of married life and his red-headed wife, he would return to New York and the extravagant bachelor life he had enjoyed for years.

It was a brilliant solution, and he'd congratulated himself several times for thinking of it. With Molly at Vanora Point, and his business and social life in New York, he would have the best of both worlds.

Marriage, without any real ties. A wife and children he could see when it suited him, and leave behind when they bored him.

He heard the humming coming from the parlor, but paid no attention as he walked down the hallway from his study.

Larkin had arranged everything. The minister, the license, the food that was—for some reason Wolf did not comprehend—required. Weddings and funerals were celebrated in much the same way, he'd noticed.

Wolf stopped as he passed the opened parlor door.

The maid was hanging ribbons from an arched trellis that had been placed in the center of the room and behind a raised dais. She hummed softly, something bright, as she fussed with a bow that was, evidently, not quite to her satisfaction.

Wolf didn't understand what all the fuss was about. It was a simple ceremony. All they really needed was the minister and a witness or two.

Women were such sentimental fools.

The maid turned and stooped down to catch another ribbon between her fingers, and when she rose she saw him standing there. The ribbon flew from her hands, and she squealed shrilly, as she often did when she caught sight of him unexpectedly.

"I'm sorry sir," she said breathlessly. "You took me by surprise."

She never actually looked at him, if she could help it. Her gaze was locked somewhere above his head, and her hands trembled visibly.

This was the reaction he usually got when he was in Maine. Terror. The maid was a young girl, and not particularly pretty but not ugly either. It wasn't just the sight of a man that sent her into this panic, it was the specific sight of her employer.

He should fire her, but it would be damned inconvenient to replace her at this particular time.

"Carry on," he instructed with a wave of his hand, but he didn't move. The girl retrieved her ribbon and tried, with shaking hands, to tie a bow to match the ones she'd already done. This time she didn't hum, and the bow she fashioned was lopsided.

Every three seconds or so the fidgeting maid glanced over her shoulder warily, and so briefly it was a wonder she didn't break her neck when she snapped her head to the front again.

Oh, well, when he returned to New York Molly could do as she wished with the staff. She might want to expand it, or to let the lot of them go and hire her own servants. If she wanted a staff of fifty servants, he would see that she had it.

Big Bad Wolf

Wolf actually found himself smiling as he walked away from the parlor where he'd be married in less than twenty-four hours.

The transformation itself would be fascinating to watch, he was certain. He would watch with great pleasure as Molly Kincaid, simple, hardworking girl, became Molly Trevelyan, rich woman of leisure. Someone else would bake her bread and wash her laundry and clean her home. She would sleep all day if she wished, and fill her leisure time with trivial and pleasurable pursuits befitting a Trevelyan.

Her only duty would be to satisfy him.

Chapter Seven

People cried at weddings all the time, but not like this. Molly looked straight ahead at the preacher, who spoke in a monotone, but she couldn't ignore the wailing that continued ceaselessly behind her.

The parlor of the mansion at Vanora Point had been sparsely decorated with beribboned vases of roses in red and pink and white. Molly and her groom stood upon a raised platform that was cushioned with a plush rug, and an arch that had been decorated with ribbons that matched the flowers curved above their heads. Several chairs had been set up behind the makeshift altar, but there were only a few guests.

It was her mother who wailed so loudly, and Grandma's sniffles were unmistakable. Except for Mr. Hanson, who had escorted the Kincaid women to Vanora Point and would take Mary and Nelda home, the only other witnesses were Wolf's servants.

Wolf was wonderfully handsome in his formal black suit and starched white shirt, even though his face had remained emotionless and even cold. Molly reminded herself that to Wolf, this was still strictly business.

She much preferred the wicked smile and more relaxed stance of the Wolf she'd met in the forest, but the well-dressed and refined man who was her groom had his own charm. No elegant suit of clothes could disguise the strength she'd felt in his arms, or contain the energy he radiated even now.

Molly was wearing the wedding dress she'd always dreamed of. It was white satin, with pearls and lace and a skirt full enough to thoroughly cover a good-sized ottoman. The sleeves were full, but not grotesquely so, and white silk flowers to match the ones in her hair were fastened to the waist.

It had been her grandmother, in the end, who had fashioned her hair atop her head. They'd been trying for an austere style, but several strands had already escaped and curled over her shoulder and down her back. Before Grandma had taken over, Mary Kincaid had tried to secure Molly's hair for her—declaring it a mother's duty—but her hands shook horribly, she cried so hard.

Molly had told them of Wolf's offer, and they thought she was sacrificing herself for their sakes. Nothing she said would change their minds. They trembled when she told them she loved Wolf, and then they reminded her of his first wife's death. On this one point they finally agreed. Nelda and Mary Kincaid had never, that Molly could remember, agreed on anything.

They reminded her again and again of the fate of the first Mrs. Wolf Trevelyan, until Molly forbid them to speak of it. It was the only time in her life she'd forbid anything, and she'd been rather surprised to find it so effective.

Molly smiled as Wolf took her hand and slipped a ring onto her finger. It wasn't a plain gold band, but a cluster of sapphires and diamonds in a gold setting. His mother's, he'd said. There had been no time to have rings specially made, though he'd promised her any sort of ring she desired. He'd have it made in New York.

Looking down at her hand as Wolf placed the ring on her finger, Molly was perfectly satisfied. She didn't need or want any ring but this one. The one he promised his life with.

Everything was grand, but it would be nice if the groom would smile, just a little.

When the preacher pronounced them man and wife, Mary Kincaid sobbed loudly, and Wolf closed his eyes. This had been an ordeal for him, Molly knew. Subjecting himself to inlaws who openly detested him. Holding his temper. She had an urge to take his hand and comfort him, to thank him for his patience. It couldn't be pleasant to have your bride's relatives wailing in the background.

The preacher's solemnly spoken, "You may kiss the bride," brought a new howl, which Molly ignored as she leaned forward to accept her first kiss as Wolf's wife.

For a moment she thought Wolf would refuse to kiss her. He hesitated before lowering his lips to hers, and when he did finally place his lips against her mouth it was not in a burning kiss like the price he'd demanded in the forest, but rather a cool brush of his lips against hers. She felt a touch of comfort in his mouth on hers, but it was short-lived and passionless.

When he pulled away from her she searched his hooded eyes for a clue to his thoughts. In spite of the fact that this marriage was a business deal to him, she wanted to see some joy in his eyes. There was none.

The magnificent wedding feast went all but untouched. Only Mr. Hanson and the preacher seemed to enjoy the sumptuous spread. Molly was much too nervous to eat, and Wolf was apparently too angry. Mary Kincaid wouldn't stop crying long enough to take even a bite, and Grandma was just being stubborn, through her own sniffles. Molly couldn't help but notice that Wolf gave Grandma and her ever-present cane a wide berth.

Molly had invited no one else. Her friends from Kingsport, especially Hannah and Stella, had been as horrified upon hearing the news as her small family had been, and she would have none of that distrust and anger in Wolf's own home. There would be no whispers of the first wife or ridiculous notions of mummies on the third floor, and there would certainly be no suspicious glaring at the groom.

The guests left in the afternoon, so that both the Kincaid women could be home well before dark, and Molly was glad to see them go. The constant sniffles and pitying glances were getting tiresome.

Mr. Hanson was such a dear, guiding Molly's mother from the Trevelyan house with a whisper of assurance. He'd been quiet all day, voicing neither his support for this marriage nor his disapproval.

Molly knew he was only here for her mother's sake. Perhaps now that Mary had leisure time, she'd spend some of it in Mr. Hanson's company.

Wolf closed the double doors on the retreating guests and leaned against them with an audible growl.

Molly clasped her hands at her waist. "I'm sorry," she whispered.

"Don't apologize," he snapped. "It's pretty much the reaction I expected."

"Oh."

"But it has been a perfectly hideous day," he added.

Molly had never thought to hear her groom describe their wedding day as hideous. There had been unpleasant moments, of course, but hideous?

"I'm sorry."

"You're apologizing again." Wolf passed her without even glancing down. There was no smile, no softening of his bitter expression.

"I'm . . ." Molly stopped in mid apology.

"I have some papers to go over. I'll be in the study. If you need anything, ring for Larkin."

Big Bad Wolf

Molly was left standing in the entryway alone. Her wedding gown trailed on a Persian carpet, and the ceiling was magnificently high. The afternoon sun shone through stained glass windows and left broken shards of light at Molly's feet and all around. She was surrounded by beauty, fine art in gilded frames and furniture so delicate she was afraid to touch any of it. It was like standing in a castle, wearing a princess's gown.

The problem was, Molly was no princess. It had never been her ambition to live in a castle, to have servants to ring for when she needed anything. Her dreams were simple, attainable, and realistic. At least, they'd always seemed realistic. She'd never counted on Wolf Trevelyan stepping in and changing everything.

Molly could get lost in this big house, and she felt more than a little lost already.

What on earth had he done? Wolf shuffled the papers before him needlessly, barely glancing at the figures. There was nothing here that couldn't wait another day or two, but he'd had to get away from Molly.

Good God, married. Again. And there was no guarantee that this marriage would work out any better than the first one had.

Like a lovestruck boy, he'd allowed himself to rationalize until he found a way to get what he wanted, Molly Kincaid. Until now he'd been perfectly content to allow this branch of the Trevelyan family to end with him. To be honest, he'd never even considered his responsibility to carry on the family name.

It had certainly never bothered him that there was no one to leave his fortune to. Until now.

The little redhead had gotten under his skin, had made it perfectly clear that he couldn't bed her unless he married her, and like a well-trained lap dog he'd willingly done just that.

She was a clever, mercenary witch. Not only had he actually married her, he'd promised to care for her dreadful family for the rest of their pitiful lives.

And all the while she watched him with those wide, gray, innocent eyes. For all he knew, she wasn't even a virgin, as she'd claimed. It could have been part of a wickedly clever machination to trap him into marriage. Was Molly as innocent as she'd have him believe? He'd find out soon enough.

This faltering uncertainty was unlike him. He didn't like it. Not at all.

Wolf tossed the papers into the top drawer and slammed it shut. What was done was done. He didn't have to actually *live* with her. Nothing had to change. He'd go back to New York when he felt like it, and he'd leave Molly here. She'd be waiting whenever he came back.

Nothing had to change.

Wolf was unaccustomed to doubts of any sort, and he hated indecision of any kind, in himself as well as in others. He went after what he wanted and got it. Simple enough. But when the preacher had uttered his solemn "you may kiss the bride," he had looked into Molly's eyes and seen something impossible.

Hope.

It had to be an act.

He had a stiff brandy as he stood at the window and watched the last light of day die.

Somehow, someday, he would peel away the disguise and find the real Molly Kincaid . . . the real Molly Trevelyan. She hid it well, but Wolf knew they were two of a kind, that Molly was more like him than she cared to allow. There was a mercenary streak in her heart, just as there was in his, and when they wanted something they took it.

For the first time that day, a smile crossed his face. This marriage was likely to send a shock wave through New York to rival the first one. Foster would get a good laugh out of it, at the very idea of Wolf Trevelyan marrying a sweet, poor, simple girl. Adele would be furious to be sure, but he'd never promised her anything. Their relationship didn't have to end just because he was married.

Unlike Molly, Adele could be bought. A bauble or two, and all would be forgiven.

Actually, Molly could be bought. Her price was high, frightfully so, but she was waiting for him, right now, he imagined. Her mother and her grandmother would be cared for for life, and Molly herself would certainly never want for anything.

Wolf poured himself another brandy and downed it quickly. Molly was waiting.

The house was quiet. Everyone had been bustling well before sunup, cooking and arranging flowers, cleaning the bedroom he had chosen to be Molly's. It was next to his, and there was a connecting door.

Only the butler remained, to no surprise, standing stiffly at the foot of the stairs.

"Go on to bed, Larkin," Wolf said as he passed the stern old man.

"Yes, sir."

Larkin showed no indication that he might move from his post at the foot of the stairs.

Wolf smiled bitterly as he climbed the stairs, bravely presenting his back to the butler. Perhaps Larkin would stay there all night, in case another Trevelyan bride decided death was preferable to marriage.

The door to Molly's room was slightly ajar, and Wolf pushed it open with a hard shove. The door crashed against the wall, and Wolf stepped into his wife's room.

Molly was indeed waiting for him, sitting up in her plush, wide bed, candlelight illuminating her face and a cascade of red curls, shining bright on the white nightgown she wore and on the blue spread that covered her to the waist.

He closed the door behind him quietly.

"I thought maybe you wouldn't come," Molly said softly.

Wolf grinned at her as he began to unbutton his shirt. "Not a chance, Red."

"Oh."

Her voice was soft, but she didn't appear to be

afraid. Her gray eyes were wide, but not with fear, as she watched him shed his wedding suit. The hands that rested on her lap didn't tremble, until he stood before her completely naked, and then it was more of a faint quiver that rippled through her.

Molly looked him over boldly, curiously, her eyes raking over him from his grin to the arousal that had grown and hardened as she'd watched.

"My," she whispered softly. "What a . . ." Molly lifted her gaze sharply, meeting his stare at last. "Never mind."

When he placed a knee on the side of the bed and yanked back the covers to toss them to the floor, Molly didn't protest, but licked her lips slowly in a way that made Wolf impatient to feel her beneath and around his body. He couldn't allow her to steal his control with such a simple maneuver of her tongue.

"Worried, Red?" Wolf growled as he slid her nightdress upward slowly, allowing his fingers to trail across the warm, soft skin of her legs.

"No," she whispered, and she lifted her eyes to his. "I know you would never hurt me."

His hands stilled, and in spite of his resolve not to let himself be fooled by her masquerade, Wolf leaned forward to kiss her waiting lips.

She raised her hands to his face, touched his cheeks tenderly as she parted her lips for him, moved her mouth instinctively against his.

Damn her, she was right. He wouldn't hurt her for the world.

* * *

There was such a strong, strange beauty about her husband. Even in candlelight his features were harsh, his eyes too sharp to be called tender . . . but his hands were gentle, and his lips moved over hers so tenderly she wanted to cry with it.

Wolf scooted her nightgown up slowly, until he apparently lost patience and made short work of ridding her of the cumbersome thing.

Without it, she could feel the heat of his chest against hers, the wondrous sensation of flesh against flesh.

His body was so unlike hers, so hard and rough, with rippled muscles under dark skin and tiny, soft, dark hairs on his arms and chest. She should have felt weak beneath him, powerless, but that was not true. There was more power within her than there had ever been before.

"Red?" he whispered against her mouth.

"Yes?"

"I don't want to hurt you, but I might—"

Molly silenced him with a kiss. "No, you won't," she breathed against his mouth.

"Dammit, Red," he growled. "The first time . . ." He drew away from her slightly, and looked down at her with a strange expression on his face. Desire, frustration, maybe even a little embarrassment. "Didn't your mother tell you anything?"

"She tried, but she was crying so hard I couldn't understand a word she said." It wasn't funny, not really, but Molly started laughing. "Well, I did understand a few blubbery words. *Close your eyes and lie very still.* Does that sound about right?"

Big Bad Wolf

Wolf buried his face against her shoulder and groaned lowly.

"I'm afraid it does hurt the first time, Red. There's nothing I can do but try to make it easy on you, and that's going to be difficult."

"Why?"

He lifted his head to look down at her. "Because I want you too much."

"That's good, isn't it?"

He grinned crookedly. "I haven't decided yet."

Molly lifted her head and kissed her husband. His smile disappeared as he parted his lips and yielded his mouth to her. He forced her legs apart with his knee, and Molly spread her legs wide.

Wolf settled between her spread legs, deepened the kiss that could heal any hurt, and touched her.

It was shocking and wonderful, his tender fingers stroking her softly, and then thrust inside her.

Molly wanted more. She couldn't understand why, or how, but she rocked against Wolf and wrapped her arms around his neck. She tingled where he touched her, and she was warm—hot—everywhere.

When he took his hand away she wanted to object, but she never got the chance. In one swift thrust he entered her, and in another he filled her. And it *did* hurt.

Wolf lay very still atop her, his swollen manhood buried inside her, filling her, stretching her.

"Oh," she breathed. Wolf kissed her again, softly, deeply, and the pain faded.

It took a moment, but Molly felt herself relaxing, her body adjusting to Wolf's inside her. As if

Linda Jones

he felt her response, as if he knew that the pain was gone, he began to move again, rocking back and thrusting. Slowly at first, and then quicker, harder.

It was a most shocking invasion, more powerful than she'd expected. Molly lifted her hips instinctively, clasped her hands against Wolf's muscled back, and closed her eyes. What a magnificent and unexpected sensation this was, and it grew with every stroke.

As he moved above and inside her, Molly was certain Wolf would devour her, with his mouth, with his tender invasion of her body. The thought of being consumed by Wolf wasn't frightening. It was exhilarating.

Just days ago she had accepted the fact that she loved him, and now she had to admit that it was more than that. He had made himself a part of her, and she would never be content to be alone again. Wolf possessed her, owned her body and soul.

And heart.

Wolf drove so deep it took her breath away, and then he shuddered above her, inside her. His lips, his arms. The completion shot through him, and she could feel it.

For a long moment he was very still, wonderfully heavy atop her, and when he lifted his head from his shoulder he kissed her again. "I'm sorry. I did hurt you . . ."

"Never apologize," she whispered. *For loving me.* She kept that last to herself. Wolf wasn't ready to admit that there was any love between them. Not yet.

Wolf woke with a start to find that he'd fallen asleep in Molly's bed. She was snuggled up against his side, with her face buried against his ribs and one bare leg thrown over his.

She'd extinguished the candle earlier, and the only light in the room was pale moonlight that broke through the window. It was just enough to reveal the blurred outlines of the room, and the soft shape of his bride.

Unable to stop himself, Wolf lifted a strand of curling red hair that had fallen across his chest and caressed it easily before he released the strand and allowed it to fall back into place.

He wanted to wake Molly and take her again, but he knew it was too soon for her, his virgin bride. Still, he was tempted. Her chest rose and fell steadily against his side, and the sensation of her heartbeat and her breath were oddly stimulating.

Wolf extricated himself slowly, gently, so he wouldn't wake her, and slipped from the bed. Molly moaned softly, rolled onto her stomach, and clutched her pillow.

He stood by the bed for a long time. The air was chilly against his bare skin, and he was uncommonly tired, but he wouldn't allow himself to crawl back into the warm bed with Molly.

The bed that was waiting for him in the room next door was no more appealing than the idea of standing here and watching Molly as the night passed. Less appealing, and that was something Wolf wouldn't allow.

He turned away from her, and gathered his clothes as he approached the door that separated his room from hers. Separate. He had to remember that he and Molly would lead separate lives, that only when he desired her body would he think of her as a real wife.

If he weren't so tired, he thought, as he tossed his clothes over the back of a chair in his own room, he wouldn't be forced to remind himself of that fact.

The wide bed looked unappealing, at the moment, so Wolf fixed himself a brandy at the small bar that was always well-stocked, and took his favorite chair to stare into an empty fireplace.

A few more nights like this one, and his obsession with Molly would surely vanish. At the very least it should fade to a manageable condition. He'd been infatuated with women before, and it never lasted.

He had to admit, grudgingly, that it had never been this strong, either.

He also had to admit, every bit as grudgingly, that he'd never known a woman like Molly before.

Wolf finished his brandy and glanced warily to the bed that awaited. After a few hours with Molly in his arms, the uninhabited bed was vastly wide, and cold, and empty, and extraordinarily repugnant.

There was a hint of light in the sky when Wolf finally dozed off there in the chair, wondering as he drifted off why Molly had married him.

Chapter Eight

Molly smiled brightly at the man who waited stoically at the foot of the stairs. "Good morning, Mr. Larkin," she greeted cheerfully, hoping for a returning smile. She didn't get one.

"Good morning, madam."

"Have you seen Wolf this morning? I thought we might have breakfast together." She'd been disappointed to find her husband gone when she'd awakened, but she couldn't stay disappointed for long. She was much too happy.

Wolf's butler watched her every move as she descended the staircase, his stern, unblinking eyes following her intently. "Mr. Trevelyan doesn't take breakfast, madam."

"Oh. Well . . ." Molly held her head high and continued to smile, refusing to allow the forbidding man to ruin her happiness. "I'm always starving when I wake, and I find that I have a particularly beastly hunger this morning."

"Yes, madam."

Mr. Larkin was awfully uncooperative this morning, and Molly wondered if he was always so cross. "Where's the kitchen?"

She could almost think that she had shocked the man. His steely eyes widened, just slightly. "If you'll wait in the dining room, I'll serve your breakfast shortly, madam."

Her first morning as Mrs. Trevelyan, and already she'd made a mistake. Was the lady of the manor forbidden from entering the kitchen? "Of course, Mr. Larkin."

Molly turned to make her way down the long, echoing hallway. Perhaps Wolf didn't eat breakfast, but she still wanted to see him. Would he give her a good morning kiss? A smile bloomed across her face at the very thought.

She peeked into the parlor where they'd been married. Every sign that a ceremony had taken place in the room was gone: the makeshift altar, the roses, the neatly arranged chairs. Still, it was a nice room, the only room in the house she'd seen thus far that had even a hint of a feminine influence.

It was empty, but that didn't surprise her. She couldn't imagine Wolf in this brightly lit room. When she thought of him, when she imagined him, it was in the shadows of the forest, or by soft candlelight in a darkened room.

The next room was a library, as dark as the

parlor was bright, as masculine as the parlor was feminine. She'd never seen so many books in all her life. The bookshelves that lined the walls were filled with leather bound books, and there were several comfortable-looking leather chairs and lamps with colored shades.

It might be a very nice room, if those heavy drapes were opened, and a vase of roses was placed here or there. Light and color, that was what this house needed.

Molly closed the door silently and moved to the next room. She swung the door inward, as she had the others, and found herself face to face with her husband.

Wolf jerked his head up from the papers on his desk, a scowl on his face. "Don't you know how to knock?" he grumbled.

Molly closed the door, took a deep breath, and rapped her knuckles lightly against the heavy wood. And waited. After a moment of silence, she knocked again. Nothing.

She opened the door and stepped into the study. "Don't you know how to say 'come in?'"

Wolf leaned back in his chair and stared at her. "What are you doing here?"

"I thought you might like to have breakfast with me." She wasn't going to allow his sour mood to spoil this lovely morning.

"I don't eat breakfast." He dismissed her with a wave of his hand and returned his attention to the papers on his desk.

"That's what Mr. Larkin said."

Wolf lifted his eyes slowly.

"But perhaps if you had breakfast you wouldn't be such a grumpy old man in the morning."

"Molly, I have work to do."

She stepped forward until she could see the stack of papers on his desk. Figures and scribbled notes filled much of the paper. "Oh. Well, I guess I should leave you alone for a while."

"I guess you should."

"We'll do something later?"

Wolf lifted an impatient face to her. "I don't think I'll have time."

She'd already learned that she wasn't allowed in the kitchen, and now Wolf was dismissing her with an indifference she didn't care for at all.

"Well, what am I supposed to do all day?"

His indifference quickly changed to exasperation, but Molly didn't particularly care. Wolf Trevelyan might scare grown men with the look he was giving her now, but he couldn't scare her.

"Whatever it is women do with their time. Sew. Read. Take a nap."

"I just got up."

"Molly!"

He might be exasperated, but he did like her. A little. He'd proved it to her last night, with his tenderness and his concern. She gave him a smile to offset his scowl.

"I thought maybe we could take a picnic into the woods this afternoon."

Wolf threw up his hands and leaned back in his leather chair. "What are you going to do while I'm in New York? Even when I'm here I can't be expected to entertain your every waking moment!"

This was a snag she hadn't thoroughly considered in her hasty decision to accept Wolf's proposal. "I remember you mentioning that after the children came I would be staying here with them, but am I to stay here even now, while you're in New York?"

"Yes." It was a curt and dismissive answer, meant to end this uncomfortable conversation. Molly couldn't let it go.

"You'll be leaving next week, won't you?"

"Yes." His affirmative answer was sharp, biting.

Molly bit her bottom lip, but only briefly. She didn't want to appear to be insecure. "And how long will you be gone?"

She waited for an answer, but none was forthcoming.

"A few days? Weeks?"

Still, Wolf stared at her silently.

"Months?"

"I don't know." He returned his attention to the papers spread before him. "Perhaps."

She should leave with a smile, pretending that she didn't care. But she did care. Very much. This house would be a lonely place without Wolf in it. It was beginning to look as if it could be a lonely house even when he was home.

"I have an idea," Wolf suggested. "Have Larkin contact a dressmaker in Kingsport and arrange for a few decent gowns to be made. That should keep you occupied for a while. Besides, I'm damned tired of seeing you in nothing but brown and gray and white."

He managed quite nicely to make his suggestion sound like an insult.

Molly reminded herself that Wolf had been entirely honest in his assessment of their marriage. Of all the women he might have married, he'd chosen her in part because she was undemanding. He wanted a wife who could be easily left behind, a woman to share his bed at night and give him redheaded children. He wanted nothing else from her. Not companionship, and certainly not love.

This was going to be harder than she'd thought.

Wolf managed to waste the entire day in his study, reviewing figures that could wait. Hiding. He couldn't remember ever hiding from anyone.

Molly had done it again.

He had known, as she'd watched him come to her last night, that she was as innocent as she claimed to be. Innocent, but not timid.

And she was his. All his. Good God, he'd never actually had a virgin before.

She hadn't intruded into his study again, after her invasion of this morning when she'd offered him breakfast. On occasion he had listened for her, and had heard her a couple of times in the library next door, moving things around, humming to herself.

But for a while, now, all had been quiet. Too damnably quiet.

When Wolf opened the study door, Larkin was there, waiting in the hallway.

"Where is Mrs. Trevelyan?"

Larkin was silent for a long moment. The old

man disapproved of the match, Wolf knew, but he would never say so. It was not his place, and Larkin was very well aware of his place in the household. "Mrs. Trevelyan went out for a walk some time ago, sir."

"And you let her go?" Wolf snapped.

"She insisted," he said.

"You should have gone with her." Wolf headed down the long hallway.

"She forbid it, sir."

Wolf stopped in the middle of the hallway and glanced over his shoulder. "She forbid it?"

"Yes, sir," Larkin sighed.

Wolf hurried down the long hallway and out the front door. There were gardens to explore, the stables, the woods not so very far away. Surely she wouldn't venture there without an escort.

Of course she would.

There was also the cliff and a breathtaking view of the Atlantic.

Wolf rounded the house, not quite running. As a rule, he avoided the jutting cliff and magnificent vista.

He slowed his step when he saw her. Molly sat on a blanket not far from the edge of the cliff, her legs tucked beneath her, her long red hair free and fluttering in the wind.

The red curls fell past her waist, bright and beckoning in the sun that shone on her. He was almost upon her when he noticed that her shoulders were shaking. Another step, and he could hear her soft sobs.

He'd never felt like such a heel. Why had he

married her and ruined her life? Because she tempted him? The world was full of easy women. Because she wasn't afraid of him? That had been the initial attraction, he knew, but there were plenty of women in New York who weren't scared off by his own personal horror story.

In truth, he knew he'd married her because he wanted her and because he could. Because he was so damned determined to get what he wanted. Money was power, and Wolf didn't mind using his to obtain whatever he craved at the moment.

He'd craved Molly from the moment he'd seen her.

She must've heard his step, because she glanced over her shoulder and swiped away her tears.

"You're too close to the edge," Wolf said, his voice too sharp.

"No I'm not," she said defensively.

Wolf didn't move nearer. It had been seven years since he'd looked over the cliff to the rocks and the surf and what was left of his bride below. This was as near as he'd been since that morning.

"What's wrong?"

Molly scooted around to face him, but didn't move farther away from the cliff. She drew up her knees, clutched an opened book to her chest. "*Little Women*. It's just so sad."

In spite of his resolve to remain distant, separate, Wolf smiled down at her without a hint of his usual cynicism. "That's why you're crying?"

She nodded her head, and red curls danced. He had to admit that he loved her hair. The color, the soft curls, the heavenly thickness of it.

"Did you get all your work finished?"

"Most of it," he conceded.

Molly scooted to one side and patted the blanket beside her. "Come sit with me."

Wolf hesitated, but he stepped forward slowly and lowered himself to sit next to Molly. Like her, he sat with his back to the ocean. "Larkin says you forbid him to accompany you."

"I did," she said sternly. "Every time I turned around today, he was there. Watching. Waiting. If I sneezed he had a handkerchief. If I was thirsty he had a glass of lemonade. It was really . . . uncanny."

"Larkin's very good at what he does," Wolf admitted. "What did you do all day?"

Molly looked askance at him and wrinkled her nose. "Not much. Harriet won't allow me into the kitchen, it seems."

"Who's Harriet?"

Her eyes widened. "Your cook, Wolf. Don't you even know the woman's name?"

"No."

"Dreadful," she said. "I tried to putter around the house, but I kept running into Shirley."

"And she is . . . ?"

"The maid. She's awfully skittish." Molly placed a small scrap of paper in her book and closed it carefully. "After a couple of uncomfortable encounters, I closed myself in the library."

"I heard you."

Molly sighed deeply. "See? I can't do anything right. I didn't mean to disturb you—"

"You didn't disturb me," Wolf interrupted, compelled, for some unknown reason, to assure her that listening to her moving about in the library hadn't disrupted his day.

"What will I do while you're gone?" Molly stared at the big house. There was a hint of pleading in her soft voice that he tried to ignore. "I'll likely have read every book in the library before you come back."

"I doubt that."

"But you said it might be months." Molly frowned. She actually pouted. The pleading in her voice, the wide eyes, the thrust out lower lip. One could almost think that she would . . . that she would miss him while he was gone. Impossible.

"It probably won't be that long," he confessed. "We can hardly start a family with me in one state and you in another."

A smile stole over her face, ended the childish pout and brightened her eyes. "I want lots of children."

"Lots?"

"At least six," she confessed. "And there won't be any nursemaids or governesses raising my children." She sounded quite adamant. If this was the voice she used to forbid Larkin to accompany her, it was no wonder he had obeyed. "I'll raise them myself. We can't expect a stranger to love our children the way we will."

"Of course not," he agreed gruffly, and in his mind he could see it. Just what he'd said he wanted. Six redheaded children, running through the house with their mother chasing merrily—or

not so merrily—after them. The Trevelyan house
would never be the same.

What had he done?

"Do you think six will be enough?" she asked
conversationally. "To carry on the Trevelyan
name?"

"More than enough," Wolf growled.

"Unless, of course, they're all girls."

The picture running through his mind intensified. Six little redheaded Mollys, turning the house
upside down. Ghastly.

"Are you all right?" Molly bent her head to study
his face more closely. "Goodness, you look rather
pale all of a sudden. If you'd eat breakfast I'm sure
your disposition would improve."

"There's nothing wrong with my disposition,"
he insisted through clenched teeth.

Molly simply smiled.

He wanted to take her right there, on the cliff-
side blanket, and he might have if he hadn't been
certain that Larkin was watching.

Watching to see if Wolf Trevelyan would toss
another bride off the cliff. Watching to see if Molly
would prefer death to another night in his bed.

It hadn't bothered him for a long time, the tales
people spun. His immunity to the hate and the lies
had grown slowly, and he was stronger for it. He
knew the truth, and he didn't care what anyone
else believed.

With a start, he realized that Molly had invited
him to join her there by the cliff, that she leaned
into him without a qualm.

Of course, she had told him last night that she

knew he wouldn't hurt her. How did she know? Why did she trust him?

Molly's refusal to accept the horrid tales as truth had at first attracted and then intrigued him. Depending on his mood he alternately thought her brainless or brilliant or brave.

The easy trust that would make a woman like Molly place herself in his hands and in his bed without a qualm only made him suspicious. Everyone wanted something from him. Including Molly.

The dining room was much too big for two solitary people. The table had been set formally, and candles burned brightly from a silver candelabra that had fresh flowers arranged at the base. It was lovely, but it blocked much of Wolf's face.

Molly felt as if she were dining all alone. Wolf was seated at the head of the table, and her place had been set at the foot. Mr. Larkin had filled their wine glasses regularly, and carried in course after course. There was fish and red meat and potatoes and greens and bread that was not quite as good as her mother's but would do nicely.

Mr. Larkin was downright spooky. As soon as she finished with one course, he was there to take her plate away and deposit another one before her.

There had been nothing so far that could pass for dinner conversation. When Molly commented on the food, Wolf nodded and that was it. When she tried to ask him about his work, he gave her a stony glare and ignored her. Of course, she felt as if she had to shout to be heard. Wolf was so far away he might as well be in Kingsport.

When Mr. Larkin placed a huge piece of cake before her, Molly almost groaned. There was no way she could eat another bite. Once he had left the room Molly stood, picking up the dessert and what was left of her wine.

Wolf stared at her as she approached, narrowing those eyes and frowning. Was this an infraction of the rules? Well, he was always telling her that she should break the rules more often.

She placed the plate and glass next to Wolf's, and took the chair to his left.

"I hope you don't mind." She ignored the fact that he looked as if he did mind, very much. "I feel as if you're already in another state."

"It's a big room."

Molly picked at her cake, but Wolf ignored the dessert and finished off his wine.

She felt that she was making Wolf nervous, just by moving close to him. "Maybe we can take that picnic tomorrow," she suggested. "Since you've finished most of your work."

"Perhaps," he said with a casual shrug of his shoulders.

"Could we go to that stream, do you think? Is it very far from here on foot?"

"It's a good walk, but not too far."

Molly smiled, but her smile only seemed to make Wolf cross. It didn't take much, she'd discovered, to rub him the wrong way.

What she wouldn't give to see that wicked grin of his.

"Why didn't you accept the gifts I sent?" he asked abruptly, and she knew the question had been on his mind as he'd sat there and stewed all through dinner.

"I didn't want them," she said simply and truthfully.

"You didn't even want to know what was in those boxes?"

"Not particularly," Molly said, popping a small piece of cake into her mouth.

Wolf lowered his wine glass and placed it carefully on the table, and without warning he leaned close. "That's not natural."

It was an accusation of some sort, an indictment against her femininity. "Well," she confessed. "I did try to guess. I assumed the bracelet you tried to force me to take was in one of those boxes."

His frown confirmed her suspicion.

"And I guessed that there was jewelry in some of the other boxes, also. Several of them were quite small."

"Don't you like jewelry?" he asked.

"Well, of course I do."

"But . . . ?"

"That doesn't mean," she said, "that I'll willingly make a fool of myself over something pretty. Nor does it mean I can be swayed or bought with something just because it's expensive."

"Remind me never to give you jewelry for our anniversary."

He sounded so bewildered that Molly had to laugh. "I think there was a music box in one package. It made a silvery sound when Willie dropped it."

Wolf winced.

"I hope it wasn't broken," Molly added quickly, "And if it was it was all my fault. Not Willie's. I slammed the door in his face."

"He told me," Wolf growled. "Tell me, just so I'll know, what it would have taken to get you to take those gifts. The information might come in handy in the future."

Molly mused as she sipped her wine. Another bite and she would surely burst. "Well, I might have taken them if . . ." She shook her head. "Never mind. It doesn't matter now, anyway."

Wolf glowered at her in a way that told her very clearly to continue.

"If you must know, if you'd brought them to me yourself instead of sending that poor boy, who always thought that you were going to kill him if I sent everything back." She stopped abruptly. Somewhere along the way Wolf's irritation had turned to pure anger. She saw that fury in his eyes, in the set of his mouth.

And she remembered why Wolf never set foot in Kingsport.

"You ask too much, Molly," he said, standing.

"I didn't mean . . ." her words trailed off as he exited from the dining room in long strides.

Chapter Nine

Molly waited rather patiently, sitting up in bed as she had the night before, wearing her prim nightgown even though she thought it was a waste of time to slip it on.

Wolf would just remove it impatiently, as he had the previous night.

Candles burned softly, giving the room a warm and pleasant glow. In the room next to hers, Wolf's footsteps echoed thinly, and Molly listened as he opened and closed drawers, and scraped something heavy, a log perhaps, across the stone fireplace.

She waited a while longer, even after the sounds in the room next door ceased altogether.

Surely he didn't intend to spend the night in his own room, and just because she'd suggested that he might have delivered his offered gifts himself. She hadn't meant it, not really. Well, she'd meant it, she just hadn't been thinking straight.

Without a qualm, Molly slipped silently from under the covers, moving cautiously and not even allowing the big bed to squeak. She didn't exactly understand her husband, not yet. Last night he had been tender and sweet and wonderful, and today he had been cold and dismissive.

If they were to have a chance at happiness, there had to be something of Wolf she called her own. Something to bring them together. She certainly couldn't allow him to ignore her all day and all night.

The door that separated her bedroom from Wolf's was unlocked, and she swung it open before she would allow herself second thoughts.

Wolf sat in a wide upholstered chair before the fireplace, dressed in nothing but his trousers, and brilliantly illuminated for her eyes by the light of a blazing fire. There was a brandy snifter in one hand, and a cigar in the other.

He looked maddeningly content as he turned his head to her.

Molly grasped the doorknob and pushed the door shut, took a deep breath, and knocked softly.

"Come in."

Wolf was staring at the fire, not at her, as she opened the door again and stepped into his room.

She was drawn to the warmth of the fire, and to Wolf, and without saying a word she crossed the wide room and settled herself on the rug. The small blaze was at her face, and a surprisingly cold husband was at her back.

Molly looked over her shoulder to her husband, at the harsh planes of his face that were not softened by the firelight.

"I'm sorry if I said something to upset you."

He glanced down at her, and Molly realized that all his earlier anger was gone. "You certainly didn't upset me. If I snapped at you it's because I haven't been sleeping well. I'm tired, that's all."

He did look awfully tired, Molly conceded, and she hated to bother him, but . . .

"Why do we have two bedrooms?" she asked casually, though it wasn't a casual question at all.

Wolf hesitated. She heard him sigh—such a human reaction for a man like Wolf. "I don't sleep much, and you'll rest better in your own bed and your own room."

"You don't sleep, you don't eat. Don't you need anything besides brandy and those smelly cigars?"

"No," he answered quickly.

Molly drew her legs up and leaned back against Wolf's chair, settled herself comfortably between his widely spread legs. "Would you be terribly disappointed if I told you that I didn't want my own bedroom?"

He didn't answer right away, so Molly tilted her head back so she could see his face. Wolf was smiling, just a little.

"No," he finally conceded. "I wouldn't be disappointed."

"Good." Molly returned her gaze to the fire. All in all, this was very nice.

She relaxed, once she realized that Wolf wasn't

going to be angry, and leaned her head against his knee. He didn't seem to mind. A few minutes later he put out his cigar—because she had said it was smelly?—and then she felt his fingers in her hair.

"What do you want, Red?" The easy stroking in her hair continued, as Wolf asked his soft question.

"I don't know what you mean."

"From me," he clarified. "What do you want from me?"

The question was easier to consider facing the fire than if she'd had to look Wolf in the eye. What Molly really wanted was love. She wanted more than anything for Wolf to love her.

But it was much too soon for that.

Still, she had to be somewhat honest with him. "I guess," she admitted, "that I want you to need me."

"Why?"

Molly wrapped her arm easily around his leg. What else could she say? That need was as close to love as she was likely to get? That if he needed her he wouldn't leave her behind for months at a time, and he wouldn't ignore her for an entire day and even into the night?

The fingers in her hair tightened, and with a tug Wolf forced her to look at him. "Why?" he asked again.

"Because you don't need anything else."

He smiled, that wicked grin she had first spied in the forest. "It's power you want?"

"Power?"

"Over me," he clarified.

She already recognized that grin as a defense. It was nothing like a true smile. Poor Wolf, he expected the worst of everyone. "No." His fingers tightened in her hair, but she remained calm. "Everybody needs something or someone. Everybody but you."

"And what do you need, Red?" he asked sarcastically.

His voice was so harsh, so cold, that Molly shivered deep down. How much could she safely give of herself?

"I need you."

The simple and truthful answer broke his defenses, and the false smile died.

"You need my money, for your family."

"No."

Wolf found it so difficult, perhaps impossible, to accept the fact that anyone could need him. He would never believe her if she told him it was so much more.

His hands in her hair relaxed, and with an easy motion he leaned forward and lifted her from the floor and onto his lap.

"You're going to be the death of me, Red," Wolf muttered as she settled her head against his shoulder.

"Am I, now?" She smiled against the warmth of his bare chest. It hadn't sounded particularly kind, but she considered his words a sort of compliment.

Instinctively, she pressed her lips against his warm skin. He wouldn't admit it, but he did need her.

Wolf set his brandy aside with a sigh, and wrapping his arms around her he stood. He carried her to his bed and tossed her gently on top of the satin coverlet.

"You're a witch," he grumbled.

Molly laughed as he fell beside her. "A witch, am I? What does that make you?"

Wolf was already sliding her nightgown up, trailing his hands over her flesh from ankles to hips, to sensitive breasts. "Cursed."

She laughed again, and lifted her arms so he could dispose of her nightgown. He smothered her laughter with his mouth over hers, with a kiss that satisfied her and yet made her yearn for more.

Wolf pressed her back against the soft bed, never breaking the thrilling hold of his kiss, and Molly wrapped her arms around his neck.

He could ignore her all day, swear he didn't need her, but there was a hunger in his kiss that belied his indifference.

Wolf drew his mouth from hers slowly, lifted his head with a marked reluctance. He removed his trousers quickly and tossed them aside as he had her nightgown, and then he was above her again. This time he lowered his mouth to her breasts, closed his lips over a nipple and sucked gently. She felt the power of his touch through her body, shooting through every part of her.

When he spread her thighs and stroked her, Molly caught her breath. When he raised his mouth to hers again, she caught his face in her hands and parted her lips. This was more intoxicating than any brandy, more brilliant than any gem he could offer her.

She throbbed, achingly empty, and the ache grew at an alarming rate. Every touch, every heartbeat took her to a new urgency.

With a surge he filled her, and Molly deepened the kiss. She was lost. Searching. She closed her eyes, and savored the sensation that intensified with every passing second, with every stroke of Wolf's body inside hers.

She felt as if she had no control over her own body. Wolf had all the control, over his body and hers.

"Relax," he whispered as he surged to fill her completely. "Let it happen, Red. Let go."

Surely she was going to break. Shatter into a thousand pieces beneath the tender and demanding onslaught.

And then she did, or so it seemed. Lightning flowed through her body, given to her by Wolf. She clung to him, lifted her hips to take all of him.

The same lightning coursed through him. She could feel his release, as she had last night, inside her and in the trembling muscles beneath her hands, as Wolf finally lost control.

For a long moment Wolf lay very still atop her, the only sound his ragged breathing in her ear. He was heavy, and warm, and this was heavenly.

She couldn't breathe, she couldn't move. Her body was drained completely of all energy.

Wolf rolled onto his back, but he didn't release her. "I think I've finally found your vice," he said, sounding as breathless as she felt.

"My vice?"

"I tried drink, I tried gambling, I tried diamonds and sapphires. But it seems that your vice is entirely of a physical nature."

Molly should have been insulted, but she didn't have the energy. "It seems so." She snuggled against Wolf's side, and for a while he held her. If he knew how much she loved this, he would surely move away.

"Wolf," she lifted her head as her strength returned. "Why were you searching for my vice?"

"Because everyone has a weakness for something, and I wanted to know what yours was."

Molly rested her chin on Wolf's chest and tried to decipher the stony expression on his face. "This is a weakness?"

The dying firelight flickered on his face. He wouldn't look at her, wouldn't acknowledge that what had just happened was anything more than a moment of pleasure. "Yes," he finally said.

Molly knew what had happened was more meaningful than Wolf was willing to allow. Surely he recognized it, though, deep down, just as she did.

But now was not the time to ask more of Wolf than he was ready to give.

"Will you teach me to be wonderfully lascivious?" she asked.

Wolf turned surprised eyes to her, and Molly smiled.

"If I am to be as sinful as you," she continued, "I might as well be truly wicked."

Molly was brushing one flat nipple on Wolf's

chest with an indolent finger, and he caught that wrist in his fast grip. "Witch," he accused again, and with as little venom as earlier.

As he moved his mouth to hers, Molly wondered how long it would be before she could tell Wolf that he was her only vice.

She fell asleep in the exact position he'd awakened to find her in the night before. Her face pressed against his ribs, her leg thrown over his, as if she'd found the one place in the world where she fit perfectly.

Molly did seem to fit perfectly there, and she certainly didn't have any problem sleeping.

He did, though, as always. Only now he was wondering if he'd disturb Molly if he moved around too much in his sleep. If he rolled on top of her or rolled away. Either was a distinct possibility.

Wolf had never considered himself the kind of man who'd make a good candidate for husband. He liked his freedom too much, and he'd never intended to settle down.

But right now his cold, wide bed was warm, and Molly was breathing softly against his side, and he liked it. Too damn much.

It wouldn't last, he was certain. His nature was too restless. But for now, it was nice.

He should apologize to her, for erupting when she'd suggested he should have delivered his offered gifts himself. She'd been a child seven years ago, and she certainly wouldn't remember what had happened the last time he'd made an appearance in Kingsport.

He tried not to remember it himself.

He'd gone to Kingsport to fetch the doctor for his father, never suspecting what sort of furor he would cause just by appearing in town. Oh, he knew very well that there were those who suspected him of causing Jeanne's death and even of killing her outright, but he hadn't known how vicious they would be, or how hard it would be to face their hate, and such open hatred it was. Stones thrown, along with shouted words of loathing that had hurt more than any rock.

After he'd spoken to the doctor, as he tried to leave Kingsport peacefully, the crowd had grown. A young girl had stared up at him as he'd ridden past, with such fear in her eyes it had startled him. You would have thought she was looking into the face of an untamed man-eating beast. That had been the moment he'd realized that there was no hope for him, that no one would ever forget.

The stones had hit him steadily as he'd left town. His pride wouldn't allow him to race away, so he'd ridden back slowly and endured the abuse.

Not long after he'd looked into the terrified face of that pretty little girl, a small stone had hit him in the center of his back. He'd known the girl had thrown it, as soon as it hit.

He hadn't been to Kingsport since.

Molly didn't know all that, and Wolf suspected that if she knew the memory was keeping him awake she would pat him on the head and give

151

him a kiss and tell him to get some sleep.

In the dark Wolf smiled, gathered Molly close, and fell into a deep and dreamless sleep.

The man apparently never slept. Molly lifted her head from the pillow, brushing the tangled hair out of her eyes. A thin stream of sunlight broke through an opening in the heavy drapes, lighting Wolf's bedroom where she was all alone.

Just like yesterday. A smile crossed her face, even though he had deserted her without so much as a morning kiss. Already she'd decided that Wolf might be hers by night, but by day he was his own man. He would never admit by the light of day that he needed her.

One of the luxuries of the Trevelyan house that she had already learned to appreciate was the private bath that was connected to her own bedroom. Running water that was occasionally heated, if her timing was good, awaited at the twist of a handle.

Since she knew Wolf wouldn't have breakfast with her, Molly sat in the tub as the water cooled. Her stomach was growling, just a little, but this was an extravagance she would not quickly leave behind, not even for breakfast. Her hair was piled on top of her head, but a few errant tendrils fell past her shoulder and into the bath water.

When she'd arrived at her new home, she'd found the bath well equipped with scented oils and sweet smelling soaps. Thick, splendid towels hung from a rack by the door, and every day they were replaced with fresh ones.

Big Bad Wolf

Molly leaned back and stared at the high ceiling. In a few days, Wolf would return to New York. That thought stole her smile and her comfort. This would be such a lonely house without him in it. Harriet wouldn't allow her in the kitchen, Shirley scurried from the room whenever she entered, and Mr. Larkin . . . well, Mr. Larkin would be no company at all.

Just a few more days, and he would be gone.

Her daydreaming was interrupted by the sharp din of Wolf calling her name. Impatiently, as if it weren't the first time.

"I'm in the bath," she shouted, and a moment later he threw open the door.

He glared down at her, a flash of anger in his eyes, a hint of impatience. It didn't take long for his expression to change, to soften so slightly perhaps no one else would have noticed. But Molly did.

"I'm leaving for New York today," he snapped, lifting his eyes to hers.

"What?"

"A telegram was just delivered. It seems there's been a minor crisis with the steel mill."

"Oh," she gasped, feeling as if she were having a major crisis herself. "It's awfully sudden."

His face was so impassive. He didn't seem to care at all that their time together had been so short. "I'll have to pack and be out of here in less than an hour, if I'm to make the train."

"Less than an hour?" She tried not to sound as if she were complaining. Wolf didn't want a demanding wife, she remembered. "When will you be back?"

"I don't know." He left the bath, closed the door before he quite finished his sentence.

Molly dried herself sullenly, no longer hungry, no longer content. She dressed in her best gray dress, to see her husband off. There had never been time to even see about having new clothes ordered, much less for them to be made and delivered.

And she remembered that Wolf was tired of seeing her in gray and brown and white. He would leave for the exciting city of New York, with all its beautiful women, and this was how he would remember her. A dowdy wife in a plain gray dress.

Molly watched Wolf pack his bags, standing back and out of the way. She remained silent because he was silent. He didn't want a demanding wife, so it wouldn't do for her to make a spectacle of herself. She'd never been one to cry, but she felt like it now.

She would make a fool of herself if she cried because he was leaving, when he so obviously didn't care. In fact, he seemed anxious to return to New York, and she shouldn't be surprised. It was undoubtedly a much more exciting place than Vanora Point.

"So long, Red," he called as he hurried down the stairs with his two small bags.

Molly followed at a discreet distance, hurrying to match his step. So long, Red? That was it? "Wolf?" she called as he threw open the front door.

He stopped, turned to her slowly, and gave her

an unreadable stare from hooded eyes as he waited.

"Aren't you even going to kiss me good-bye?"

She didn't mean to pout, not really. It took him a moment, but Wolf finally dropped his bags in the doorway and returned to the foot of the stairs where she waited.

"You want a good-bye kiss?" he growled.

"I don't think it's too much to ask," Molly said defensively.

He kissed her quickly, impatiently, and no doubt simply to shut her up. His mouth barely touched hers, a cold brush of his lips like the poor excuse for a kiss he'd delivered on their wedding altar.

But before Wolf had completely raised his head, he relented with a low growl deep in his throat and kissed her again. A real kiss this time, with parted lips and hands that stole around her back.

"So long, Red," he said again as he drew his mouth from hers.

"Good-bye, Wolf." She reached up to straighten the lapel of his gray suit as he backed away from her. "Be careful."

He turned his back on her and headed for the door and his waiting bags.

"Don't forget that you must eat and sleep on occasion."

He picked up his bags and left the house, slamming the door shut behind him.

Molly hated this house without him, already. It was too big, and too dark, and too empty. With a sigh, she sat down on the bottom step. Minutes later, when Larkin rounded the corner, Molly was sitting there dejectedly with her head in her hands.

"Can I get you something, madam?" he asked formally.

"No thank you, Mr. Larkin," she sighed.

"Tea? Should I ask Cook to prepare your breakfast?" he offered again.

"I'm not very hungry," she said.

"Should I fetch the doctor from Kingsport?"

Molly lifted her eyes to the persistent man. "I'm not sick, Mr. Larkin. I just miss my husband already, that's all."

He raised a normally steady eyebrow. Did she shock him with her honesty, or was he surprised that she missed Wolf?

The front entrance exploded, both doors flying inward and crashing against the walls.

Wolf looked—furious was not the word. Savage, like the animal he was named for. "You have five minutes," he snapped. "Pack your bag."

"What?" Molly didn't even rise. "Where am I going?"

"You're coming to New York with me."

Chapter Ten

They traveled inland by speeding carriage, the silent driver, Willie, was at the reins, and Wolf said nothing at all. There was no explanation for his sudden change of plans, and Molly was afraid to ask for one.

She was afraid his explanation would spoil her good mood.

They were just in time to catch the train to Boston, and once they started moving, Wolf seemed to relax. Molly was certain that if Wolf had missed the train because he'd changed his mind about leaving her behind, he'd blame it all on her. Very unfair, but she was grateful they were on their way.

Molly had never been any farther from Kingsport than Vanora Point, and she peered through the window for a long time. Lulled by the speeding train, she finally fell asleep with her head on Wolf's shoulder.

In Boston they transferred to the steamer that would take them to New York, and Wolf carried their three bags to their stateroom.

It would be silly, wouldn't it, to let her husband see how excited she was? Perhaps so, but she couldn't help herself.

"Oh," she said suddenly, when an unpleasant thought struck her.

"Oh, what?" Wolf asked impatiently. They'd hardly said half a dozen words all day.

"I just wondered," Molly said uncertainly, "if I'll get seasick. I've never been on a ship before."

He gave her a look of disbelief. Did he think she would lie about such a thing? "Never? You live on the ocean, Red."

"On it, not in it," she said with a smile. "I've never actually been anywhere before, so there's been no opportunity for me to discover if I suffer from seasickness. My friend Hannah sailed to Charleston last year to visit relatives, and she said she was deathly ill the entire time. She really thought she was going to die."

Wolf crossed his arms over his chest, and there was, perhaps, the beginnings of a smile on his face.

"It's not amusing," Molly said indignantly.

The stateroom was comfortable, but small. In two strides Wolf was with her, his smile widening and his eyes sparkling wickedly.

"You won't get seasick," he rumbled as he

wrapped his arms around her.

"How can you be so sure?"

"I won't allow it."

Unreasonably, there was comfort in his assurance, and Molly smiled as she placed her head against his chest.

"I'll keep you so busy, you won't have time to be seasick," he continued. "Before you know it we'll be in New York and on dry land."

"You said we'd be nearly twelve hours traveling to New York. All night long, Wolf. What if I can't sleep? What if the rocking of the ship makes me ill? What if—"

Wolf slipped his fingers beneath her chin and forced her to glance up at him. He was more relaxed, happier, than he'd been all day. When he looked at her like this, it made her heart swell and beat fast.

"We'll be too busy to notice, Red. Trust me."

Molly kept her face lifted, her gaze on the tall buildings their carriage passed, and Wolf couldn't take his eyes off of her.

He would never know what had possessed him to go back, when he was well down the road and determined to leave her behind as he'd planned all along. How had she made him change his mind? With the request for a good-bye kiss, so unexpected and sincere? With the kiss itself? God, he couldn't get enough of her. Had his incentive been those soft words Molly had uttered as he'd turned his back on her? *Be careful. Don't forget to sleep and eat.* As if she actually cared.

Finally, he accepted the fact that he'd been gripped by the same madness that had possessed him to marry her, but he accepted this truth with a smile. It was quite safe to let down his guard and let go of the scowl he usually presented to his bride. Molly's eyes were devouring the city, the people and the buildings, and she had barely given him a second glance since they'd docked.

The madness that had driven him to such extremes was intensified by the fact that two nights at Vanora Point with his new wife were not enough to satisfy his hunger for her. The passion would die, he knew. It always did. Until it burned out he intended to put his obsession to good use, just as he had last night, on board the steamer that had carried them from Boston to New York.

It made no sense that he wanted Molly so hard it hurt to look at her, that a smile aroused him, that those little catches in her throat when he kissed her drove him over the edge.

When they pulled up to the Waldorf and two bellboys appeared to take their bags, Molly's eyes, impossibly, grew wider.

"Where are we?" she asked as he held her hand and assisted her from the carriage.

"Home sweet home," Wolf muttered.

"You live here?" At last she looked at him, studied him as if he were completely daft.

"Not normally, but I don't think you'd be welcomed at my gentlemen's club, where I keep a room."

"It's going to be terribly expensive," she whispered as he led her through the front entrance and into the ornately furnished lobby.

Wolf was able to make arrangements for a suite rather quickly, and a brass-buttoned bellboy led them to the elevator. Inside the box, Molly gripped his sleeve and held on as if for dear life.

"Wolf?" she whispered, her soft words loud in the small space. "What floor are we on?"

"Our suite's on the third floor."

"Are there stairs?"

"Of course."

She seemed to relax, but the grip on his sleeve didn't diminish. "Good," she breathed.

The bellboy led them to their suite, and at last Molly's vise-like hold relaxed. They would be quite comfortable here, until the time came for Molly to return to Vanora Point. His obsession, his uncontrollable passion for her would surely fade as the days passed.

Their bags were placed in the bedchamber, a sumptuous room dominated by a wide bed with an ornately carved bedstead and a canopy of figured mahogany.

As the boy nodded curtly at the opened door, Wolf stopped him.

"My wife is in need of a dressmaker," he said. "Someone reputable and quick. Can you make the arrangements?"

"Yes sir."

"Have her here at four o'clock this afternoon. I'll be back by that time." He reached into his pocket for a generous tip.

"Where are you going?" Molly asked softly.

"My office," Wolf answered as he peeled off a bill.

"What am I supposed to do while you're gone?"

Wolf paused with the single bill in his hand. "Did you ever finish your book?"

"No, but I don't have it with me. You didn't give me much time to pack, you know."

Wolf smiled at the bellboy and peeled off another bill. "Have a copy of *Little Women* delivered to Mrs. Trevelyan." His smile widened. "And while you're at it, pick up a copy of *Fanny Hill*, and *The Strange Case of Dr. Jekyll and Mr. Hyde*, as well." Wolf grinned down at his wife, at the innocent expression on her face. "A volume of Poe, I think, and if you can get your hands on an English translation of Balzac, that would be splendid."

He peeled off more than enough bills, and the bellboy nodded as he accepted the cash.

Molly waited until the bellboy was gone and the door to their suite was closed.

"Another copy of *Little Women* would have been sufficient," she protested.

"No, I don't believe so. Red, my dear, your education has begun."

"My education?"

Wolf brushed the back of his hand against her chin and her neck. "It was you who asked me, is it not true, to teach you to be truly wicked. Those were your words, Red. Not mine."

"Oh," she breathed.

"There's no better place in the world for such an education than right here in New York."

"Is that why you came back for me?"

She had no right to look so innocent, her clear gray eyes as guileless as a child's, her hair down and curling over her shoulders like a country maid's.

But she was no child, and she was no simple country maid.

"Yes," he said with certainty, even though he knew his answer was a lie.

Molly turned away from him, headed for the bedchamber to unpack, but Wolf caught her from behind and pulled her back against his chest.

"Wolf," she protested softly as he teased her breasts with gently rocking thumbs. Through the fabric, he felt her nipples harden. "It's the middle of the day."

"I know."

"But it's . . . it's . . . the middle of the day."

"You already said that." He propelled her toward the bedroom with a gentle shove, keeping his body against hers so she couldn't help but feel how he already wanted her.

"But—"

Wolf spun her around before she could protest again, silenced Molly with a rough kiss she responded to almost immediately. As he backed her into the bedroom, he slipped several buttons of her gray dress through his fingers, so that she was halfway undressed even before they fell to the bed, knocking the bags to the floor.

"Oh, my," she whispered breathlessly when he took his mouth from her to finish the job. "I didn't know a businessman could act with such a lack of decorum." She tried to sound serious, but broke

163

into a giggle before she'd finished her sentence.

Wolf shucked off his shirt and leaned over Molly, giving her his most wicked grin. "My great-grandfather was a pirate."

"Well that explains—"

Again, Wolf silenced Molly with a kiss, and her laughter died. What a sweet transformation it was. Swift, complete, magnificent. He savored it, as her merriment was replaced with a passion that matched his own.

Molly couldn't sit still. She paced to the window, glancing down at the bustling scene below. Carriages and pedestrians crowded the street, and everyone seemed to be in a hurry.

She'd never seen a carriage as elegant as the one that had carried them from the dock to the Waldorf, but vehicles as fine and even finer passed regularly beneath her room.

It was another world, so unlike Kingsport and even Wolf's grand house at Vanora Point.

This suite was as elegant as any room in the Trevelyan mansion, and larger than the house Molly had shared with her mother. It consisted of three rooms. The chamber she paced impatiently in was a sitting room, complete with a desk and straight-back chair, a settee, and two plush wing chairs, with a small table in reach of any chair. Unlike the Trevelyan house, this room was decorated brightly, all in gold and white.

There was a landscape hanging on one wall, and a gilt framed mirror on another. Fresh flowers, yellow and white, were arranged and displayed on the long table nearest the settee.

The bedchamber was as distinctive as the sitting room. Molly had never seen anything like the intricately carved canopy. There was also a huge wardrobe for storing their clothes, a piece that would have easily held everything Molly had ever owned. There was a vanity and mirror, rich wood that matched the bed and the wardrobe, and more yellow and white flowers were placed there.

Molly was afraid to touch anything.

The bath was similar to the one she'd used at the Trevelyan house, with running water and a supply of scented soaps and fluffy towels.

After wandering through the rooms, exploring but not touching, Molly made herself comfortable on the settee and picked up her new copy of *Little Women*. The same bellboy who had delivered their bags had brought her everything Wolf had requested, less than half an hour after Wolf had left for his office.

Molly tried to follow the story, but she was so excited she didn't do it justice. After several wasted minutes, she closed that book and picked up another one. She leafed through the pages, curious as to what sort of reading material Wolf had chosen for her.

Fanny Hill was a far cry from *Little Women*, she decided rather quickly.

Molly removed her shoes, tucked her feet beneath her, and started at the beginning.

The minor crisis at the steel mill, an expensive piece of broken equipment that had to be replaced, was easily taken care of. Horace, Wolf's assistant, had most of the paperwork taken care of. All that was needed was Wolf's approval and signature.

But the manager of the lumber mill was threatening to quit, and a summer storm had battered one of his best ships, so Wolf found himself with those problems to see to, as well.

Wolf came up with an offer the manager of the lumber mill couldn't refuse, and made arrangements for repairs to the ship. Fortunately, none of the crew had been lost, but there were bumps and bruises and a couple of broken limbs. By the time the ship was ready to sail, the crew likely would be, too.

Horace brought Wolf a small stack of papers to be signed, and without a word placed them on the desk.

Without his assistant, Wolf would be lost. Horace managed everything, had a brilliant mind for business, and as far as Wolf knew, the man had never been sick a day in his life. He'd certainly never missed a day of work.

Wolf signed the papers Horace had placed before him.

"I'm staying at the Waldorf, if you should need me." Wolf kept his eyes on the papers. As he signed each one, Horace whisked it away.

"Is there a problem at your club, sir?"

"Only that they're unlikely to allow my wife to stay there." He signed the final paper and handed it to Horace.

Horace still gripped the stack of papers, but

didn't take the last document. His normally placid face was strained, his eyes wide with surprise. Above his starched white collar, his neck turned red, and the color seeped up and into his normally pale face.

"Congratulations, sir." Horace's voice was calm, and while his face was slowly returning to a normal color, he couldn't erase the surprise from his eyes. "I had no idea you were planning to be married."

"Neither did I," Wolf revealed with a smile, as he continued to offer the last signed document.

"Would I know her, sir?"

Wolf shook his head, ignoring Horace's attempt to discover the identity of the newest Trevelyan bride. "Not a chance."

Horace recovered his composure and took the offered paper. He cleared his throat and straightened the papers unnecessarily. "We've another dispatch from Mr. Young's office, requesting a meeting."

"I've told Clarence a hundred times the steel mill is not for sale," Wolf said tiredly.

"He seems quite determined to have it," Horace observed.

His assistant had recovered quite nicely, Wolf thought. He'd dismissed the obviously shocking news about his employer's marriage and returned to the business at hand quite smoothly.

The word would spread. Horace was no gossip, but this was big news. Soon everyone in New York would be clamoring to meet Molly, the second Mrs. Trevelyan.

* * *

Molly fidgeted as the seamstress measured, teetering for a moment on the stool she stood upon. Wolf was facing her, seated quite comfortably in a plushly upholstered chair, his legs stretched out before him as he stared up at her.

They were talking about her as if she weren't in the room.

"She'll need two velvet dresses," Wolf instructed, "Four walking dresses, three ball gowns, six dresses suitable for receptions or parties. A silk evening robe, three nightgowns, five rather simple dresses for breakfast and lunch."

"Wolf!" Molly whispered, trying to get his attention. This was ridiculous.

He ignored her. "Whatever undergarments she needs, slippers, boots, stockings. Oh, and two shawls, one silk and one lace. That should get her started."

"I don't need so much . . ."

"Use a light hand where the lace and frills are concerned. And as for color, I have only one instruction. No brown and no gray. That monstrosity she's wearing is the best dress she owns, and when you're finished with your work I'm going to burn it."

The dressmaker sighed loudly, seemingly unaffected by the large order. "She should have a black silk dress. Something sturdy and practical."

"No black, either," Wolf snapped. "Nothing sturdy, nothing practical. I think I should like several things in blue and green. No pastels. No blasted pink."

"I like gray," Molly said, raising her voice just a little.

Wolf locked his eyes to hers. "You like gray. Well, I don't. Not on you."

"I don't want to be too . . . too flashy."

Wolf grinned, and the light in his eyes warned Molly he was up to no good. "All right, Red. One gray dress."

When the dressmaker was finished taking her measurements, Wolf lifted Molly from the stool and set her on her feet. Then she was excluded while decisions about her wardrobe were made. Wolf gestured with his hands, spoke so softly on occasion that Molly couldn't hear, while the seamstress made notes and nodded furiously.

She'd been afraid to ask why he'd come back for her. Why he hadn't left her at Vanora Point as he'd planned. And then he'd told her, to see to her *education*.

It was a game for him, she knew. Entertainment. She'd glanced through the books he'd requested for her, and knew he wanted to shock her, or else to transform her.

He wasn't as wicked as he pretended to be, she knew. *She believed*. Was she blinded by love, or did she see something others missed? From first glance she'd seen more than an immoral animal. She'd seen loneliness, and pain, and just a spark of hope.

He needed her. He might never admit it, but he *needed* her.

While he was teaching her to be totally wicked,

she was going to teach him what it was like to love and be loved.

When he closed the door on the dressmaker, Wolf turned to Molly. The smile he'd been wearing was gone, but it hadn't been a real and true smile, anyway.

"It'll be tomorrow morning before a delivery of any consequence can be arranged, but she's promised one decent dress within the hour."

"That's not possible. It took four women from Kingsport three days to make my wedding dress."

"Ready-made, Red," Wolf said sharply. "Not what I would have liked, but I can't take you out in that."

Molly glanced down at her gray dress, a plain but perfectly good garment. "There's nothing wrong with—"

"It's unsuitable for this evening."

She waited for Wolf to explain, to tell her where they would be going, but he turned his back on her and strolled to the window.

"Where are we going?" she finally asked.

Wolf glanced over his shoulder and grinned. "A gambling hall that happens to be a favorite establishment of mine. You'll love it, Red. Drinking, gambling, smelly cigars, and loose women."

"I'm awfully tired, Wolf. Can't we go another night?"

"No."

"But I could hardly sleep last night. I'd never slept on a ship before, and it was quite disconcerting."

He raised his eyebrows slightly. They both knew

that her sleepless night was attributed to more than the rocking of the ship.

"I don't believe New York can wait another night to meet the new Mrs. Trevelyan. What a sensation you'll cause, Red."

"Why?"

Wolf walked away from the window, and straight to Molly. "Why? Surely you appreciate the absurdity of this marriage."

"Absurdity?"

"There are those who believed that I would never marry again, and there are those who believed that no woman of sound mind would have me." Molly tried to look at a button on his waistcoat, but he placed a finger under her chin and lifted her face so that she had no choice but to meet his stare. "I go to Vanora Point for a few days and return with a wife I haven't known a full two weeks. They will all want to know what kind of a woman would marry me."

"Wolf . . ."

"And they'll all know that you married me for money."

"I did not—"

"They'll wage bets on how long the marriage will last, and perhaps even on how long you'll last." His green eyes glittered, hard and unrelenting. "And we'll smile through it all, you and I, and we'll create a scandal to rival that of my first marriage."

"And how will we do that?" Molly whispered.

Wolf lowered his face so that it almost touched hers. "Proper ladies don't go where I'm taking you

171

tonight. There will be a few daring and curious socialites in the crowd, hiding their features discreetly under a floppy hat, peeking from dark corners, seeking a thrill. Not you, Red. You're going to march into that club on my arm with a smile on your face. You're going to gamble, you're going to drink, and when someone tells a bawdy joke, you're going to laugh."

She couldn't possibly do any of that. This idea of an education was quickly losing its appeal. Molly knew she could get all the tutelage she would ever need in this very room.

"I don't want to go."

"It doesn't matter what you want," Wolf growled. "If you don't walk in on my arm, you'll be carried in over my shoulder."

He would do it, too, of that Molly was certain. Wolf was an awful lot like the great-grandfather pirate he'd told her about. He took what he wanted, and didn't care about the consequences.

That wasn't entirely true. Wolf did get what he wanted, but he'd never taken anything from her. He bargained, he cajoled, he seduced, until she gave in.

Molly grasped the lapels of his jacket as Wolf pulled her close. "Why? Why do we have to do this?"

A grin split his face. "It's going to be great fun."

Chapter Eleven

Once more, in the carriage that carried them from the Waldorf, Molly tugged at the bodice of her new emerald green gown. And again, Wolf laughed at her.

"She made a terrible mistake," Molly said, horrified at how much of her skin was exposed to the night air.

"It's exactly what I ordered," Wolf said calmly. Casually, he reached across to brush the back of his hand against the soft rise of flesh above the low neckline. In reflex, Molly shivered pleasantly, but she was still mortified.

There was nothing she could do about the indecent gown. All the tugging and pulling she'd done since first donning the gown, and there was still much too much skin exposed. She couldn't even bring her hair forward to cover herself. Wolf had insisted that she twist her hair up in a fashionable psyche knot, so that her bare shoulders and a good portion of her chest was exposed.

The carriage stopped in front of a red brick building. There were no windows, no fancy awning like the one in front of the Waldorf. There was not even a sign indicating that any sort of business was conducted within.

Wolf grinned as he helped her from the carriage, and Molly clung tenaciously to his arm as he led her to the red door. She wondered if he could feel her shaking. It was a deep tremble that wouldn't cease, no matter how hard she willed it.

At the door Wolf stopped and stared down at her. His grin was gone, and so was the amused sparkle in his eyes. "You look splendid, you know," he said softly. "Beautiful, in fact."

"I feel half naked," she whispered, and the grin reappeared on his harsh face.

"Wonderfully shocking," he confirmed as he threw the door open.

They were greeted by a somber faced man who recognized Wolf, and who merely nodded in Molly's direction.

"Good evening, Phil," Wolf greeted the man enthusiastically. "Have you missed me?"

"Terribly, sir," the gloomy-faced Phil replied dryly.

The fact that the man didn't give her a second glance warned Molly that she was not the first woman to walk into this gambling hall on Wolf's arm.

Big Bad Wolf

"Phil," Wolf said as he drew Molly close to his side. "Allow me to introduce you to my wife."

Molly watched with a grain of satisfaction as the man finally looked squarely at her. His eyes grew wide, and his mouth dropped open.

"My bride, actually," Wolf clarified with a grin.

"Congratulations, sir." Phil pulled his eyes from Molly and glanced up at Wolf. He had regained some of his composure, but was not yet completely recovered. "Enjoy your evening."

As Wolf led her into the smoky game room, he lowered his mouth to her ear. "Within five minutes everyone here will know."

They created a mild but noticeable stir as they walked through the gambling hall. Heads turned, men nodded to Wolf, and a few even spoke briefly before they returned to their cards or dice.

The room was crowded, with tables and chairs, with a crush of patrons. Worst of all, the air was horrible, thick with cigar smoke, bay rum, and cheap perfume.

Molly wasn't the only woman in the room, but the others were different from her. Brassy, bold-eyed women stood beside or behind the gamblers and clung to broad shoulders just as Molly clung to her husband's arm. A number of the women nodded and smiled at Wolf, and he returned their greetings.

In shady corners, a few women sat and watched. Broad brimmed hats shielded their faces, and they sipped champagne from long-stemmed crystal glasses.

Without instruction, a man appeared bearing a

tray laden with glasses. Wolf took his customary brandy, and handed Molly a glass as well. She started to speak, to refuse the strong drink, but the stormy look Wolf gave her stopped any protest.

"Well, well."

Wolf turned toward the sardonic greeting, and Molly turned with him. "James," he muttered, breaking into a distant and chilling smile that warned Molly this James was no friend.

"What's this I hear about you marrying? Another one of your jokes?"

"Not at all." Wolf sipped calmly at his brandy, but he was anything but relaxed. Beneath his jacket his arm was tense, and that tic in his jaw was working. "This is my bride, Molly Trevelyan."

The man turned his attention to her, and Molly stiffened. She didn't like the way he looked at her, as if she were a strumpet like the other women in the room. Of course, what was he to think, when Wolf insisted on dressing her this way?

"Well, well," he said again. "Brave little girl, aren't you?"

"Whatever do you mean, James?" Wolf asked casually.

James didn't take his eyes from Molly. "Doesn't she know about the first Mrs. Trevelyan? Perhaps I should enlighten her."

"You'll have to excuse James's horrid manners, darling. He's still angry because I almost bankrupted him in this very room, not much more than a month ago. He's always been a poor loser."

James ignored Wolf's revelation and insult.

"Money is a great motivator, isn't it Mrs. Trevel-yan? It can even induce a young woman to risk her life. To make great sacrifices. Particularly if the sum is great enough. With enough money, any man can buy himself a beautiful wife, even Wolf. Let's face the truth. In this country, if a man has enough money, he can get away with murder."

James finally pulled his eyes from her chest and looked up at Wolf. Wolf smiled, but beneath her hand his muscles were tensed, and he was ready to spring.

Their first night in New York, and already they were facing disaster.

"Sir?" Molly leaned forward slightly, placing herself between Wolf and the insulting man who had so angered him, and James returned his attention to her. "If you insist on making such outrageous assumptions, I will be forced to consider that it is you who are so very brave."

Someone in the back of the growing crowd laughed, and the tension was diffused. Even Wolf seemed to relax.

James had no answer for her, but turned away abruptly.

"Really, Red," Wolf said softly. "Things were just getting interesting."

"A little too interesting for me."

Wolf led her to a table where he sat across from a dealer, and he instructed her to stand at his side as he played. Molly felt as if every eye on the room was on her. The dress, the scene that had been narrowly diffused, the fact that Wolf kept her

177

close, all combined to produce exactly the reaction he wanted.

He played his game, faro, winning more than he lost. At times Molly thought he'd forgotten about her, but if she moved her hand from his shoulder or sighed too deeply, he turned to silently chastise her.

"My God, Wolf," a young man said as he took the next chair. He looked like a dozen men in this room. As young or younger than she, well-groomed, aloof in an annoying superior way. "What would possess you to bring your bride into Phil's?"

Did the man think she couldn't hear? How very rude.

Wolf didn't seem to think so. He smiled widely at the man. "She's lucky," he said brightly. "My new good luck charm. How could I possibly leave her behind?" He captured her wrist lightly, and turned her palm to his mouth for a quick kiss.

"Lucky?" the man muttered.

Wolf raised his eyebrows and turned to the dealer. "A fresh deck, before we continue," he instructed.

The dealer laid a deck of cards on the table before Wolf. He shuffled them several times, then he placed the deck in front of the brash young man at his side. The young man cut the cards, and then Wolf spread them across the table, a wide fan of cards.

"Five hundred dollars says she'll draw high card," Wolf said calmly.

"Wolf!" she protested. He ignored her.

Big Bad Wolf

The young man was excited by the challenge, and smiled widely. "Just five hundred? Really, Wolf, you have no confidence in your lucky charm at all. Double it, and you're on."

"Done." Wolf kissed her palm again.

"Ladies first," the young man insisted.

At Wolf's urging, Molly reached past him to choose a card. A thousand dollars on the turn of a card! Her fingers hovered over the fanned deck.

"Go ahead, darling," Wolf muttered softly.

Molly closed her eyes and flipped over a card. Wolf laughed, and the young man who had insisted on doubling the bet cursed. She opened her eyes slowly, to see that she had turned over the queen of hearts.

"Another red queen," Wolf said, glancing over his shoulder.

The young man reached out and turned over his own card, a ten of spades, and with a grimace he reached into his pocket and withdrew a thick wad of cash. He peeled off ten bills and placed them on the table in front of Wolf.

Wolf gathered up his winnings and folded the bills neatly, before offering the fortune over his shoulder. When Molly didn't take the cash right away, he glanced up and waved the cash.

"Take it, Red. It's yours."

Molly leaned forward. She didn't want to cause a scene, though she knew Wolf would be pleased if she drew even more attention to them. "I don't want it," she whispered.

"Ill-gotten gains," Wolf answered, apparently not caring who heard. And there was quite an audience. "But you won it, fair and square, darling. Don't be a spoilsport."

He had never called her darling before this evening, and it was becoming a trying habit. The endearment was delivered with no real affection, and in fact there was a sarcastic bite to the word that was beginning to irritate Molly.

"No thank you, dear," she answered coolly, and with enough sarcasm of her own to force Wolf to twist his head and look at her.

In a smooth and powerful motion, he stood. Somehow he was taller, wider, more forbidding than before. The cash was clutched in one hand, and in a smooth motion Molly didn't see coming, he tucked the wad of bills into the bodice of her decadent gown.

Then with a smile he gave her an almost innocent kiss on the cheek. "Don't ever defy me in public, Red," he whispered before he pulled away.

Molly was almost asleep on her feet, and Wolf watched her through narrowed eyes that he hoped wouldn't give him away. She yawned, covered her mouth with one hand, and blinked sleepily.

When the yawn had passed, she used the hand that had covered her mouth to push away a column of smoke that wafted past her nose.

No low cut gown or sophisticated hairstyle was going to make her appear to be anything more or less than what she really was—an unsophisticated and beautiful woman whose only fault was her bad taste in men.

He had finally allowed her to leave the table and

to sit in one of the vacant chairs that lined the wall. As he studied her, she caught his eye and gave him a look that was pleading and tired and impossible to resist.

"Tell me what I hear is not true."

Wolf turned toward the familiar voice and gave his old friend Foster a grin.

"Married? Wolf Trevelyan? It's blasphemy, that's what it is," Foster said as he took the vacant chair at Wolf's right.

"And true," Wolf added.

"What happened? You were drunk out of your mind and woke up married, right?"

"Actually, I was sober as a judge," Wolf declared.

"You got her with child and had to marry her? Why didn't you tell me?"

"Wrong again."

Foster leaned back in his chair, his fair features colored with too much drink and his hair mussed, no doubt by one of his many women. Women loved Foster Williams as easily as they were frightened of Wolf.

"She tricked you," Foster hissed, horrified. "How ghastly."

Wolf leaned back and wondered if Foster would remember any of this conversation in the morning. He was pretty far gone already. "If you must know," he revealed, "I married Molly on a whim. I wanted her, and marriage was the only way I could get what I wanted."

Foster looked terribly puzzled, completely uncomprehending. "Where is she? I heard the ridiculous story that you brought her here."

"Over there," Wolf nodded in Molly's direction, and Foster turned his head.

A smile split Foster's face. "Over there by the redhead? Forget the introductions, Wolf old boy. I'll meet this Molly later. Right now I think I'll introduce myself to the redhead. She's new isn't she?"

As Foster tried to rise, Wolf grabbed his arm and pulled him back down. A glance showed him that some lady out for a thrill, complete with proper gown and wide brimmed hat, sat next to Molly.

"Actually, Foster my old friend, Molly *is* the redhead."

Foster leaned back and studied Molly with more regard than was proper. "I see," he muttered wisely.

"What do you see?" Wolf growled.

"Your motivation for such a drastic measure as marriage. She's enchanting, Wolf, even though she appears to be colossally bored at the moment."

Molly yawned again.

"So, when do I get a proper introduction?" Foster began to rise from his seat again, and Wolf yanked him back down.

"When you're sober."

Truth be known, he didn't want Molly to meet Foster at all. Foster had the kind of good looks that drove women wild. Blond hair and blue eyes, features regular and perfectly proportioned. A smile that had been known to knock many a lady off kilter . . . and directly onto her back.

Foster was one of the few men who had stood by Wolf after Jeanne's death. At one time, Wolf had thought his friend believed him innocent. It had been years before he'd realized that Foster simply didn't care if he was guilty or innocent.

"Don't be a bore."

"She's tired," Wolf said as he stood. "We just got in this morning. Another time, Foster."

Molly stood as he approached, a look of pure hope on her face. "Are we leaving now?" she asked softly.

"Yes, we're leaving." He nodded to the woman under the broad brim, and took Molly's arm. Before they'd reached Phil and the door, she was yawning again.

A carriage was waiting, and Wolf practically lifted Molly into it. Once they were inside the coach she snuggled against him and closed her eyes.

"You smell," she said softly, wrinkling her nose but not moving away from him. "Like brandy and cigars and terribly sweet perfume."

"Thank you."

"That is not a compliment, Wolf," she insisted. "Do we have to go there again?"

He smiled down at the top of her head. The once tight knot of red hair had relaxed, and curls fell across his chest. "I go to that particular gambling hall almost every night."

Molly lifted her head and gave him a despairing glance. "Every night?"

"Almost."

She sighed against his chest. "I think we should go back to Vanora Point. I think I prefer the company of that uncanny Mr. Larkin to most any of the men you introduced me to tonight."

"I have business here, and besides, Vanora Point gets dreadfully monotonous after a while."

"I like monotony," Molly muttered as she closed her eyes again.

"I suppose you could stay at the hotel tomorrow evening, and I could go to Phil's without you."

She lifted her head slightly and opened one eye. "I don't think so. Those women were entirely too . . . too familiar."

There was a hint of petulance in her voice. Wolf could almost convince himself that his wife was jealous, but it was a ridiculous thought.

"What are you going to do with your winnings?" He slipped one finger into the bodice of her gown and withdrew the cash.

"I don't know," she said sullenly. "He wouldn't take it back."

"What do you mean," Wolf lowered his head so it was close to Molly's, "he wouldn't take it back?"

"I didn't want it, so when you finally allowed me to leave the table I tried to give it back to that rude young man. He seemed very upset when he lost."

"It would have been dishonorable for him to take that money, darling," Wolf droned. "You no doubt embarrassed him greatly. Very good," he added.

"Wolf," Molly said, and from the sound of her voice she was almost asleep. "Don't call me darling."

"Why not?"

She sighed once and placed an arm across his midsection, making herself quite comfortable. "Because you don't mean it."

Within seconds she was asleep.

The literature Wolf had provided was most interesting, but Molly couldn't possibly sit still all day. After a delivery of several new dresses, Molly put on one of the simpler outfits and laced up her walking boots.

There were throngs of people on the street, so it would certainly be safe for her to take a short walk. Wolf had told her to leave the suite only for lunch in one of the dining rooms downstairs, and while Molly was quite sure he had meant for her to return directly to the suite, he hadn't actually ordered her to do so.

The dress she wore was lightweight and simple in design, and the color was a pleasant blue, not a pale pastel and not dark, but the color of a robin's egg. Unlike her silk gowns, the neckline was decent, and she could leave the suite with her head held high.

She took the stairs briskly, slowing to a more sedate pace when she passed another resident.

She ate lunch as quickly as was proper. She watched the other diners, some families, some single diners like herself, and wished that Wolf were with her. Even when he didn't say a word, she was comforted by his presence. She had always enjoyed her quiet time in the forest, but she'd never wished to spend an entire day alone.

Her view from above, from the window of their suite on the third floor, had protected her from the noise, but as Molly walked down the promenade she couldn't help but make note of the riot of sounds. Horses' hooves against the road accompanied by the turn of well-oiled wheels was rather rhythmic, while the shouts that came from all around punctuated the rhythm irregularly.

She took in everything, turning her gaze up to the tall buildings, behind her to the awning at the entrance to the Waldorf, and even occasionally ahead.

Molly was looking up when she bumped into a woman who was peering through a shop window. She apologized profusely to a sour-faced lady who didn't seem inclined to forgive the infraction.

In order not to get lost, Molly stayed on the same street, even though she glanced longingly down unexplored avenues. Perhaps one day . . .

She was looking up when the boy ran into her, almost knocking her down. She grasped his shoulders, even as he tried to spin past her, mainly to keep either of them from falling to the ground.

A whistle sounded, a shrill intrusion to the sounds Molly was becoming accustomed to, and a second later a burly policeman in a wrinkled blue uniform grabbed the boy by the collar and dragged him backward and off of Molly.

The child squealed, and the policeman, a brutish looking man who was taller even than Wolf and twice as wide, lifted the boy so that he stood on tiptoes to keep from being choked by the grip at his throat.

"Excuse me," Molly called. The policeman ignored her and turned away, and she called again, louder this time.

A crowd was gathering.

The policeman turned slowly, and there was no hint of patience at all on his round face.

"Let me go!" the child screamed, struggling fruitlessly against the firm grip. The child's struggles didn't affect the policeman at all.

"What do you want, miss?" the policeman snapped, ungracious and impatient.

Molly stood tall and stared up into the policeman's face. Goodness, Wolf would be furious if she were arrested, but she couldn't allow that child to be manhandled.

The boy was filthy, his hair too long and matted, his clothes no better than rags. His screams had turned his face a bright shade of red, and he was clearly terrified.

"What are you doing to my brother?" Molly asked calmly.

The child stopped squirming, and turned inquisitive green eyes up to Molly.

"Your brother," the policeman repeated, obviously unbelieving as he looked up and down her expensive dress.

"Yes. You see," Molly turned her gaze to the little boy and smiled sweetly. "It's been just Ralph and me ever since the accident." She whispered mysteriously when she said *the accident*, and allowed the policeman to wonder at the circumstances. "Ralph ran away several weeks ago, and we've been so worried. I was recently married, you see, and poor Ralph was afraid he wouldn't be welcomed in my new home, but that's not the case."

"He's a thief," the policeman thundered.

Molly tsked loudly. "Ralph! I'm so ashamed." She turned her gaze back to the policeman, and tried to look properly contrite. "I'll be glad to pay for anything Ralph stole, and for any damages that might have resulted from his crime spree."

"It was an apple," the boy said, angry and beginning to struggle again. "And I only took it because I was hungry."

Molly reached out and took the boy's arm, and the policeman reluctantly released his grip. "You may send the bill to me at the Waldorf," she said calmly. The child and the policeman stared at her as if they were seeing her in a new light. "Molly Trevelyan, and please have the bill sent directly to me," she said, thinking of the fortune she'd won. "There's no need for Wolf to know about this."

The policeman grudgingly turned over his prisoner to Molly, and when the boy tried to break free she tightened her own grip.

"What did you do that for?" he asked, struggling, but just a little. "Are you crazy?"

"Of course not. I just couldn't let that angry policeman carry you off, and all for an apple!"

"Well, thanks," he said, every bit as grudging as the policeman had been. "But you can let me go, now."

Molly didn't let go. "What's your real name?"

Big Bad Wolf

He pressed his lips together.

"I suppose I shall have to continue to call you Ralph," she said with a sigh.

"Arthur," he muttered.

"How old are you, Arthur?"

Again, he clammed up.

"Ten?" she guessed.

"Fourteen!" he said indignantly.

She wanted to launch into a lecture on stealing, but his excuse rang in her ears. He'd been hungry.

Maybe he'd rather have a meal than a lecture.

Before she could make the offer. Arthur broke free and took off down the street. Molly thought about calling out, but she knew it would do no good. Arthur was quick, and Molly held her breath as the child crossed the street, barely avoiding being hit by a carriage.

Exhausted, Molly turned and started back toward the hotel. Children shouldn't be living like that, but she knew that many did. Hungry, dirty, with perhaps no one but a make-believe sister to protect them from the world.

On the way back, she didn't glance up once.

Chapter Twelve

Molly stared in dismay at the gray dress that was spread across the bed. This was Wolf's idea of a joke, the reason he had smiled so widely when he'd given in to her request for just one gray dress.

First of all it wasn't exactly gray. It was more of a pewter, and was shot with silver threads that sparkled when the light shone on the fabric. And she could tell very well that the neckline was every bit as low as the emerald gown, though it was more square than rounded.

The lines of the ball gown were simple, the skirt full but not flowing, and the bodice free of decoration. The pewter sleeves looked as if they would fit her tightly, from shoulder to wrist.

She was supposed to wear the monstrosity tonight, to a ball that was being held in this very hotel. Wolf had commanded it.

At least they wouldn't be going to that gambling hall Wolf insisted on frequenting. On occasion, Wolf would demand that she play a quick game of high card, and her luck had been good. There were several thousand dollars stashed in a new pair of shoes, money Wolf forced on her.

She didn't need it and didn't want it, but he wouldn't allow her to give it back. Of course, she'd used a bit of her initial winnings to pay the man who'd called on her to pay for the apple Arthur had stolen, and when he'd declared that he was sure the boy had stolen from his market before, and not been caught, Molly had paid him again.

That had been a very expensive apple.

She'd walked down Thirty-third Street several times since her encounter with Arthur, but she hadn't seen him again.

They'd been in New York less than a week, and already they'd fallen into a routine. Wolf was gone when Molly woke in the morning, and stayed away until late afternoon. Molly slept late, because Wolf kept her up half the night. She smiled as she fingered the pewter fabric that covered half the bed.

At night, when Wolf loved her, Molly knew that he needed her more than he would ever admit. He lost himself, forgetting to scowl, and he even smiled on occasion, a real smile, not his familiar wicked grin.

And Molly forgot herself, as Wolf did. She forgot that this marriage was a business deal, that her husband's obvious intentions were to corrupt her totally. He proved that every day with the shocking books he provided, the scandalous clothes, the late evenings in his gambling hall.

But what happened between them when all that was forgotten, when Wolf took her in his arms, was much too beautiful to be corrupt.

So Molly slept late, usually missing breakfast. She had a noon meal in one of the many dining rooms in the Waldorf, and spent the afternoon reading or stitching on a sampler she was making for Wolf. It was a wedding sampler, with their names and the date of their marriage embroidered in silk, and with a border of flowers in yellow and blue. Most afternoons she took a short walk. It was impossible for Molly to sit all day long.

When Wolf returned later in the afternoon, they changed clothes, dined in one of the smaller, more private rooms, and then the evening of debauchery began.

Well, to Molly their evenings at the gambling hall were debauchery. To Wolf they were business as usual.

Knowing it was scandalous, Molly donned the gray dress. She had known that the neckline was horribly low, but she wasn't prepared for the sight of her breasts pushed up and together until they practically spilled over the top of the square neckline.

"Wonderful."

Molly spun around at the sound of her husband's supremely satisfied comment. He was ready himself, clothed in black evening dress that made him look dashing and civilized, with just a hint of the Trevelyan pirate in his eyes and the set of his mouth to contradict the image.

"Wolf," Molly groaned. "I can't possibly leave our room in this gown. It's positively disgraceful."

"I know," he said with a grin. "And you're beautiful in it."

"Must we shock everyone in the city of New York?" It took all Molly's control not to stamp her foot like a displeased child. "Can you not leave me just a single grain of dignity?"

"Not a grain," he said casually, stepping forward with a predatory and wicked gleam in his eyes. "But there is something missing."

"You mean besides the top portion of my gown?"

His grin grew. "Besides that," he said lowly, reaching into the pocket of his dress jacket. "Turn around."

Molly did as he commanded, turning her back on that insolent grin.

"I like your hair twisted up this way," Wolf said, lowering his mouth to the back of her neck. "It makes this so easy."

Molly shivered. "This is what I was missing?"

She felt the cold weight of the jewels against her throat before she realized what Wolf was placing around her neck.

"Diamonds," he whispered against her ear. "Nothing else would do for this gown, don't you agree?"

Molly laid her fingers atop the cold stones that dangled against her skin. "It's too much—"

"You can never have too much, Red." Wolf spun her around and dangled matching earrings in front of her eyes. "Tonight, all eyes will be on you."

"And therefore," she said cynically, "on you."

"You know me too well," he admitted, fastening on one earring and then the other. When he was done, he stepped back and studied her with open admiration. "Splendid. You do dance, don't you?"

"Yes," she shook her head at him, making the diamonds at her ears sway. "Believe it or not my life was not a complete wasteland before you came along."

"Come here." Wolf reached out and captured her hand, and pulled her against him solidly. In his arms she felt safe, and warm, and happy. "You do look shockingly magnificent, Red," he said as he lowered his lips to hers.

She couldn't help but respond, as she did whenever he touched her. Her anger and frustration evaporated when Wolf molded his mouth to hers and teased her with his tongue.

Molly wrapped her arms around his waist and pressed her body against his. When he kissed her like this she felt it to her toes, to the very center of her body and her soul. Maybe they could forget the ball and stay right here.

Wolf pulled away from her abruptly, and grinned down at her wickedly. "That's better," he whispered.

"What?" she whispered dully as he stepped away from her. "What's better?"

"You were looking much too pale, but now

there's a nice glow to your cheeks and color to your lips."

"You're despicable," Molly said as he took her arm.

"I know."

Normally, Wolf avoided these occasions like the plague. Society accepted him because he had the Trevelyan fortune, but he'd always been just on the outside. He heard the whispers that followed him wherever he went, the rumors that had quieted over the years but had never died.

So he flaunted his unconventional life-style, threw their silly rules right back in their faces.

Just as he was throwing Molly in their faces tonight.

She clung to his arm as she had when they'd first entered Phil's. Did she look to him to protect her? Surely she knew better by now.

There was not another woman in the room to rival Molly. In the gray dress that matched her eyes, she cut a striking figure. And with that fabulous red hair piled high on her head, the bare flesh beneath it pale and soft, she would take the breath away from any man.

The jeweler who had sold him the diamonds had tried to sell a hair ornament to match, but Wolf had declined. He wanted nothing in the curls. Molly's red tresses needed no adornment.

All eyes turned to them as they entered the Grand Ballroom, and Molly's grip on his arm tightened.

"Don't be afraid, darling. I'm the only one here who bites."

His comment brought a smile to her lips, and Wolf was struck with the sudden urge to kiss her again. An urge he denied, because it revealed too much.

"Shall we dance?" he asked softly as he led Molly onto the dance floor. The crowd parted for them, and heads craned to get a better look at Wolf Trevelyan's unfortunate wife.

"I'm not very good," she revealed in a whisper when he took her in his arms for a waltz. "If I step on your toes will you let me fall?"

"Never," he answered in a voice as soft as her own, and she smiled up at him. Brilliantly. Beautifully. Bright as a summer day.

And he wished for a moment that he had forgotten his purpose for tonight. That on this evening he was alone with his wife in the solitude of their suite. And he wished, for a moment, that he knew how to love her.

Only for a moment.

"Wolf, darling." The husky, syrupy and insincere voice came from directly behind them, and Molly turned her head as Wolf did to see a tall, dark haired woman with a false smile on her face bearing down on them.

And she called Wolf darling.

"Adele." Wolf took the woman's outstretched hands and kissed them, one and then the other. "You're gorgeous, as always."

Molly noted the emeralds around the woman's

neck, at her wrist and her earlobes, and she wondered silently if Wolf had given the jewels to this Adele. If he had kissed her neck and placed the jewels around her throat.

Adele turned her wide brown eyes to Molly. "And this must be your bride." She all but gritted her teeth when she spoke, and Molly knew that this woman had been one of the mistresses Wolf had so casually spoken of.

"You've heard," Wolf said casually.

"Of course I've heard. The entire city is agog with the news."

Adele stood several inches taller than Molly, and her height, along with her striking black gown, provided her an imposing presence. The woman looked at Wolf as if she intended to kiss him right then and there, and made it clear with her proprietary stare that she wouldn't think twice about shoving Molly aside and taking her place.

Sometimes Wolf called her beautiful, but Molly had never believed it. This woman was truly beautiful.

Molly took Wolf's arm, and Adele noted the move with a cold smile.

"You're such a scoundrel, Wolf. All this time you've been sneaking off to Maine by yourself, and now we find you've been keeping this little country girl there all along."

Wolf just smiled.

"Actually," Molly said, leaning forward to gain Adele's attention. "We just met a couple of weeks ago."

"Really." The look Adele gave Molly was cutting,

and she wished she'd kept her mouth shut. "How charming," she added dryly.

Before Molly could think of a response, Wolf's strange friend Foster arrived, sneaking up quietly. "I don't want to miss this," he muttered as he took Adele's arm. Already, it seemed that Foster had had much too much to drink. He held a half empty glass comfortably in one hand, as he leaned against Adele.

"You've met Wolf's country girl?" Adele asked, a condescending tone in her husky voice.

"Briefly," Foster answered with a lift of his glass in Molly's direction. "It seems I always appear just as they're headed out or off or something of the like." He gave her a wide smile. "You put every woman in the room to shame, Mrs. Trevelyan," he toasted, and then he turned to Adele with a start. "Except for you, of course, dear Adele."

Adele was not appeased.

"If you'll excuse us." Wolf led her away from the odd couple. "I promised Molly the next waltz."

He spun her away from them, and onto the dance floor. "Thank you," she whispered.

"For what?"

Molly sighed, content for a moment in Wolf's arms. She wasn't a great dancer, but she hadn't yet stepped on Wolf's toes. "For rescuing me, of course, from your . . . your very strange friend."

"Adele or Foster?"

"Both." She wondered if she should ask Wolf about his relationship with Adele, but she was afraid he would be brutally honest with her.

"Most women find Foster irresistible," Wolf

said, narrowing his eyes slightly.

"And why is that?"

Wolf almost smiled. "His looks, I suppose. He's such a pretty boy. Of course, his money doesn't hurt, and he can be quite a flatterer, as you well know."

"Well, I think he's very odd."

"You do?"

"He drinks more than you do, and he smiles like a complete idiot, and . . ." She couldn't tell Wolf that there were times she just didn't like the way the man looked at her. "And how do you know him, anyway? Does he do business with you?"

"No. Foster inherited a lot of money, and decided to live like an English lord instead of an American financier. He doesn't work, and doesn't pretend to. I met him at the gentlemen's club where we both keep a room."

"You still keep a room there?" For the first time that evening, Molly slipped and stepped on Wolf's toe.

He seemed unconcerned. "Yes. I'll need it when you go back to Vanora Point, and it gives me a place to change clothes and rest after a sparring match."

"After a what?"

"There's a boxing ring at the club, and occasionally I spar with another member, or a boy they hire to fight with the members."

"You fight?"

Wolf leaned in close. "Shocked?"

"Nothing you do shocks me anymore," Molly revealed, her voice purposely droll.

"Actually, I haven't been to the club since we arrived. There's been no time." He spun her around, and Molly smiled. If she had her way, he wouldn't ever have the time or the energy for such a dangerous and unworthy pursuit.

"How long do we have to stay here, tonight?"

"Tired?"

"No."

Molly stared into his deep green eyes, telling him silently that she didn't need all this. The diamonds or the fancy balls, the shocking and expensive gowns, the luxurious suite. All she really needed was Wolf.

Wolf grinned. Perhaps he could read her mind, after all. "You are becoming as shocking and bold as your husband Mrs. Trevelyan."

"That should please you greatly," she said as he led her from the dance floor before the waltz was finished.

Molly had refused since their arrival to take the elevator, and in this Wolf indulged her. He even seemed to find it amusing that she was uncomfortable in the boxy device.

They climbed the stairs slowly, arm in arm. Away from the crowded ballroom, Molly could truly relax.

Wolf waited until they were behind the locked doors of their suite before he kissed her. He claimed her mouth, trailed his lips over her throat, past the diamonds and to the rise of pale flesh above her decadent gown.

"Wolf?" she whispered as she turned to allow him to unfasten her dress. "That Adele woman—"

"Hush." He trailed his lips along her spine.

"But . . . I didn't like her at all. Is she one of the mistresses you told me about? I mean, you told me there had been . . . and I never expected that you were a monk before we met, but . . ."

Wolf spun her around and glared down at her. "You're stammering, Red. Stop it."

"But the way she looked at you, I'll have you know I didn't like it at all."

He grinned. "A little sympathy, darling. Adele's just recently been widowed."

"I didn't realize." Of course, if Adele had been married it wasn't possible that she had been one of Wolf's women. "How very sad."

Wolf slipped the unfastened gown from her shoulders. "Well, old Tidwell had lived a long life, and he died happy, from what I hear."

"How does a man die happy?"

"In bed, and not alone."

"Oh." She frowned as she began to work the buttons of Wolf's shirt. "He was older? A lot older?"

"Old enough to be her grandfather."

"Adele's very beautiful," Molly admitted wistfully. "Why would she marry a man so old?" She lifted her arms, and Wolf whipped the chemise from her body.

"For the same reason you married me, Red. The old man had amassed quite a fortune."

She was tiring of this argument, and gave it little energy. "I didn't marry you for your money," Molly insisted softly.

"Then why, Red?" Wolf turned her around and unfastened the diamonds. His question was light-hearted, and she knew he took none of this conversation seriously.

"You were very persistent," she whispered.

"I was, wasn't I?" He dragged the necklace slowly across her bare flesh, allowing the cold stones to fall into the valley of her breasts before he took them from her completely and dropped them on a nearby table. "What was it that finally convinced you to have me?"

The tone of his voice remained nonchalant, and Molly knew her husband didn't yet believe there was any love between them. Life was a game, to him, and this was just another part of the sport.

"Three things, actually," she revealed as she turned to watch Wolf shed the last of his evening clothes. "The wildflowers, your hesitant request for redheaded children, and that first kiss."

He came to her and took the pins from her hair, allowing the curls to fall over her shoulders and down her back. There were moments, moments like this, when she felt she could tell him anything. Everything. Even that she loved him. He desired her, if nothing else, and he couldn't deny it. There was such hunger in his eyes, and even a hint of vulnerability.

"I still say it's sad," she whispered as Wolf reached beneath her hair to remove the diamond earrings. He trailed his fingers and the earrings slowly down her neck before dropping them to the table with the necklace.

"Being my wife?" He asked with a lift of his black eyebrows.

"No, that poor Adele. It's horrible. I don't ever want to be a widow."

"Trust me, Red." Wolf lifted her easily and headed for the bedchamber. "I don't ever want you to be one."

Molly slept nestled against his side, as she always did, and Wolf stared at the canopy above their heads, as he often did.

He wanted to rouse her slowly, to make love to her again, but he couldn't bring himself to disturb her when she was sleeping so peacefully.

Besides, waking her now would be proof that he needed her, and that wouldn't do.

Why did she continue to insist that she hadn't married him for his money? He knew that was the reason, and didn't care. Marriages had been arranged for hundreds of years, with the parties gaining something they wanted or needed. Land. Alliance. Money. Heirs.

Molly would never again have to work hard just to get by, and neither would her mother. She'd have everything a woman could want. Clothes. Jewels. Servants. The best of everything.

What Wolf got from the deal was Molly herself. She'd always said she couldn't be bought, but he'd proved her wrong. The price had been high, but she was his.

She'd seemed genuinely distressed to learn that Adele was a widow, and even more distressed at the possibility of finding herself in that situation.

Wolf hadn't wanted to remind her, as he'd propelled her toward the bed, that when that day
came she'd be a very rich widow.

He had tried to joke about dying happy himself,
when the time came, as he'd tossed Molly to the
bed, but Molly had made it clear she didn't find
his joke amusing.

She stirred against him, and lifted her leg
slowly, brushing it against his.

Forgetting his earlier concern that waking
Molly as he wanted to would prove that he needed
her, Wolf stroked her side slowly, bringing his
hand to a breast she'd pressed against his ribs. She
murmured in her sleep, and shifted slightly so that
her breast rested fully in his hand.

Eyes closed, she lifted her face to him, and the
faint moonlight that broke through the window
illuminated a small smile for him.

"You never sleep," she murmured.

Wolf took his hand from her breast, letting his
fingers linger and drag across the silky skin. "I
didn't mean to wake you."

Molly's eyes opened slowly. She took his hand
and put it right back where it had been when she'd
awakened, and then she placed her small, delicate
hand low on his belly. "Of course you did," she
said, her voice low and sleepy. "And since we're
both awake . . ."

The sentence trailed off as Molly brought her
face to his and kissed him gently.

When Wolf rolled Molly onto her back and entered her, he knew he would never have enough
of this. Of *her*. When she arched against him and

cried out, he knew she was his, and his alone. When his own completion came, with an intensity that drove away all rational thought, he knew that he needed her, just as she'd always planned.

And when Wolf fell asleep in Molly's arms, he knew this marriage was more real than he'd ever intended it to be.

Chapter Thirteen

Molly was well into *The Strange Case of Dr. Jekyll and Mr. Hyde* when the knock at the door sounded, and she nearly jumped out of her skin and off the settee. She hurried to the door, anxious to prove to herself that there was no reason to be shaking so.

She remembered well the face of the policeman, and she'd never forget little Arthur. Once again, the policeman gripped the boy by the collar, and Arthur struggled to no avail. A nervous bellboy stood a few steps back, wringing his hands in an uncustomary display of anxiety.

"I wanted to send up a card, Mrs. Trevelyan," the bellboy said defensively, "But this officer refused to wait."

"That's quite all right." Molly smiled at the fidgeting bellboy to ease his discomfort, and then turned her attention to the stern police officer.

"What's he done now?" Molly asked wearily.

"Stealin' again," the policeman growled.

"He's a difficult child," Molly revealed. "I'm afraid he ran away again, almost immediately after you returned him to us such a short time ago."

"There are places for boys like this."

Molly shivered at the policeman's words. *Places for boys like this* couldn't be very nice. "One moment."

Molly collected a sum of money from her shoe that would surely cover whatever Arthur had stolen. She left the door to the suite open while the policeman and the child waited in the hallway.

"Here we are," she said brightly as she returned to the policeman. "Would you please take care of paying for whatever it is Ralph's stolen?"

The policeman held his hand out, palm up, as Molly counted out what was certain to be more than enough for whatever Arthur had filched this time.

As she added a couple of extra bills, the man's glum face broke into what was almost a smile. With a mighty shove, he sent Arthur stumbling into the room.

"If you see him on the street again, would you be so kind as to keep an eye on him for me?" Molly asked sweetly. "He's been a trial, but he's a good boy at heart."

Stuffing the bills into his pocket, the policeman agreed.

Molly closed the door and leaned against it, giving the defiant Arthur a shake of her head.

"Stealing again?"

"I was hungry," he insisted, eyeing the door as if he were trying to find a way past her and to freedom.

Molly didn't move. "Perhaps you should join me for lunch," she suggested.

Arthur narrowed his eyes suspiciously.

"I do get tired of eating alone," she added, as if he would be doing her a great favor by agreeing to dine with her. "You'll have to have a bath first, of course, and I suppose you could wear something of Wolf's." Anything of Wolf's would be much too large on the boy, but a definite improvement over the rags he wore.

"I ain't takin' no bath."

Molly leaned against the door, refusing to be intimidated by the urchin. "That's too bad. The food here is excellent. Yesterday there was steak an inch thick, and the most delicious rolls, warm from the oven, and potatoes, and chocolate cake for dessert."

Arthur didn't quite trust Molly, but the promise of such a feast was too much for him to resist. She ran the bath while an amazed Arthur looked on, and left behind towels and soap and one of Wolf's more worn shirts and a pair of trousers. The cuffs of the shirt were just beginning to fray, and the trousers were sturdy but not among his best. With a belt cinched tight they'd do just fine.

It was a handsome and completely transformed boy who descended the stairs with her. His hair was much too long, but it was clean and Molly could see that it was a medium honey brown. In the new clothes that were too large, Arthur held himself tall.

She'd expected him to devour his food, but Arthur ate slowly, savoring every bite.

Arthur was not quick to answer her questions, but as the meal wore on and a few tidbits were divulged, Molly came to understand the urchin who continued to steal. He had no family. His mother had died the year before. For a while he'd worked for a chimney sweep, but at fourteen he was already too big for the job.

Since being dismissed by the chimney sweep, he'd been living on the street and stealing or begging for food.

That just wouldn't do, Molly thought.

She considered, for a moment, taking the boy in. How would she ever convince Wolf to take on this kind of responsibility? It would never work. Besides, Wolf would be a terrible influence on such a young boy.

Before the meal had ended, she'd arrived at a solution.

Arthur didn't need to be taken in, he needed a real and stable job, a place to stay and food on the table.

The Waldorf was just the place for him.

"What's wrong with you, Wolf? Married life going sour so soon?" There was a smile in Foster's voice, and Wolf scowled at his friend.

For the first time since his return to New York, Wolf had stopped at the gentlemen's club when his day was done at the office. Every day he found that he was all but rushing to the Waldorf to see his wife, smiling as he contemplated the night to come. How totally inappropriate and unlike him that was.

Today he'd forced himself to stop. He needed time to think, he told himself.

"Not at all," he confided as Foster joined him. This was a man's room, a place for cigars and brandy and all the pleasures Molly turned her nose up at. "It's going, in fact, disgustingly well."

He had indeed found Molly's vice. In his bed she held nothing back. In his arms she melted. They laughed in bed—a first for Wolf—and Molly cried out as Wolf brought her to the ultimate pleasure.

He should have been pleased, but there was a nagging voice in his brain that had become quite insistent, a voice that told him, again and again, that Molly could find that same pleasure in the arms of another man.

It was ridiculous. He didn't love her, but this insistent doubt was too close to jealousy for comfort. He told himself it was his right, and nothing more. Molly was his wife, after all. He had every right to feel a certain possessiveness.

"You don't look very happy for a man whose marriage is going disgustingly well."

Wolf returned his attention to Foster and sipped at the brandy. "I have my suspicions," Wolf revealed.

Foster grinned widely. "What sort of suspicions? She doesn't look the sort you'd have to worry about, but they're often the ones you have to watch most carefully. Has she already been un-faithful?"

"No," Wolf said softly. "At least not yet. I won-der, though, what she would do if she were tempted. She has such—" He stopped abruptly. There was no need to share with Foster that Molly hid an incredible passion beneath her veil of pro-priety.

"You could always hire a man to watch her," Foster suggested. "That's what Celia's husband did when he suspected that we . . . well, you re-member how unpleasant that evening was."

Foster had never lacked for women in his life, in spite of his obvious failings. Few women could resist the combination of his charm, his money, and his good looks. There had been a time when Wolf and Foster spent many evenings together, and more than one woman had commented that they made an odd pair.

The pale and almost pretty Foster. The dark and harsh Wolf. Adele had said that the two of them together could fulfill any woman's fantasy. Some-thing for everyone, she said, but Wolf had never doubted that the charming Foster came closer to any woman's dream than he ever had.

Molly had claimed not to like Foster much, but was that the truth?

"Actually," Wolf said casually, "You could do me a tremendous favor."

"And what would that be?"

Wolf studied Foster's immaculately groomed blond hair, the even features, the bright blue eyes. Foster Williams was everything Wolf was not, everything a woman wanted in a man. "I want you to flirt with my wife."

Foster's smile faded. "I don't think I heard you correctly."

"I want you to flirt with Molly, and then I want to know how she responds." *And if she tells me about it.*

He was still certain that Molly wanted something from him, something she had not yet revealed. It wasn't in him to trust any woman, but he would rest easier if he knew Molly would be faithful and honest.

"Tonight," he said. "At Phil's. You'll be there?"

"Of course," Foster said dully. "Aren't I always?"

What had he done? He didn't love Molly, so why did he care if she was faithful? Why did the thought that she might respond to another man the way she responded to him make him more than a little crazy?

Molly's hold on him was too secure. Her appeal was growing instead of fading as it should, and he couldn't allow it. When he had to remind himself again and again that this was no ordinary marriage, that she was no ordinary and devoted wife and he shouldn't be expected to be an ordinary and devoted husband, then he knew he was losing control of the situation.

Molly had done nothing to hint that she was or would ever be anything less than faithful, so why did he feel compelled to test her this way?

Wolf eased his conscience by reasoning that he wanted to make certain any redheaded Trevelyans were his.

Big Bad Wolf

*   *   *

Molly clutched the lace shawl over her rising cleavage, hoping that just this once Wolf would allow her to keep herself covered for the evening. At first she thought he would, and then he whipped the lace shawl from her shoulders and handed it to Phil, leaving her standing there in another of the outrageous gowns, a sapphire blue creation that was cut low both front and back.

By now she knew many of the regulars at Phil's, and they recognized her as readily as they did Wolf. They didn't stare at her so boldly as they once had, and she'd even heard that they called her Wolf's red queen. She preferred that description to Wolf's country girl, the title Adele had so ungraciously offered.

Wolf was distracted tonight, not his usual self. He said he'd had a difficult day in his office, but he wouldn't share any details with her, and he wouldn't even consider spending the evening in their suite and forgoing another evening at Phil's.

She sat beside him as he gambled, winning as he did most every night. The money didn't seem to mean anything to him, but the winning ... Wolf loved to win. It didn't seem to matter if it was a game of cards, or business, or a battle in their constant gentle war. Winning was everything to Wolf. It was a characteristic Molly didn't quite understand.

Adele came in not long after they'd arrived, dressed in black and wearing a broad brimmed hat that shadowed her features. She was unmistakable, though, in her bearing and her signature

Linda Jones

black. Adele walked along the wall, stood alone for a moment and watched the patrons who played and drank and laughed, and after a while she disappeared into the crowd.

As long as she stayed away from Wolf, Molly didn't care where the woman was or how she passed her evenings.

Wolf was quickly bored tonight. He took his winnings and left the faro table, taking Molly's arm as she stood.

"Why don't we just leave," Molly suggested softly. "It seems you don't feel well tonight."

He glanced down at her, and the spark in his eyes was cool, distant. "I feel fine. Why don't you sit here and rest for a while, and I'll search out another game."

"Rest from what?" Molly complained in a low voice as Wolf led her to the chairs against the wall. "Sitting and watching you gamble is hardly tiring."

"I'll be back," Wolf said shortly as Molly lowered herself into one of the comfortable chairs. She watched her husband walk away, watched as he disappeared into the crowd and the cloud of smoke.

At times like this, Molly wondered if she hadn't made a terrible mistake. No matter how fiercely Wolf believed it, marriage was not a business deal. It was a commitment, a pledge, a partnership of the highest order. It was a joining, of heart and soul and body, and there was nothing businesslike about it.

At least, not to her. On occasion, Wolf made

mention of the day when she would return to Vanora Point. She had known all along that was his intention, but she didn't like to think about returning without Wolf. If only he would go back with her, conduct his business from the Trevelyan house and live a normal life.

But to Wolf, this was a normal life.

"I thought I should never catch you alone."

Molly glanced up and saw Foster easing himself into the chair next to hers. He seemed not quite as tipsy as usual. His smile was not so wide, and he didn't wobble at all as he took his seat.

"Wolf will be back soon," she said. "He's looking for another game."

"I can't imagine why he continues to spend so much time here when he has you." Foster locked those blue eyes on her. "You are gorgeous," he whispered. "Fascinating. I wish there was some way you and I could spend more time together. Get to know one another better."

"Perhaps when Wolf returns the three of us can have a nice long talk," Molly suggested, trying to ignore his improper comments and the nasty gleam in his eyes.

"How wonderful it would have been if I had met you first." He leaned close, too close. "If I had a woman like you, Molly, I'd never leave her sitting alone."

Molly searched the room quickly for Wolf. Foster made her nervous. Actually quite uncomfortable. "He'll be back in a minute."

"I don't think so. I saw him headed to one of the private rooms in the back."

"He wasn't feeling well," Molly confided. "I hope he's not ill."

"Shall we go see?" Foster stood and offered his arm, but Molly rose without his assistance.

"Where are these private rooms?"

"Down the hallway, beyond the ladies' salon." Foster took her arm and led her through the crowd. Even when they were through the crush and approaching the hallway, he held her arm and leaned much too close.

As they passed the ladies' salon, they heard a low feminine laugh from one of the private rooms, and Foster stopped suddenly. "You wait here, while I look for your missing husband."

Molly breathed a sigh of relief as Foster moved away, and she leaned back against the wall and the fancy wallpaper that was shot with gold and blue. All she wanted was to go home. Not just back to the Waldorf, she realized, but back to Maine. She missed the woods, and her mother and her grandmother, and fresh air, and wildflowers. The only problem was, she wanted Wolf to go home with her, and she didn't think he ever would.

"No sign of him." Foster reappeared to interrupt her thoughts. "I guess I was mistaken."

"Oh, well." Molly tried to turn away, but Foster's arms, placed beside her and effectively pinning her to the wall, stopped her.

"It's such a nice change to escape the noise and the smoke," he whispered. "I know the smoke bothers you, Molly. I've seen you brush it away from your eyes at the end of a long evening. Why don't we enjoy the peace and quiet for a while?"

Big Bad Wolf

"I really should find Wolf—"

"As a matter of fact, if you really want to escape this madness for a while I could secure us a room of our own." Foster lowered his face, as if he planned to kiss her, and Molly ducked down and under his arm. She wasn't fast enough, though, and he snagged her arm before she could steal away.

"Come on." Foster tugged on her arm, hard, and pulled her body against his. "Don't be a prude. Wolf and I have shared women before."

One hand held her arm tight, and the other brushed the flesh that rose above the low neckline of her gown.

"Oh you have," she said in a low voice, and she felt Foster relax. Just enough.

Molly kicked his shin, pushed against his chest and turned as he fell. She saw just a glimpse of the surprise on his face before she went in search of her husband.

Where was he? Why had he left her alone to fend off that drunken idiot? Of all evenings for Phil's to be so crowded! The place was thick with gamblers and their ladies, curious onlookers, Phil's own employees bearing trays of filled glasses. Smoke hung over the room, blurring her vision like fog as Molly looked for Wolf.

He was taller than most, and she should have been able to see his head above the rest, unless he had found another game and was seated somewhere in this room.

Her heart beat in panic. She'd never expected that Wolf's own friend would attack her! Wolf would be furious, but she wouldn't feel safe until she was with him, until she could lay her hand on his arm and beg him not to leave her alone in this place again.

She walked past the tables, but Wolf could not be found. It took all her restraint not to lift her head and scream his name. Not that he would mind. He loved it when she made a scene.

"Wolf's red queen," someone shouted coarsely, and before she knew what was happening someone at the faro table had grabbed her wrist and held tight. "I need a bit of luck myself right now," a vaguely familiar man said with a smile. "Stand here while I win this hand."

"I . . . I can't," Molly said, yanking her hand from the man she recognized as one she'd won more than a thousand dollars from on the turn of a card.

As she spun away she saw Wolf's head, on the other side of the room and headed for the hallway where Foster had attacked her. It seemed everyone in the room was determined to get in her way as she headed back for that side of the room. She weaved her way through the crowd, slipping through with a gentle shove here and there, until she saw the entrance to the hallway.

Wolf was just entering a room at the end of the hall, and Foster was, thankfully, absent.

Molly took a deep breath and hurried down the hallway. Wolf would be furious, but she had to tell him what had happened. More than anything, she wanted him to hold her, and tell her that everything was going to be all right, and promise her that he wouldn't ever leave her alone again.

She heard the voices coming from the room long before she reached the door that Wolf had left ajar.

"Darling, I thought you would never come."

That husky voice was unmistakable. Adele.

"What do you want?" Wolf asked casually.

There was a pause, a long pause, and Molly's imagination ran wild. What were they doing? Should she burst in and stop whatever was happening?

"I want to know why you married that . . . that girl."

She recognized Wolf's low laugh, the one that held no real humor. "Jealous, darling?"

Molly felt her knees go weak.

"It's time to see that the Trevelyan name doesn't die with me. Molly's going to give me children."

"I could have given you children."

Molly's stomach turned.

"You don't have a maternal bone in your beautiful body, Adele," Wolf said with a laugh.

There was another long silence, and Molly clenched her fist and fell softly against the wall.

"Don't worry," Wolf said casually. "As soon as she's with child I'll take her back to Vanora Point and leave her there. Then you and I can continue as we always have."

But she'd been married. Molly hugged herself tightly, trying to chase away the chill. It had never occurred to her that Wolf would sleep with another man's wife. How could he? It was so . . . so wrong.

If he would sleep with a married woman, he would never be faithful to her. Wolf had never made her promises he didn't intend to keep, and he had certainly never promised to be faithful. He'd said it himself. She'd heard the horrid words from his own mouth.

As soon as she was with child, he was going to ship her off to Maine and return to New York and Adele.

She shouldn't be crushed to find that a man who didn't love her would betray her with another woman, but that was how it felt. As if Wolf was literally crushing her from the inside out.

"I still say you didn't have to go to such extremes," Adele purred. "Really, Wolf."

"I must admit, Mrs. Sloane had something to do with this."

"Christine Sloane?"

"There's nothing more tenacious than a mother with five plain unmarried daughters. It had gotten to the point where I half expected to wake one morning, hung over from a spiked drink, to find that I was wed to the eldest and ugliest of the five."

Adele laughed. "I guess I have no choice but to forgive you."

"I guess you don't."

"Wolf, darling, you didn't even close the door."

Molly turned away, flinching as the door was slammed shut. She didn't know if Wolf or Adele had swung the door so viciously, but it didn't really matter.

Had she ever really hoped that Wolf could love her? Molly didn't stand in the hallway for long, but turned away from the private room her husband and Adele shared. She had. In spite of all his talk of businesslike marriages and corruption, she'd hoped for love. She'd even fooled herself into believing that she saw it in his eyes, on occasion.

She made her way through the crowd again, headed for the front door. She slowed when she saw Foster collecting his hat from Phil, having no wish to come face to face with the man ever again.

By the time she reached Phil, Foster was gone.

"May I have my shawl, Phil?"

He fetched it for her quickly, and looked over her shoulder with an anxious widening of his eyes. "And Mr. Trevelyan?"

"He'll be leaving later," Molly said absently. "Much later."

"Let me see you into a carriage, Mrs. Trevelyan," Phil offered.

Molly held the shawl tight. It was a warm night, but she was chilled to the bone. "No. I think I'll walk."

"You can't—"

Molly hurried out the door, unable to stand there and carry on a conversation with Phil or anyone else.

Carriages lined the sidewalk, some private and some for hire. The drivers visited, their voices soft in an otherwise silent night.

They turned their heads to look at her expectantly, and Molly turned away, headed in the direction of the hotel. It shouldn't be a terribly long walk, and she needed to clear her mind.

Wolf had never promised to be faithful, except

in wedding vows he obviously didn't take seriously. He'd never said he loved her, never even said that he liked her.

All these nights she'd spent in his arms, she'd thought there was something there. Love, passion, need. And all he'd been thinking of was getting her with child so he could have his heir and go on with his life of debauchery.

She shouldn't be surprised, but she felt as if he'd reached into her chest and crushed her heart. Tears welled up in her eyes, even though she willed them away.

She crossed a street without even looking for approaching carriages. This wasn't where she should turn, was it? The next street, or perhaps the next.

Streetlamps cast circles of light on the sidewalk, but most of the neighborhood Molly walked through was in shadow. There was enough light to see that much of what she passed was dirty. Her nose told her it was no illusion.

She missed the shadows of the forest, the green of the trees, and the clean smell of pine and an abundance of fresh air. She didn't belong here, not on this street, or in this city. For the first time she considered that marrying Wolf had been a mistake.

It didn't take her long to realize that she was lost.

The dark street was suddenly ominous, more forbidding than the forest had ever been. And here, there was no magic. No Wolf.

"Hello there, pretty lady." Molly started, nearly

jumped out of her skin, as a man stepped from the shadows and into the light. "Are you lost?"

"Yes. No," she said.

The man was dressed in clothes that needed mending and washing, and his beard and hair were untended. When he grinned at her, she saw that he was missing a front tooth.

"I'll help you find your way home," he offered. "But it'll cost you."

Chapter Fourteen

Wolf left a pouting Adele behind, closing the door softly. His grin died as he stepped into the hallway, a reaction he hadn't wanted Adele to see.

The explanations had come naturally enough to his lips. He *had* married Molly with the intention of bedding her until his obsession had faded, and then leaving her in Maine to raise his children. He *had* reasoned that with a wife in Vanora Point, the Mrs. Sloanes of New York would have no more reason to harass him.

And he had *never* intended to be a faithful husband. It had always seemed unnatural, the prospect of spending ones life with one woman. Hell, he'd actually laughed at men who'd allowed a slip of a woman to lead them around by the nose, and he'd sworn more than once that he'd never . . .

Of course, Molly wasn't exactly leading him around by his nose.

But as Adele offered herself to him, Wolf realized that he didn't want her. Not in the least. It was a turn of events neither he nor Adele had expected.

Good God, all he wanted was to find Molly and get out of this place.

She wasn't sitting where he'd left her, and he searched the room for that familiar and striking head of hair. When he didn't spot her immediately, as he should have, he looked for Foster's pale head.

His heart sank when he realized that neither of them were in the room, and his imagination ran wild. Were they occupying one of the private rooms like the one Adele had secured? Had they stepped outside, perhaps for what Molly had demurred would be no more than a kiss?

As he searched the room as inconspicuously as possible, another, more horrible scenario occurred to him.

They were really gone. Not outside and not in a private room. But gone.

Well, he'd asked for it, hadn't he? Literally.

Adele emerged from the hallway with her head high and her disguising hat in place. He couldn't see her face as she made her way through the crowd and to the front entrance, but he knew she was still angry. Adele didn't like not getting what she wanted any more than he did.

Wolf took a brandy from a passing waiter, and downed it in one shot. He'd known all along that no one could be as innocent and pure as Molly had always pretended to be. He'd tried from the beginning to corrupt her, to introduce her to the pleasures that lay off the path.

How well he'd succeeded.

A seat was vacated at a nearby table where a rousing poker game was going on, and Wolf took it. Smiles faded as he glared at each and every one of his opponents.

He won the first hand, but there was no joy in it. The man next to him gathered the winnings and placed the money before Wolf, when it became obvious Wolf wasn't going to do it himself.

The second hand was terrible, and Wolf folded early. While the hand was played out he glanced around the room, unconsciously and then consciously searching for Molly or Foster.

The third hand nearly gave him heart failure. A pair of queens, diamonds and hearts.

Before the hand was finished, Wolf tossed his cards into the center of the table and abandoned the game.

He made his way through the crowd, ignoring friendly greetings and vigorous challenges. The noises and the images around him blurred, turning Phil's into a gray nightmare. Dammit, she was his *wife*.

Wolf was headed for the door with a single and unbending purpose.

"Good evening, Mr. Trevelyan," Phil said formally as Wolf passed. "I do hope Mrs. Trevelyan reached her destination safely."

Wolf stopped in mid-stride and spun around. "What do you mean?"

"She left here not long ago, and said she was going to walk." Phil sounded rather horrified at the prospect. "I did offer to see her into a carriage, but she left rather quickly."

"Alone?" Wolf asked with a lift of his eyebrows.

"Yes, sir. She seemed, if I may say so, rather anxious."

"She would," Wolf muttered.

"Excuse me, sir?" Phil leaned forward to hear more clearly.

"Never mind. Foster Williams wasn't with her? I rather expected him to see her home."

Phil shook his head slowly. "No, though I do believe he left just before Mrs. Trevelyan. Perhaps she did catch a ride with Mr. Williams, after all."

"Perhaps." *Just like Molly, to be concerned about appearances.*

Molly took a step back and the man stepped forward, bringing that horrid grin into the light.

"I'm not lost," she said again, and a bit more forcefully. "My husband is right behind me."

"I don't think so, missy," he said softly. "I've been watching you stumble along for the past three blocks, and as far as I can tell you are all alone." His voice was menacing, and more than a little crazy.

Molly spun around and ran back in the direction she'd come from. If she could just make it back to Phil's she'd be all right. Anger had carried her from the gambling hall, anger and a certainty that she couldn't face Wolf again, couldn't look into his eyes and see the same man she'd loved since she'd met him in the forest. She should have waited for her inconstant husband, rather than running away like a spoiled child.

If she could just make it to Phil's, a hired carriage would take her to the hotel. She thought of this and nothing else as she listened to the plodding footsteps that were gaining on her steadily. Before she made it to the corner, an insistent hand grabbed her arm and stopped her in her tracks.

"Where are you going in such a hurry, missy?"

Molly tried to jerk away from the man, but he held her fast. When he forced her to turn and face him, she was assaulted by the strong odor of unwashed clothes and fetid breath that made her hold her own.

"Let me go," she insisted softly.

"No." He leaned close to her face, bringing an unkempt beard and that terrifying smile much too close.

There was a thwack at his back, and in spite of his refusal to release her, the man removed his hand from her arm quickly, jumping back and away, and Molly got her first view of her savior.

The woman was shorter than Molly, and appeared to be younger as well. Her clothes were plain, her straight hair hung loose, and she wielded a long broom with both hands.

"The lady asked you to let her go."

She had a strong voice for one so small and delicate. Faced with the unusual weapon, the man who had accosted Molly slunk away, crossed a deserted street and disappeared in the shadows.

"Thank you," Molly began, and the girl turned a disapproving face on her.

"What are you doing out here this time of night and all alone?" the girl snapped. "If I hadn't been sitting at the window unable to sleep, there's no telling what that man might have done."

"You're right, of course," Molly said with a sigh. "I feel so foolish. You see, I lost my temper, and stormed off without thinking. I thought I could walk home."

"And you got lost," the girl finished, finally lowering her broom. She looked Molly up and down, disapproval in her eyes and in the shake of her head. "Well, why don't you come on up to my room, and in the morning we'll get you back to wherever it is you belong."

"I couldn't impose," Molly began.

The girl turned away from Molly wearily, raising her eyebrows only slightly. "Do whatever you want. That bum is probably watching us right now, you know. He'll run from a broomstick, and when the odds are against him even if we are only women, but he won't hesitate to follow you if you leave here on your own. You can try to make it home tonight, but I wouldn't recommend it."

Molly fell into step behind her rescuer, who was moving rather quickly. "Thank you so much. My name's Molly Trevelyan," she said as she came alongside the girl.

"Bridget Brady."

They stepped into a narrow building, and climbed steep, narrow stairs.

"Wolf will be worried," Molly mumbled to herself as she followed Bridget up the steep staircase.

"Who's that?" Bridget asked casually.

"My husband," Molly said softly, and Bridget glanced over her shoulder.

"He's the reason you're out by yourself in this part of town at this time of night?"

"Yes," Molly admitted as they turned on the landing and began to climb to the third floor. "Well, Wolf and my own stubbornness, if I'm to be truthful. I could have taken a carriage, but I just started walking."

Bridget made a low sound.

"Why did you help me?" Molly asked as they reached the third floor.

Bridget turned to Molly after opening the door to her room. "We women have to stick together, don't we?" With the light from a lamp that was burning near the open door, Molly saw a deep sadness in the young and brave Bridget's eyes.

Bridget's room was small, and the window that looked down on the street was still open to the night breeze. There was just the single room, with a small bed in one corner, and a stove in the other, and a ragged sofa in the middle of it all. Everything was clean, though, and an attempt had been made to brighten the small room with cheerful yellow check curtains that fluttered in the wind.

The small room reminded Molly of home.

"It's not much," Bridget said as she closed and locked the door behind Molly, "but no one will bother you here. In the morning it will be safe for you to be on the streets alone."

"It's very nice," Molly said, and Bridget cut her a glance that clearly conveyed her disbelief. To emphasize her disbelief, Bridget looked pointedly at Molly's dress, the indecent gown that probably cost more than everything Bridget owned put together.

"Take the bed, if you'd like to lie down," Bridget said sharply.

"I can't possibly take your bed," Molly said, clutching the lace shawl around her shoulders.

"It's clean," Bridget snapped.

"I'm sure it is."

Bridget returned to the chair that was next to the open window, and presented Molly her back. "I can't sleep, anyway," she said softly.

Molly stood behind Bridget and looked past the girl's dark head to the street below. She didn't think she'd be able to sleep for a long time, herself.

She'd become accustomed to sleeping beside her husband, in his arms or curled against his side. If Bridget's bed had been wide and deep and soft, sleep still would have been impossible.

Marriage to Wolf had never been ideal, but it had never even crossed her mind that he might be adulterous. Foolishly, she had ignored everything he'd told her about this marriage being a business deal, and she'd seen only what she wanted to see in Wolf and in herself.

"Why can't you sleep?" Molly dragged a mismatched hard back chair across the room, and placed it by the window, where she could see Bridget's delicate profile.

"You don't want to hear about my troubles."

231

Bridget didn't even look at Molly as she took her seat.

Molly followed Bridget's riveted gaze into a night that was dark, into the black shadows that were broken only by the sporadic glare of a street-lamp.

Bridget was petite, and fragile in appearance, but Molly knew she had strength in those arms, and perhaps in her spirit as well.

No one should be so sad. Or so alone.

"I have a thought." Molly leaned forward slightly. "You tell me why you can't sleep, and when you're done I'll tell you why you're going to have sleepless company tonight."

Wolf took the familiar stairs two at a time, unable to stop, unable to try to keep his step soft. He'd never been a patient man, but this was unconscionable. Molly had left Phil's hours ago. *Hours.*

He'd gone to the Waldorf first, and there he had waited, an hour, two, three. His imagination and his anger had kept him pacing the entire time. He'd tossed Molly's precious books about the room, cursing her and Foster and himself—himself, most of all.

This was exactly what he'd wanted, wasn't it? To prove that even Molly could be corrupted. That every human had a fatal weakness. That no one was perfect.

But dammit, why had she given in so easily?

Foster's room was on the second floor of the exclusive gentlemen's club, two doors down from

Wolf's own. Women were not allowed, but it was not unknown for a resident to sneak a female companion in late at night, and down the stairs early the next morning. Foster had done it before. So had Wolf, for that matter.

At the door, Wolf hesitated. It wouldn't do for him to break in and kill them both, his wife and his best friend, but that was exactly the frame of mind he found himself in.

A soft, feminine giggle drifting to him from the other side of the door sent him over the edge, and Wolf put his shoulder to the locked door and forced it open.

The bedspread was on the floor, and the mound of white sheets on the bed moved furiously as Foster sat up and pale, feminine hands pulled those sheets over her head.

"You son of a bitch," Wolf growled. "I'll kill you for this."

Foster's eyes grew wide, and the sheet flipped back with a snap, revealing a head of dark hair that was most definitely not Molly's.

"Wolf, darling?" Adele turned her head toward the broken door, and she smiled seductively. It was very clear that Adele thought he was here for her.

Already, the hallway was filling with residents he had awakened when he'd battered in the door. Old and young men, Wolf knew them all. He ignored each and every one of them, and disregarded the censuring words of one crotchety old man he'd awakened.

For the moment, all Wolf felt was relief. All this

time he'd been imagining Molly in another man's bed, and Foster had been here with Adele all along. Wolf felt almost comforted, and then panic took over, a panic as strong as the anger that had simmered as he'd waited for her.

"Where's Molly?" He shut the damaged door as best he could, and leaned back against it.

"I don't know." Foster sighed and reached for the half empty bottle beside his bed. "I haven't seen her since I left Phil's." A flash of realization transformed his face. "Don't tell me you thought she was here."

"She left right behind you."

If not to follow Foster, then why? Phil had said she was walking, and suddenly Wolf realized that was exactly what had happened.

"Good God," he muttered. "She's lost." Molly had the worst sense of direction, and she never would have found her way from Phil's to the Waldorf.

"Don't you want to know what happened?" Foster called as Wolf rushed from the room, past one frowning old man who remained in the hallway.

Beyond the bright curtains, the sun was coming up. Molly wasn't tired at all, and evidently neither was Bridget.

They'd talked all night, about their problems and the men who were at the center of them all, and it had been strangely comforting, trading confessions with a complete stranger.

Well, Bridget had been a complete stranger a few hours ago, but not anymore. Last night Molly had felt so all alone, and now she had an ally. She was still hurt, but she knew that she'd done nothing wrong, except perhaps to overestimate her husband.

"What are you going to do?" She asked, placing a comforting hand on Bridget's arm.

"What can I do?" Bridget didn't whine or wail, but there was a desolate finality in her words. "I have no choice in the matter. I'll likely never leave this room. For the rest of my life I'll work in that factory, sewing until the day I die. And I'll certainly never marry, because no man will ever have me, not after all this."

Bridget's words were hopeless, but her eyes were brighter than they'd been a few hours ago. Perhaps she, too, had been helped by the long night of talking.

Molly's problems were insignificant compared to Bridget's, and she had options the younger girl didn't have. There was always Vanora Point to return to.

There was Vanora Point, and Kingsport, and her family and friends there. She could bake bread like her mother had for years, if she had to. Near home there was the comfort of the ocean and the forest.

None of it sounded inviting at the moment, but at least she had a place to go.

Options. They made every difference.

In spite of the long and harrowing night, Molly smiled. "I have an idea."

Bridget turned to her in anticipation. "Are you going to leave him?"

Molly waved her hand in distraction. "Not that. I don't know what I'm going to do about Wolf. I hope he didn't get a wink of sleep last night, wondering where I was. He probably didn't even miss me . . . but I'll think about that later."

She couldn't bear to think about it now, Wolf and Adele and the horrid slamming of that door. Wolf might as well have slammed the door in her face.

With a shake of her head, Molly pushed her problems aside and took Bridget's hand. "Will you come with me to the Waldorf?" She could almost manage a smile. "I've had the most wonderful idea."

Chapter Fifteen

The sun was shining on them as they walked down Thirty-third Street, and Molly was relieved to see the Waldorf awning and entrance. She would never be able to think of the hotel as home, but after a long night it was a comforting sight, nonetheless.

Bridget slowed her step. "I'll be going now. Remember what I said. Don't let that husband of yours take you for granted."

"It's much too late for that, I'm afraid."

Bridget had come to a complete stop on the sidewalk.

"Come on, Bridget." Molly took the girl's arm and persuaded her to continue forward. "I have a surprise for you."

Bridget balked again, and Molly had to stop. "I

don't want a reward. That's not why I helped you."

"I know that, and it's not a reward," Molly pleaded. "Really, it's not."

Molly had to give Bridget's arm a tug to force the young girl to move forward again. For someone so petite, she was quite stubborn and strong, but Bridget eventually came along reluctantly.

They had almost reached the awning that covered the sidewalk in front of the Waldorf, when Molly heard her name being bellowed. That voice was unmistakable, and she lifted her head to see Wolf coming toward her, on foot and from the opposite direction.

His jacket was unbuttoned, and his tie was missing, and his normally flawless black hair was mussed. But it was the savage expression on his face that stopped Molly where she stood.

Wolf took three long strides, and then he was running toward her slowly as if those long strides were not adequate. Before Wolf reached her he seemed to grab hold of himself. He no longer ran, but the clenched fists at his sides told her he was controlling himself at great cost.

"Is that your husband?" Bridget whispered as they waited, a touch of awe in her voice.

"Yes, I'm afraid so. He doesn't look very happy at the moment, does he?"

"No," Bridget breathed the reluctant answer. "I really can't stay."

Molly refused to release Bridget's arm.

"Where the hell have you been?" Wolf stopped several feet away.

Big Bad Wolf

"Where have *you* been?" Molly lifted her chin as she asked the question.

He lifted his eyebrows, taken aback at her insolence, apparently. "I've been looking for you. All night, Red. Where the hell have you been?"

"Can we finish this conversation inside? The doorman is staring."

Molly passed Wolf without actually looking at him, and she wondered, with each and every step, if he would try to forcibly stop her.

He didn't. Wolf turned and followed them into the hotel lobby. Molly turned to the stairs, and then made an abrupt about face. She nearly ran Wolf down trying to get to the desk, but managed not only to avoid running into him but also to slip past him before he could stop her.

"Good morning, Mrs. Trevelyan," the clerk greeted politely, without even a raised eyebrow to indicate her unusual time of arrival or her disheveled appearance.

"Good morning. I was wondering if you would do me a tremendous favor."

The clerk nodded crisply. Molly had already learned that—short of murder—the clerks and bellboys in the Waldorf could arrange anything, and they'd do it with great precision.

"The dressmaker that visits our suite on occasion, Mrs. Watkins. Could you please contact her and ask that she come to my suite at her earliest convenience? It's rather an emergency."

"Of course."

"And I'll need a railway ticket, but I'm not quite sure of the destination. Could you send someone to the suite, oh, shall we say after Mrs. Watkins departs?"

He nodded again.

"But first, we're all terribly hungry. Could we have breakfast delivered to the suite as soon as possible?"

"Red," Wolf growled, and she realized that, of course, he'd been listening closely to every word. "What the hell is going on?"

Molly glanced at Bridget. "Forgive him. His rudeness seems to come naturally, but he's not always so crude." Bridget stared at the floor, and the clerk pretended, quite well, that he hadn't heard a word of their conversation.

Molly slipped away from the desk with Bridget on her arm and headed for the stairs.

"Train ticket?" Wolf said softly, and from directly behind her. "Where the hell do you think you're going?"

Molly ignored him.

"And who is this woman?"

"See?" Molly glanced at Bridget. "He's feeling better already. A moment ago it would have been 'who the you-know-what is this woman?' "

"Red." There was a warning in his voice, and Molly glanced over her shoulder. Wolf had thunder in his eyes, and his fists were still clenched.

"This is Miss Bridget Brady." Molly whipped her head around so she didn't have to look at Wolf. "I'll be happy to tell you how we met, but not until I've had a chance to bathe and change clothes and we really should have breakfast first."

Wolf took a very deep, very slow breath, but

Molly didn't turn to watch him exhale it.

Inside the suite, Wolf took a corner chair, thrust his legs forward, and crossed his arms across his chest. His silence was disconcerting, and with that scowl on his face he really did look quite beastly.

Bridget refused to be left alone with him, and Molly couldn't blame her.

Molly bathed and changed into a suitable morning dress, with Bridget waiting and fidgeting on the edge of the bed while Wolf waited even less patiently in the other room. When Molly was refreshed and wearing a suitable and decent dress, Bridget tried to excuse herself once again. Molly wouldn't let her go. Not yet.

Breakfast was delivered. Molly and Bridget both ate well, they were starving, but Wolf didn't take anything but coffee.

When they were finished and feeling better, Molly forced herself to look squarely at Wolf. He glared at her through narrowed eyes, and looked as fierce as she'd ever seen him.

"Red, darling," he said coldly. "Now."

It all came back in a rush. Wolf and Adele, making plans Molly couldn't bear to think about. Wolf calling the horrible woman darling. And he wanted an explanation.

"Don't," she said coldly, "call me darling."

Wolf glanced at Molly's new companion briefly.

"She knows all about it," Molly said sharply.

He wanted to kiss her, he wanted to shake her. Instead of giving in to either impulse, Wolf re-

241

mained in his chair. Motionless. "She knows all about what?"

"You and Adele," Molly snapped. "Did you think I wouldn't find out? Or did you expect that I'd be a quiet little mouse and let you have your infidelity without question?" Molly turned to Bridget. "What do you expect of a man who believes you married him for his money? Sometimes I think he believes I should simply be grateful that he married me and accept any slight without a word of protest."

"Over here, Red," Wolf instructed, and she turned her face to him once again. "What are you talking about?"

Molly lifted her chin. "I heard you. I went looking for you because I was upset, and I heard everything."

"You heard me talking to Adele."

She turned to Bridget Brady again. "See? Calm as can be. As if nothing happened."

"Nothing did happen."

Molly sighed deeply. "We'll have to finish this conversation later. We're upsetting Bridget."

Bridget didn't seem at all upset, but he'd never seen Molly so agitated.

"And how did you meet Miss Brady?" Wolf asked.

"After I left Phil's, I got lost."

"That's a surprise," Wolf muttered. Both women gave him a cutting glance.

Molly tried to be calm, but her eyes got wider, clearer. "This . . . this horrible man attacked me."

Wolf came out of his chair, without intending to. "Are you hurt?"

"No. Bridget rescued me, with the help of her broom handle."

"You should never have been out alone at night." Wolf took a deep, calming breath and turned to Bridget. "You have my thanks, Miss Brady."

"Sit down, Wolf," Molly commanded. "If you hadn't upset me, I never would have been in that predicament."

"I didn't—"

"We'll discuss it later."

Her crisp instruction cooled his blood, and Wolf sat. For the first time in hours a smile crossed his face.

"Bridget asked me to stay the night in her home, and this morning she was kind enough to walk me here."

"So you wouldn't get lost again."

"Exactly."

Wolf reached into his pocket and withdrew a wad of bills. "We are grateful, Miss Brady."

"I don't want your money."

Bridget Brady refused his offer of reward with just a touch of distaste. What had Molly told her? There was no telling. Just a bit of the truth would turn any decent woman against him, he supposed.

When the dressmaker arrived, Molly effectively and coolly dismissed him. Wolf could not remember a time in his life when anyone had treated him as if he were insignificant.

It had been a hellishly long night. His bones

ached, there was a pounding throb at one temple, and his heart had been through an exhaustive workout. As he'd searched the streets for Molly, he'd thought it would burst through his chest, and every time his imagination ran away with him he could feel every hard and quick beat.

Now that Molly was here where she belonged, his anger and frustration dissolved into a bone melting weariness. He leaned back in his chair and watched.

"Mrs. Watkins, this is my good friend Mrs. Brady, and she's in desperate need of your talents."

Bridget shook her head and tugged at Molly's sleeve, but it was a useless gesture. Wolf recognized that futility immediately, but it took the younger girl a moment.

"Mrs. Brady has recently been widowed," Molly confided. Bridget's eyes widened, and Wolf knew something was wrong. "She needs, for personal reasons, to leave New York immediately, but her entire wardrobe was destroyed in a horrid fire."

Mrs. Watkins nodded her head sympathetically. "I heard about that tragedy."

Well, there had evidently been a fire somewhere, Wolf surmised. He almost laughed, but it would have ruined whatever Molly had planned.

"My friend must have three good black dresses, and she must have them today."

Mrs. Watkins looked skeptical.

"Ready-made will suit," Molly conceded, "I suppose. Oh, and," Molly leaned close and whispered an aside to Mrs. Watkins. The dressmaker glanced briefly, and with great sympathy, to Bridget Brady.

"Should I put these on your bill?" Mrs. Watkins asked as she walked to the door.

"No." Molly went to the desk, and withdrew from the bottom drawer . . . a shoe. Several bills were withdrawn from the toe and placed in the dressmaker's hand.

Bridget didn't protest until Mrs. Watkins was gone. "I can't accept any of this."

"You can," Molly said with assurance. "Where do you want to go. South? West?"

"It's a lie," Bridget protested.

"Yes," Molly conceded. "But it's a *good* lie."

Molly tried to avoid looking at her husband as she made all the preparations for Bridget's journey. Bridget protested, but Molly had been able to convince her, at last, that this little lie would be best for the baby.

A new life. It was the least she could do for the poor girl. After all, Molly reminded herself. It could have happened to her.

Some wealthy and charming man had promised to marry Bridget, but when she'd discovered that she was with child, the coward had deserted her, leaving her with a low paying job in a factory sewing ready-made garments, a small rented room, and a baby on the way.

With a little of Molly's winnings and a good story, Bridget and her child could start fresh, out West, Bridget had decided.

Wolf had finally come to understand what Molly

was trying to do, evidently, and while he watched closely, he said little. There had been a moment, when Molly had mentioned the baby, that a light of understanding had come over his face. And something else. Something akin to pain.

Wolf had adamantly refused to allow her to leave the hotel alone, and so together Molly and her husband had put Bridget on the train. Dressed all in black, and with her dark brown hair secured severely at the nape of her neck, Bridget Brady had appeared every bit the grieving widow. The fact that she was just a little terrified didn't hurt the pretense.

As bad as Bridget's situation was, it wasn't as scary as the unknown. Molly recognized that fact, as she squeezed her new friend's hand and whispered words of encouragement.

It was late afternoon before the two of them returned to the Waldorf, and the fact that she'd spent a sleepless, and for the most part horrible, night was catching up with Molly. Every bone in her body was weary.

The trip from the depot had been horribly silent and tense. All Molly wanted was to crawl into bed and sleep for a week. But of course, Wolf would demand that they finish their conversation, and perhaps it was best to get it over with.

Inside the suite, Molly lowered herself into the most comfortable chair in the room. She closed her eyes, just for a moment, and almost drifted off before Wolf placed his own chair directly in front of hers and claimed her attention by placing his hands on her knees.

"I looked for you all night," he said. "I walked every route I could think of from Phil's to the hotel." He looked every bit as tired as she felt, and Molly almost felt sorry for him. Almost.

"I missed my turn," she explained.

"Dammit, Red, why didn't you wait for me?"

She could lie, she could tell only what she wanted Wolf to know . . . or she could tell him the truth, and all of it. If they had no honesty between them, if their marriage was based on nothing but lies on both sides, they had something less than a loveless marriage. They had nothing. For Molly, the truth was the only way.

"I suppose I should start at the beginning."

"Please do," Wolf said impatiently.

After a deep, calming breath, Molly told it all, beginning with the moment Wolf had left her sitting alone to go search out another game. Amazingly enough, he listened without interruption, up until the moment when Foster grabbed her.

"He did what?"

"I was trying to walk away, to find you, and he stopped me rather forcefully. If you didn't insist that I wear those indecent gowns, he wouldn't have had much to paw, but as it was . . ."

"He touched you?"

"I thought I made that rather clear," Molly said sensibly.

The thunder she'd seen in Wolf's eyes that morning was back, and that little tic in his jaw started jumping.

"And then he made the most vile suggestion. He said that you had shared women before, and apparently he thought that debauchery would continue with me. So I kicked him, and pushed him down, and then I went to look for you." Molly gave him a chastising glare. "I was very upset. You should have been there."

Wolf said nothing in defense of himself, but leaned back and appeared to relax.

"After a while I saw you, heading toward the back rooms, and I followed you."

"Red . . ." he began, apparently deciding the time to try to excuse his actions had finally arrived.

"Let me finish," she insisted. "I heard everything you said to that woman, Adele. It's bad enough that you insist you only married me to provide heirs and to get those persistent mothers off your back, but to share that with someone else . . . to tell her . . ."

"The truth?" Wolf finished.

Molly didn't want to believe that was the truth, but Wolf had never told her any differently. "That's not the worst of it. I can't believe that you had a . . . a relationship with that woman while she was married, and that you actually plan to continue that . . . that . . ."

"Affair."

Her face burned, and Molly knew she was blushing brightly. "Yes," she whispered. "I couldn't stay after hearing that. It hurt, Wolf, more than you know. And I was angry. And I didn't want to stand there and listen to any more, particularly after you slammed the door shut."

Now it was his turn, and Molly waited expectantly.

"Actually," he muttered after a moment of contemplation, "It was Adele who slammed the door."

"I really don't—"

"And if you'd stuck around a minute or two you could have lambasted me then and there, when I left the room."

"It really doesn't—"

"I have not been unfaithful to you, Red."

It wasn't much. There was no promise that he never would be, just an assurance that so far he had not strayed.

"But, when I go back to Vanora Point—"

"We'll deal with that when the time comes," Wolf said sharply.

The time would come, Molly knew, and soon. Face to face, she couldn't believe that Wolf would send her away and go to another woman, but he didn't deny that was his plan.

She believed him, though, that he had been faithful to her thus far, and that was a great relief. But he wouldn't promise her anything more. Not tomorrow and certainly not forever.

"I'm exhausted." Molly stood abruptly. "I've got to get some sleep."

"Me, too."

Wolf followed her into the bedroom.

"Did you really look for me all night?" Molly asked as she began to work the buttons of her pale green gown.

"Yes, dammit," Wolf snapped. "Don't you ever do that to me again."

He undressed, displaying as little energy as Molly felt, and together they fell into the bed. Wolf covered Molly with the thick bedspread, and drew her body against his. Some of Molly's anger melted away in his arms, even though she knew she shouldn't be swayed by the comfort of Wolf's arms around her.

She'd never realized that the softness of a bed and warm arms could be such a comfort. Her very bones melted against the mattress, against Wolf in spite of what he'd done. After a sleepless night, this was heaven.

What now? When they woke, would Wolf expect the days to continue as they had since their arrival in New York? She loved him, still, but could she trust him with her heart?

She was almost asleep when he stirred, restless even though he was every bit as exhausted as she was.

"What you did for that girl, it was very nice." Wolf's soft voice surprised her. Molly stirred a little, thinking of turning her back to her restive husband, but Wolf's arms tightened around her.

Realizing the futility of trying to move away from Wolf, she sighed and ceased her attempt to move away.

"She saved me last night."

"I know," he whispered.

"And besides . . ." Should she tell him everything? The only way to make this work was to hold nothing back. "I kept thinking, as Bridget told me her story, that it could have been me. If you had continued to pursue me, and if you hadn't married me, sooner or later . . ."

Wolf lifted her chin so she was forced to look at him. "Tell me, Red, do you really think I'd stoop so low?"

Molly considered the question for a minute or so, as Wolf stared into her eyes. She didn't know what kind of answer he expected.

"Yes," she whispered.

He didn't defend himself, but released her chin and pulled her close, so that her face was nestled against his chest and his breath was warm in her hair.

Chapter Sixteen

Molly had still been asleep when he'd left the suite, after sleeping all afternoon and through the night. He'd slept hard himself, after that long night searching the streets for his wife.

He'd wanted to wake her, to make love to her before he left to do what he had to do, but she'd looked so peaceful, he hadn't had the heart to disturb her.

It was still early and Foster was sure to be asleep. Wolf climbed the stairs without the rage that had propelled him on his last venture into this club, but with a single purpose that was just as strong.

Foster's door had not yet been repaired, and Wolf pushed it open to find his old friend sound asleep.

"Good morning," Wolf said loudly, and Foster shot up with both hands at his head.

"Softly," Foster instructed as he allowed his eyes to drift closed.

"I owe you an apology." Wolf slammed the damaged door behind him, and Foster flinched.

"And a new door," Foster whispered.

"Of course."

Foster opened one eye. "I take it you found her?"

"Yes," Wolf said casually. "All's well, for the time being, at least."

Foster covered his face with two large and slightly trembling hands. Wolf thought, briefly, of those hands on Molly, and he clenched his fists. Not now. Not yet.

"You weren't at Phil's last night. I was a little concerned." Foster sat up and kicked his legs over the side of the bed, with great effort, groaning with every move. There had been many times when Wolf had matched Foster drink for drink, and had awakened in just this condition. At the moment he couldn't understand why.

"We stayed in last night."

Foster smiled crookedly. "Well, Molly passed your test with flying colors, didn't she? Wouldn't have anything to do with me. I suppose she told you all about it?"

"Yes." Wolf grinned. "Thank you for your assistance, Foster old pal."

Foster stepped into his trousers, and turned a fading smile to Wolf. "What are you doing here so early in the morning?"

"There's never time to stop at the end of the day,

Linda Jones

so I thought I'd drop in on my way to the office. I haven't had a chance to get in the ring with anyone since I returned to New York, and I'm feeling a little edgy."

"Whom do you expect to spar with you at this time of day? The hired boys don't come in until the afternoon, and I doubt there's anyone in the gymnasium at all this early in the morning."

"How about it?" Wolf asked casually, and Foster raised his eyebrows in horror.

"Me? Now?"

"You've always been able to hold your own," Wolf said with an air of disinterest, remembering the few times he and Foster had actually sparred.

"Only because you always go easy on me." Foster pulled on a white shirt. "I've seen you light into those poor boys with a vengeance, on occasion."

"So, I'll go easy on you," Wolf said with a smile. "I always do, you know. We get into the ring, dance around a little, throw a few punches."

"You've missed it, have you?"

It didn't take Wolf much longer to convince Foster to accompany him downstairs to the gymnasium that had been added to the rear of the club, past the library and the billiard room.

Foster had been right, the gym was deserted this time of day.

"I'm not so sure about this." Foster's voice echoed hollowly through the vast and vacant room.

"It won't take long," Wolf promised.

They stripped to their trousers and socks, and climbed into the ring. Foster lifted his fists defensively as Wolf immediately took the first swing and tapped his opponent on the shoulder.

"How long have you been seeing Adele?"

Foster moved as if he had lead in his socks, but he landed a light punch to Wolf's midsection. "Couple of weeks. You mind?"

"Not at all." Wolf's right fist struck Foster in the side, and the still groggy man backed up.

Was this really going to make him feel any better?

"Did Molly tell you what happened?" Foster asked as he bravely approached again.

Yes, this would definitely make him feel much better. "Everything."

"Well then, you should be pleased. I swear, Wolf, I used every line I could think of, and I don't think she even knew I was flirting with her."

The punch Wolf landed on Foster's stomach was harder than the previous hits. "Just to be sure she did indeed tell me everything, why don't you explain what happened?"

"I tried flirting with her, as you suggested," Foster's breath was already coming hard, and sweat dotted his face. "All she did was look for you. So I told her I'd seen you heading for the back rooms, and she took off."

"Alone?"

"No, I followed her, of course."

"Of course." Wolf swung for Foster's face, but the blow was blocked by a quick forearm. "And then?"

"I got a bit bolder," Foster admitted. "I knew you wanted to be sure . . ."

"Yes, I did." He landed a glancing blow on Foster's shoulder. His own breath was coming harder now, almost as labored as Foster's, as his discipline slipped away.

Foster recognized the anger in Wolf's eyes. Wolf saw that realization come over the doomed man's face: shock and surprise, and a bit of fear, just before Foster tried to back away and shield his face.

"You asked me to do you a favor, remember?" Foster protected his face with raised and crossed arms. "It was your idea." He continue to move back and away from Wolf. "You told me to flirt with her."

Wolf dropped his arms and took a step back. He hadn't intended to chase Foster down and beat a man who wouldn't even defend himself. "You're right," he admitted breathlessly, "I did."

With a relieved smile, Foster dropped his arms. "You had me worried there for a minute." Sweat dripped down Foster's face and torso, and his breathing was labored. "I did as you asked, that's all."

Wolf returned his friend's smile, drew back his fist without a second thought, and landed a blow against the side of Foster's face. A blow that knocked the hungover and smiling man to the mat.

Wolf stood over a groaning Foster. "I never said you could touch her."

"You're not ready."

Molly lifted her eyes from the book she was reading, and into Wolf's irritated face.

"I'm not going," she said softly.

It wasn't a difficult decision to make. She'd never been comfortable in Phil's. She'd never been at ease in the daring gowns Wolf insisted she wear. For weeks, Molly had tried to become the wife Wolf seemed to want, but she was through with that.

"I'll go without you." It was a threat, one Molly was prepared for.

"I assumed that you would."

Molly returned her eyes to the book before her. It was another of Wolf's shocking novels, but she rather liked it. She jumped when Wolf slammed the door behind him, but didn't lift her gaze from the printed page.

Wolf was going to be himself, no matter what she did, and Molly had decided that she'd best be herself as well. He would either come to love her or he wouldn't. If by some miracle that happened, she wanted to be certain that Wolf loved her, and not the woman she pretended to be for his sake.

He hadn't been gone five minutes before he was back, again slamming the door to their suite forcefully behind him.

"Get dressed," he ordered. "You're coming with me."

Molly closed her book and lifted her head. How could anyone refuse a dangerous and scowling face like that? If she was to make anything of this marriage, she would have to learn. "I am dressed, actually, and I'm not going anywhere."

Wolf was not accustomed to being denied, and

the look on his face was a mixture of anger and incredulity.

"Even if you decide to drag me from here by the hair, which is, from the look of you, a possibility, I'll have to wear what I have on. The gowns you bought me are all gone."

"Gone?"

"Well, Mrs. Watkins will return them tomorrow or the next day, after the alterations are finished." Molly gave her husband a no-nonsense stare, meeting his ferocious glare. "She's finishing the bodices, adding sufficient material to transform them into suitable gowns. It seemed a waste to discard them altogether."

Wolf grabbed Molly's wrist and pulled her to her feet. "I'll do it, you know. I'll toss you over my shoulder and take you wherever I please."

"I'm sure you will," Molly said softly.

She refused to be intimidated by the glare he turned down to her.

"Are you trying to punish me?" he growled.

"Of course not. To hear you tell it, you've done nothing to be punished for." Molly took a deep breath, and tried to maintain her calm.

"The torture I've already been through is suitable punishment for any imagined wrongdoing."

"Because you had to look for me?"

"Because I couldn't find you," he snapped, "and I was worried sick."

He had to care for her, just a little, if he'd truly been so distressed. That revelation gave her a little bit of hope to hold on to.

"It still hurts." Her voice was softer than she'd

intended. "What I heard you say to Adele. If I mean so little to you . . ."

"I never said . . ."

". . . Then it should be no problem for you to leave me here while you amuse yourself at Phil's. I don't belong there, Wolf."

"I never said you didn't mean anything to me." It was a grudging confession. "Dammit Molly, I don't want—" He stopped speaking abruptly, snapped his mouth shut.

She saw the moment of surrender in his eyes, a softening of the forest green there, a spark of resignation that made him appear so human. Almost vulnerable.

"I can't leave you here without wondering if you're going to be taken by the notion to take a walk and get yourself lost again." There was just a touch of anger in his voice. "Dammit, I don't want to go anywhere without you. If I'm at Phil's, I want to be able to turn around and see you there. Yawning and bored and out of place . . ." He narrowed his eyes suspiciously. "You've ruined me."

"You could stay here with me," she suggested, slipping the hand he didn't grip behind his back. "We have a bottle of brandy, a deck of cards, and a box full of those awful cigars." With her body pressed against his, Molly raised herself slowly, until she stood on her toes and pressed her mouth against Wolf's. It began as a soft kiss, and grew into something more.

She loved his lips, so strong and gentle, so demanding and giving. When they could agree on nothing else, when it seemed they had nothing to keep them together, they had this. It was magic, it was impossible, it was real.

The hardness of Wolf's arousal pressed against her belly, and Molly arched against him. He deepened the kiss, lifted her from her feet and walked slowly toward the bedroom, Molly's feet dangling inches from the floor.

She was ready for him, aching for the fullness of Wolf inside her. All he had to do was kiss her like this, as if he offered his very soul with a silent kiss.

Wolf set her on her feet, dragging her body against his so she could feel again how he wanted her.

In this way, at least, he had come to need her.

"Seduced by my own wife," he grumbled as he unfastened the buttons of her muslin dress.

Molly laughed softly. "Is that so terrible?"

Wolf didn't answer as he slipped the gown from her body and kissed a sensitive nipple through the linen of her chemise. Her body reacted immediately, tightened and became heated.

"Yes," Wolf whispered as he pulled away from her just long enough to strip the chemise over her head.

He returned his mouth to her bared nipple, suckled and nibbled until Molly melted beneath his assault. Until her knees went weak and her thighs trembled.

They stood beside the bed, and Molly slid her hands from his hair to his shoulders, where she slipped his coat to the floor. She fumbled with his tie and the buttons of his coat shirt, until they joined the jacket at their feet.

Big Bad Wolf

His lips never left her as she worked the buttons of his trousers. Her shoulder, her neck, her lips, it seemed he was determined to devour her.

When he was naked at last, they fell across the bed, and in one swift thrust Wolf filled her.

How quickly she had come to need this, to feel as if she were incomplete without Wolf. He called their union a vice, a pleasure like all his other pleasures, but Molly knew it was so much more than that. It had been from their wedding night.

He knew her body so well. Every breath, every shudder. Every tremor spoke to him. He stroked and kissed, possessed her body and soul and heart, and when her bones quivered and her insides quaked he went with her, over the edge of a pleasure so intense it was near madness.

For a while they didn't move. Wolf lay atop her, crushing her against the soft mattress, his heavy breath in her ear, his heart thudding against hers. When he lifted his head and looked down at her, there was a trace of suspicion in his eyes, mingled with his satisfaction.

"Is this your way of getting me to stay at home?"

Molly threaded her fingers through Wolf's black hair, caressing his scalp and bringing his lips to hers for a soft kiss. "I never really thought of it that way, but if it works I'll plead guilty."

An inch at a time, Wolf pushed her to the center of the bed. "I never asked you to change my life," he whispered. Was that a touch of wonder in his voice? Perhaps he was beginning to understand that what they had was magic.

"I never asked you to change mine, but you did."

It wasn't, apparently, a satisfactory response, because Wolf scowled down at her before he kissed her again.

Molly ran her hands down Wolf's back and up again, enjoying, as she always did, the feel of him in her hands. "Guess what I did today?"

"I have to guess?"

"No."

Wolf rolled to his side, bringing Molly with him. They lay in the center of the bed, face to face, chest to chest, and Molly draped one leg over his.

"I went to the bank today, your bank, and talked to Mr. Abbott."

Wolf's eyes narrowed suspiciously. "What could you possibly have to say to Abbott?"

"I took the money I won, the money you made me keep, and I—"

"You opened your own account?" She could tell that Wolf disapproved.

"Well, not exactly." Her hesitant response alerted him. She had seen that cold gleam in his eyes before. "It's more of a fund than an account."

"A fund."

"For women like Bridget," Molly explained.

"Red, you can't—"

"It was my money, you said," she said quickly. "And I don't need it. Mr. Abbott set it up, and said he knew of some others who might be interested in contributing. Just think what a fresh start will mean for these women. Don't be angry." Wolf silenced her with a finger to her lips.

"You can't save the world," he said softly.

Molly kissed his finger before she drew his hand

away from her mouth. "I'm not trying to save the world. I'm just trying to help a few unfortunate women who really need it. That's all."

Wolf frowned down at her, and his eyes were guarded. Cool. But his hands were in her hair and resting possessively against her bare hip. He looked as if he had something to say, but he was hesitant.

"What is it?" she asked.

"You've never asked me what happened to Jeanne."

A chill climbed her spine. "I know all I need to know. I know that you don't have it in you to harm anyone, no matter what you'd have others think."

"I've never told anyone about that night. Not a soul, Red."

"Do you want to tell me?" Molly wasn't certain she wanted to hear, but she would listen if Wolf needed to explain.

"Yes." His answer was hesitant, and he waited so long before continuing that Molly thought he'd changed his mind. He drew her head against his shoulder—so she couldn't see his face?—and told his story in a soft and restrained voice.

"It was an arranged marriage. My father and Jeanne's father were lifelong friends. It was no secret that I was not ready to get married, but my father was ill, and anxious to see me settled, and after a summer in Boston with her cousins, Jeanne was anxious as well."

Molly slipped her arms around Wolf's waist, and held on. "Did you love her?"

"No," he answered quickly. "Maybe if I had that

night would have ended differently. Jeanne didn't love me, either. No surprise there. I was just as stubborn and ugly then as I am now."

Molly lifted her head and looked him square in the eye. "Stubbornness can be an admirable trait, and I happen to think you're quite handsome."

He forced her head back to his shoulder. "Maybe if I'd gone to her in a different frame of mind that night, if I hadn't been so angry . . ." He sighed, and Molly pressed a brief kiss to his shoulder. "She was waiting for me," he continued, "with her hair braided down her back and wearing that plain white nightdress. God, she was so young."

Molly didn't want to hear any more. Not a word. But she closed her eyes and melted against Wolf's shoulder.

"Her first words to me, as I burst into the bedroom, were, 'I can't do it. I thought I could, but I can't.'"

He was holding her tight, as if she could protect him from the memory, and Molly held him back, doing her best to insulate him from the pain.

"You see," he whispered, "Jeanne was in much the same situation as your friend Bridget. She'd met a man in Boston. I never knew who. Jeanne fell in love with him, but when she told him she was going to have his child, he informed her that he already had a wife and more children than he really wanted."

Instinctively, Molly placed her lips against Wolf's warm skin. She could hear the pain in his voice, but she couldn't take it away.

"She had planned to marry me and pass her lover's child off as mine, but she couldn't do it. She confessed everything and ran from the room in tears."

"Why did you never tell?"

"To what purpose? In a way it was my fault. If I had known what was in her mind . . ."

"That's impossible," Molly whispered.

"If I had followed her . . ."

"You didn't know."

"We didn't even know she'd left the house until morning. There are several guest rooms, and I just assumed she'd locked herself in one. But when we couldn't find her, someone suggested we search the grounds." Wolf threaded his fingers through her hair. "I was the one who found her, and the rumors started that very day."

"You could have told the truth."

"It was too late. Jeanne was dead, and in part the rumors are true. She did prefer death to a life with me."

Molly lifted her head and looked down at Wolf. His expression was so cold, so distant. "You don't know that. She might have fallen in the dark. It might have been the misadventure it was ruled. We'll never know."

Her hair hung forward, and Wolf tried to brush it away with his hands. "If Jeanne had had a friend like you, maybe she'd still be alive today."

Molly didn't want to cry, but she knew Wolf had never cried for himself. All these years, and he'd never told anyone. What a horror to live with, a horror made worse by the fact that he endured it alone.

Linda Jones

"I shouldn't have told you." He wiped away a single tear with his thumb. "It's more than you want to know, isn't it? Sometimes the truth is hard to take."

Molly shook her head slightly. "The truth is never worse than a lie. In fact, I'm going to tell you a fact you don't want to hear."

For a moment, Wolf looked worried, as if he expected some horrible secret from her past. Something she had hidden from him all this time.

She had kept it to herself, but it was time to give Wolf what he really needed.

"I love you."

Wolf woke with a start, escaping the dream that had plagued him over the years. Jeanne, the cliff, but in the dreams he was there, and Jeanne clutched a child in her arms as she jumped.

He could never run fast enough to reach her. Sometimes he knew it was only a dream, and he knew no matter how hard he ran he wouldn't reach her, but he couldn't stop.

As he ran toward Jeanne he kept thinking this time might be different. It never was.

Molly slept peacefully, curled against him with one leg over his, and Wolf found himself pulling her gently closer. Needing her warmth and her softness, her nearness. While she was asleep he could indulge himself and acknowledge, for a while, that he needed her.

Did she really think she loved him? Maybe she did. Maybe a good and virtuous girl like Molly rationalized that it was all right to lose control, to have passionate sex with a man, if you loved him.

Wolf knew love had nothing to do with it.

He'd come close tonight to revealing more than was necessary. When Molly had said that she didn't mean anything to him, he'd stopped himself before he could tell her that he didn't want any other woman, and if that wasn't caring he didn't know what was.

Confession wasn't normally his style, but telling Molly about that horrid night seven years ago had come easily, too easily. He'd even taken some comfort from the sharing of his secret. It was incredibly selfish, asking Molly to endure the burden with him, but the ease had been immediate. That was rather alarming, the momentary, overwhelming relief.

He didn't want or need to share his life with anyone. Not like this.

Molly had changed his life. He couldn't allow her to change who he was.

Chapter Seventeen

The air was just beginning to turn cool. Molly still enjoyed her walks down Thirty-third Street, but she had begun to wear a shawl, particularly if she walked in the morning.

Had she ever in her life been so marvelously happy? Of course not.

Wolf obviously was not ready to believe that she loved him, but she was determined to prove it. Like it or not, he did need her, and he cared for her more than he'd ever intended, she was sure.

She was several blocks away from the Waldorf when she heard someone calling her name.

Turning back toward the hotel she saw the young man approaching, calling again for Mrs. Trevelyan. Someone from the Waldorf? He was almost upon her before she recognized him.

Big Bad Wolf

"Arthur!"

Her mouth dropped open, and when she realized she was staring at the boy wide-eyed and open-mouthed, she regained her composure quickly.

His hair had been neatly trimmed, and the simple but clean clothes he wore fit nicely. Someone had been feeding him well, because he was no longer so terribly thin. And he was smiling.

"You look splendid," she said, stepping aside so other pedestrians could pass.

He ignored her compliment, but blushed just a little. "I wanted to thank you, and I'm not allowed to talk to you at the hotel."

"Not allowed?"

"Policy," he said in a very mature voice. "I'm still just kitchen help, but when they finish training me to be a bellboy that will change."

"They're training you to be a bellboy?"

Arthur grinned, and looked like a mischievous little boy once again. "Oscar says I have potential."

"You do." Molly took his arm and set off at a leisurely stroll. "I think you have great potential."

Arthur held himself tall as they walked down Thirty-third Street, and Molly found herself smiling widely.

"If not for you, I wouldn't have this job, Mrs. Trevelyan."

"Call me Molly, would you?" She glanced sideways at Arthur and found that he was blushing again. "After all, we are friends."

As they strolled down the promenade, Arthur told Molly about his wonderful new life. He had a

269

room and a roommate who had become a friend, more food than he'd seen in his hard lifetime, and several changes of clothes—hand-me-downs and uniforms.

Molly found herself confiding in him as well, telling him that she and Wolf had actually discussed buying a house in New York. She couldn't imagine living in a hotel for much longer.

For a while she had thought Wolf stayed at the gentlemen's club because he couldn't afford to maintain two residences, but he'd explained, as if she were a child, that was not the case.

She should have understood that Wolf didn't want the obligation of another residence, when a lonely single room would suit him just fine.

Sometimes, lately, he'd actually walked with her down this very street, relaxed and smiling, making plans for a house here in New York. He hadn't mentioned sending her back to Vanora Point in ages.

She didn't share all of this with Arthur, of course, but the thoughts ran through her mind as she told him about their plans for a house. They had a nice walk, turned about and headed back for the Waldorf.

Arthur had turned into such a nice young man, and was so handsome with his neatly trimmed hair and new clothes and color in his healthy cheeks. She'd known all along that he was bright, that he had potential. It hadn't been difficult to convince Oscar of that fact.

Arthur became anxious as they approached the hotel, and disengaged his arm from hers several blocks from their destination.

"I have to get back," he said in a low voice, as if someone from the Waldorf, notably Oscar, might catch him breaking the rules.

Molly watched the boy hurry back to the hotel, and after a few moments she resumed her stroll. Arthur's life had surely changed as much as hers had.

The concert was to be held in the Waldorf's Grand Ballroom, and to Wolf attending seemed a small sacrifice to make. Molly was excited at the prospect, after more than a week of somewhat quiet evenings in their suite. She had laid out her emerald green gown, one of the silk gowns Mrs. Watkins had altered to Molly's specifications, and had spent the better portion of the past hour trying to get her hair in a proper psyche knot.

Wolf was content to watch, for the moment. Good God, he was *never* content.

That was a lie. In the past several days he'd been disgustingly content. He hadn't been to Phil's, but that didn't mean he hadn't enjoyed a card game or two. He'd been teaching Molly strip poker.

She hadn't told him again that she loved him, much to his relief. He'd convinced himself that it was just Molly's way, to try to comfort him the way a wife should comfort her husband. That, or a proper lady's justification for what they had in bed.

This odd and domesticated contentment should have triggered an alarm days ago, but Wolf had let it pass. Now, watching her fiddle with that wonderful hair, it came to him like a thunderbolt. Sudden, furious, dangerous.

He knew what she wanted. After all this time, he finally *knew*. Molly didn't just want him to need her, she wanted to own him, heart and body, and he was falling into her trap very willingly.

As if to confirm his revelation, Molly glanced over her shoulder and smiled brightly. Dressed in nothing but her chemise and the emeralds he had placed around her throat almost an hour ago, she made an enchanting picture.

"How's this?" she asked, rotating her head for his inspection.

"Perfect," he muttered.

"You're tired of waiting for me. I expect you'd tell me it was perfect even if it was falling halfway down my back."

"Probably," he admitted.

Body and heart. She'd admitted weeks ago, at Vanora Point, that what she wanted was for him to need her. And now he did. More than was wise, more than he'd ever needed anyone before.

"Mr. Abbott said he'd be at the concert tonight," Molly said as she studied her hairstyle one more time.

"Did you see him again today?"

"Yes." Molly left the vanity and came to him. God help him, she already owned his body. A smile, a simple smile, and his pulse quickened. "He's been speaking to several physicians who do charity work, and they've agreed to help find suitable candidates. Two others have already made sizable donations to the fund. It's doubled already, Wolf. Can you imagine?"

"You'd think the money was yours, you're so excited."

"I don't need it." Molly stood on her toes and kissed him quickly before she turned away to fetch her gown. "I have you."

Good God, she was getting dangerously close to his heart.

It was a different, more sedate crowd than the one Wolf had introduced her to at Phil's, but it was a crush just the same. Well dressed ladies and gentlemen congregated in the ballroom, and searched for their seats. The concert wouldn't be underway for another quarter of an hour, and just a few, those who were determined to sit close to the front or close to the back, were seated.

Wolf was oddly silent, and had been all evening. Business, she decided. He'd had a difficult day and it was weighing on his mind.

She kept expecting him to complain, about the concert she'd insisted on attending, about the crowd, but he didn't say a word.

Molly turned abruptly when she heard a familiar voice calling her name, a bright "Mrs. Trevelyan," called loudly enough to claim her attention, but at a level that was civilized.

"Mr. Abbott." She smiled when she recognized the banker making his way toward her. He was not a tall man, but was broad enough in the shoulders to open a wide path through the crowd, his balding head leading the way as he leaned tenaciously forward.

He greeted Wolf, but with less enthusiasm, Molly noted, and then he turned his attention to her. "There's someone here you must meet," he said in a lowered voice. "I told Robert Hutton about your fund, and he's quite interested in making a sizable contribution, but he wants to meet the lady responsible first."

"It's supposed to be anonymous," Molly whispered. "You told me you could handle the money yourself."

Mr. Abbott grimaced slightly. "I know, but Robert's insistent, and he's offered to double the fund."

"Dammit, Abbott," Wolf snapped. "Molly gave you her answer."

"Double?" Molly whispered, and then she glanced up into Wolf's face. So often his face was like this, hard and unreadable. "All right. I don't see how I can pass up an offer like that."

Mr. Abbott led the way, and Molly followed with Wolf at her side. Beneath her hand, his arm was tense. He looked straight ahead, and she was certain there was something pressing on his mind. Still, he didn't give of himself easily, so she didn't push for an explanation.

Mr. Abbott led them to a corner where the crush of the crowd was not so great. A man was waiting, standing aloof in the corner all alone. His black evening suit was immaculate, his dark hair was as neatly styled as Wolf's always was, and he had the most perfectly proportioned face she'd ever seen on a man.

"Mr. Hutton," Mr. Abbott called as they approached. "May I present Mr. and Mrs. Wolf Trevelyan. Mrs. Trevelyan is the lady who set up the charity I was telling you about."

"Is she?" he asked, raising one eyebrow. His eyes flickered over her shoulder. "A kind-hearted woman and the miracle worker who tamed Wolf Trevelyan. I'm honored."

Molly glanced up at Wolf, just in time to see him break into that grin that held no humor. "Robert," he muttered softly. "It's been a long time."

Robert Hutton returned his attention to her, with an intensity that made her uncomfortable, even though Wolf was still with her. "What a surprise to find that the benevolent founder of the fund to benefit unwed mothers is such a beauty. Usually I find charitable workers to be a cheerless and homely lot of sour women. What a refreshing change."

She didn't like this man, not at all. He was rude and thoughtless and insulting . . . but he had offered to double the fund she'd started. "I'm going to assume that's some sort of a compliment, Mr. Hutton."

Mr. Abbott squirmed uncomfortably. Wolf, it seemed, didn't even breathe. And Mr. Hutton smiled brightly.

"Call me Robert."

Best to get right to business, she thought. "Mr. Abbott tells me you're interested in making a contribution."

"A very generous one," he said with a smile. "But first, I'd like a moment of your time." He glanced up at Wolf. "Alone."

"No," Wolf said softly.

"Double not enough?" Mr. Hutton's eyes hardened, just as Wolf's did when he didn't get his way. "I'll triple the account, for five minutes of Mrs. Trevelyan's time."

"All right," Molly said before Wolf could refuse again. Triple!

Robert Hutton led her from the ballroom, and Wolf didn't say a word. Molly got a quick glimpse of her husband as she left the crowded room, and she didn't like what she saw. Wolf was very angry.

"The Blue Salon?" Robert Hutton asked, taking her arm and leading her in that direction. "It shouldn't be crowded, with the concert about to begin."

The Blue Salon was, in fact, deserted, but for a single waiter who nodded at Robert Hutton and immediately reached for a bottle of liquor and a tall glass. Molly refused when he ordered two drinks instead of one, but the waiter ignored her and did as Mr. Hutton had asked.

"I'm looking for someone, and I think you might know where she is." Hutton took his glass and hers, and when Molly refused again he placed it on the table that sat between them. "She's . . . missing, and when I heard about your fund I thought you might know her whereabouts."

"I'm afraid I can't help you. Mr. Abbott handles the business end, along with several physicians, and I—"

"Bridget Brady," he interrupted.

Molly thought about bluffing, but she was a poor liar. From the satisfied smile that crossed Robert Hutton's face as he watched her closely, it was too late for deception. She had already given away too much.

"Are you the father of Bridget's child?" She could see how a sweet, simple girl could be fooled by a man like this, a man so handsome he was almost beautiful, a man who was good with words and had a charming smile.

"So she claims. I was never convinced that I was the only man who shared her bed."

Molly wanted to slap him, for Bridget, but she clasped her hands in her lap. "If that's the case, why are you trying to find her?" In a perfect world, he would tell her that he loved Bridget madly, that he wanted to marry her and raise their child together, but Molly didn't believe that was the case, not even for a second.

"I'm getting married in less than a month. My bride-to-be is the eldest daughter of a very prominent and wealthy family. You can see how awkward it would be if Bridget were to make an appearance. I went by her room to explain, to make things right, but she was gone, and the landlord said she'd just up and disappeared."

Instinctively, Molly knew that this handsome, charming man meant Bridget and her child harm. He didn't want an illegitimate child out there who might come to his door one day and disrupt his orderly life.

"Mr. Hutton," Molly stood slowly, with every

ounce of restraint she had in her body. "I can't help you."

His eyes flickered to the lone waiter, and then he stood to look down at her. "Think of all the women who could be helped by the money I'm willing to donate to your little fund."

The music began, the full notes drifting to them from the Grand Ballroom. Molly didn't have any desire to sit and listen to the concert, not any more. She wanted Wolf to hold her, and to tell her what to do about Bridget and this horrible man.

"I don't want your money, Mr. Hutton," she said as calmly as she could manage.

She thought for a minute that he would try to stop her. He was certainly angry enough. But instead of trying to grab her, he smiled and picked up the drink she had refused.

"There are other ways to locate Bridget, Mrs. Trevelyan," he said lazily and quite confidently.

"Leave Bridget alone," Molly insisted. "She won't disturb your cozy little life."

He ignored her plea.

"What are you going to call your little charity? How about The Wolf Trevelyan Fund For Unwed Mothers. Everyone would certainly get a laugh out of that."

Molly recognized the ploy for what it was. An attempt to hurt her, to put doubts in her mind. She straightened her spine and gave Robert Hutton a glare that would put him in his place. A glare she copied from her husband. She didn't care how much money Robert Hutton had, or how important he thought he was, he couldn't intimidate her.

Big Bad Wolf

"Wolf is not at all like you, Mr. Hutton." She left him sitting in the Blue Salon, sipping his whiskey. She'd have to get a telegram to Bridget, and advise her to change her name and move once again. Robert Hutton was certainly not going to give up so easily. He'd hire detectives, and they would track Bridget down, eventually.

Mr. Abbott was waiting for her outside the closed ballroom doors. "Where's Wolf?" she asked as she approached. She needed him now. She needed his strength and his comfort. He would know what to do.

Mr. Abbott looked very uncomfortable. He squirmed as if his collar was too tight. "Mr. Trevelyan left rather suddenly."

"Back to our suite?" Molly asked, already turning away from the banker.

"No. He said you would know where he was."

Again, he'd deserted her when she needed him. Molly's heart sank; of course she knew where Wolf was.

Wolf studied the cards in his hand with little enthusiasm. The brandy at his elbow was not as fine as the bottle in his suite, and the cigar he clenched between his teeth was not the best he'd ever had.

But he couldn't take another minute of being Molly's tamed Wolf.

This is where he belonged, where a few people accepted him for who he was. If he had to pretend enthusiasm on occasion, that was a small sacrifice. As far as anyone watching would know, the brandy was the finest he'd ever had, and the cigar was superb.

He didn't know what had broken the spell. His realization that Molly wanted to own him? Robert's offhand comment about Molly taming him? Or had the spell been broken the moment Molly had willingly left him standing in the Grand Ballroom with his banker, while she sauntered off to spend five minutes alone with the most notorious rake in New York?

Luck hadn't been with him so far tonight, but he blamed his bad fortune on his distraction. The evening was young. Wolf was certain he'd win back what he'd lost so far, and then some.

"Look who's here," Foster muttered from the chair to his right, and Wolf lifted his head to watch Molly cross the room.

She wasn't happy, but when she caught his eye he saw the relief rush over her face.

He didn't give her a chance to ask what he was doing here. "I thought you'd be enjoying the concert in Robert's company, right about now." He kept his gaze on his hand.

"How could you leave me alone with that horrible man?"

Wolf twisted his head to look up at Molly. "I didn't leave you alone. You went with him on your own, Red. Tell me, did he triple your fund? Quadruple it? What, exactly, did he want from you?"

"I told him to keep his money," she said softly.

Wolf folded, even though he had a decent enough hand. "You surprise me, Red. Most of the ladies find Robert quite charming."

"Good Lord, Wolf," Foster grumbled as he tossed down his own cards, and turned to present a fading black eye that was now more yellow and green than black. "Jealous again? She passed your little test with—"

"Shut up," Wolf muttered.

"What test?" Molly gave Foster her full attention.

"He didn't tell you?" Foster looked squarely at Wolf. "You didn't tell her? Oh dear. Look what I've done."

Wolf knew without a doubt that this was Foster's revenge for the black eye.

"What test?" Molly repeated.

"Wolf asked me to flirt with you, just to see what your reaction would be. Then, of course, he didn't approve of my methods, and gave me this." He pointed to the brightly colored skin beneath his eye. "Since you behaved so admirably, I rather did think he would congratulate you."

It would be cowardly to continue to study the cards on the table, so Wolf lifted his head and looked at Molly. She'd never been able to hide her emotions. Everything she felt was written on her face for the world to see. While it was true that he sometimes tried to deny what he saw there, he couldn't deny the pain in her eyes as she stared down at him.

Was this a worse sin than his overheard conversation with Adele? She had forgiven him that, but this . . .

"A test," Molly whispered. Wolf refused to react to the hurt in her eyes, the disbelief that came and went slowly. For a moment, perhaps, she'd wondered if he was capable of such betrayal, but of course she knew he was. "Tell me, Wolf." There was strength even in her whisper, a strength he could never match. "Was Foster to be a part of my education?"

Wolf glanced around the table, at the crowd of interested faces. "Not now, Red."

"Why not now?" she asked coldly. "You've always been one to appreciate a good shocking story. It seems you've outdone yourself, this time."

Molly couldn't maintain her icy facade. She didn't cry, wouldn't cry, he knew, but there was such pain etched on her face it made his heart ache. "Twice," she whispered, "I've needed you and you haven't been there. I turn to you for comfort only to find that you've disappeared. And now I learn that you asked your friend to test me? That you put me in that situation so I could prove myself?"

"I don't have to explain my actions to you."

"No you don't," Molly whispered. "You know, I always realized that you didn't love me. I had even accepted the fact that you might never love me, but I always thought that you trusted me. That you were honest with me. If we don't have that, we have nothing."

"We'll talk about this later." Wolf stood, and Molly backed up a step.

"No, we won't. I'm going home, Wolf." There was rebellion in her soft voice and in the stance she took, as she pulled back her shoulders and stood as tall as she could. "I don't belong in New

York, and I don't like living in a hotel. I miss the woods and the fresh air. My mother and my grandmother. I miss the quiet, and the sunshine breaking through the trees instead of past tall buildings."

"Red—"

"I'm going home." Her words were soft, but strong. Unyielding. "Are you coming with me?"

Molly stared him boldly in the eye, as if she had forgotten about the growing crowd that surrounded them, as if there was no one in the room but the two of them.

Wolf shook his head.

"I have an idea," Foster said brightly, and Wolf wanted more than anything to kill the man who had started all of this.

Foster gathered the cards that had been thrown face down on the table, and shuffled as he spoke. "One card. Molly draws high card, and Wolf leaves New York behind for the quiet of Maine. Wolf draws high card, and he stays here in the city. What do you say?"

"It's ridiculous," Wolf growled.

"I'll do it," Molly agreed softly.

Foster spread the cards across the table, fanned them evenly and widely from edge to edge.

"You first, Molly," Foster insisted.

Molly didn't hesitate, but reached out and flipped over the card at the end nearest her. The queen of hearts. There was a small collective gasp from the crowd surrounding the table.

"Wolf?" Foster prodded.

Wolf stared at the card Molly had turned over.

Perhaps it was fate. There were worse fates than living at Vanora Point with Molly—once she forgave him for testing her. And she would forgive him, eventually. She was angry now, but she wouldn't stay angry for very long.

There was something strong that brought them together, something he was not yet ready to call love.

"Come on, Wolf," Foster prodded, and Wolf looked up to see that the crowd around the table had grown, and that some gamblers were still taking bets. Who would win this time? The red queen or the black-hearted Wolf?

Molly was calm, calmer than most, as they all waited for Wolf to make his move. He caught her eye, for a second, and then he turned his attention to the cards on the table, the queen of hearts face up, and fifty-one others, face down.

Was he willing to risk the rest of his life on the turn of a card? He looked again at the queen of hearts, Molly's almost unbeatable card. His luck had been terrible all night, so perhaps he'd be lucky now and turn over a deuce.

Fate.

Wolf reached down and flipped over a card from the middle of the deck.

The king of spades.

Chapter Eighteen

Wolf followed the bellboy who carried his bags down the stairs, as he left the suite for the last time. It was out of habit that he took the stairs. Molly had never cared for the elevator, and she'd been unrelenting, no matter how often he'd tried to explain to her that the device was perfectly safe.

Since Molly was gone, Wolf was returning to the club, back to his convenient single room and the life of a bachelor.

It had taken every ounce of determination he possessed not to follow Molly to Vanora Point, to see her to the steamer and watch her sail away without so much as asking her once to stay behind.

She hadn't mentioned, not a single time, her fear of seasickness. It was just as well.

Half of New York claimed to have been there as he'd turned over the winning card. He had a reputation to maintain. He couldn't possibly relent and chase after his wife like some lovesick twit.

But he missed her already.

The bellboy placed his bags in the carriage, and when the boy turned around he stared up at Wolf with undisguised hate in his eyes.

Usually the bellboys and those who worked in the dining rooms here at the Waldorf avoided looking Wolf Trevelyan in the eye at all, and if they did it was a mistake quickly corrected. His reputation was widespread, and he had lost his temper in plain sight of the hotel employees on more than one occasion.

But this boy didn't look away. The look the frail bellboy gave Wolf was bitter, a challenge.

"Do you have a problem, boy?" Wolf leaned down slightly, placing his scowling face close to the bellboy's. Still the kid didn't back away or even blink.

The boy opened his mouth and closed it, and his fists clenched and unclenched several times. Finally, he lifted his chin defiantly. "Go to hell, sir."

Wolf was taken aback, by the suggestion and the reluctantly added "sir."

"Arthur! Are you delaying Mr. Trevelyan?"

Wolf glanced over his shoulder and raised a stilling hand to the doorman who frowned at the bellboy who blocked a guest from his own carriage. "I'd like a moment of Arthur's time, if you don't mind."

Big Bad Wolf

The doorman nodded solemnly, and Wolf returned his attention to the bellboy. "Do you have a problem with me, boy?"

"I would like very much, sir, to pound your face into the ground," Arthur said seriously.

Wolf glanced down at the small, tight fists that hung at Arthur's side.

"Any particular reason?" he asked dryly.

There was a momentary softening of the boy's face. "You made her leave, and worse than that, you made her cry."

Wolf crossed his arms over his chest, thoroughly confused. "Are you talking about my wife?"

"Yes, sir," Arthur said softly.

"Mrs. Trevelyan never cries."

Arthur narrowed his eyes. "*You* made her cry. She's a good person, you know. An angel."

"I know," Wolf said softly. "What makes you think this is any of your concern?"

"She never told you about me, did she?"

Wolf shook his head.

"She saved me from the police, and got me a good job here in the hotel, and she said . . . she said I had potential." Brave Arthur looked as if he were about to cry himself.

Molly was always trying to save the world. She said she wasn't, but Wolf knew better.

Arthur's face hardened again, as he pushed back the tears that made his eyes shine bright. "I'd love to pound you into the street," he seethed.

"Why don't you?" Wolf prodded. "I'll make certain it doesn't cost you your job, so there's nothing to stop you."

He was thinking it over, and Wolf knew the kid wanted more than anything to light into him. Maybe he should. Maybe he deserved it.

"Molly forbid me to hit you," Arthur said sullenly.

"She forbid you?"

Arthur nodded. "She said you were an old man and your heart was bad, and that if I killed you she wouldn't be here to save me from the police."

Wolf could almost smile. Molly had saved the kid from a beating and saved his pride at the same time.

Arthur finally moved aside, and Wolf stepped into the carriage.

He'd known this day would come, that Molly would return to Vanora Point and he would stay here in New York and tend to business. There was always Phil's, and the club, and all his old friends.

None of it appealed to him, and as the carriage carried Wolf to his club, he realized that like it or not, he missed his wife.

It was such a big house, and so quiet. More often than not, Molly found herself likening it to a mausoleum, rather than the castle it had first appeared to be. At the Waldorf, she'd never had to dine alone. The dining rooms had been filled with people, and even if she never said a word to anyone, at least she was surrounded by other diners.

Here, she ate her meals in isolation, in a dining room that was as large as the smaller dining rooms at the Waldorf. Wolf had, on occasion, told her about his day in the office as they shared an evening meal, but now she had no one but Mr. Larkin, who silently came and went as she ate, for company.

Molly spent much of her time in the library, because it was the one room in the Trevelyan house where she didn't feel as if she were in someone's way. She could sew or read while the staff cleaned and cooked, and she rarely even heard them. It was almost like living completely alone.

In a mausoleum.

When she'd left New York, it hadn't been her plan to return to Vanora Point to live alone. As far as she was concerned, she could move back into her mother's house, help with the baking and the mending the way she used to, and forget she'd ever met, much less married, Wolf Trevelyan.

She hadn't expected to return to Kingsport to find her mother just recently married to Mr. Hanson. Molly had sailed from New York before the telegram with the news had reached her. The newlyweds were so happy, there in Mary Kincaid Hanson's little house, and there was no room for Molly.

So she'd pasted on a smile, and told her mother that she just didn't care for New York City, and that was why she'd returned to Maine. It was the truth, after all. In a way.

Grandma Kincaid was getting along very well with the live-in companion Wolf had arranged. The woman was Mr. Larkin's sister, and she had lived all her life in Maine. She'd been widowed less than a year, and already she and Grandma were good friends. Molly didn't want to get in the way there, either.

Molly was certain she could adjust to her new circumstances, and she told herself again and again that it could be much worse. She had a roof over her head, a very nice roof, and food on the table, more than she could possibly eat, and she would eventually adjust to living alone.

It wasn't as if she expected Wolf to return to Vanora Point. He'd made his intentions very clear, on more than one occasion. Molly had chosen to disregard those intentions, until she couldn't ignore them any longer.

She'd have this house all to herself.

Molly put down her book, and lifted the sampler she didn't have any enthusiasm for. Once she had worked feverishly over the wedding sampler, but now that it was almost finished, she found she couldn't bear to look at it. The names and the date were complete, and most of the border was finished. A few hours of work would finish the piece, but then what would she do with it?

She'd intended the sampler to be a gift for Wolf, but she knew now that would be a mistake. Their marriage meant even less to him than she'd thought.

For three weeks she'd been at Vanora Point. The only time she'd been able to forget her own problems was when she was embroiled in Bridget's dilemma. Molly's telegram had found her friend, and warned her about Robert Hutton. Bridget's reply, a long letter Molly had slipped into a favorite book, had eased her fears.

Big Bad Wolf

Bridget had found, in San Francisco, the real man of her dreams. Someone sweet, and caring, and kind. A man who loved Bridget completely. Even when Bridget had told him the truth, that she was no widow, he hadn't deserted her as she'd feared he might.

They were probably already married. Molly suspected, from Bridget's glowing description of her beloved, that Robert Hutton would have a fierce battle on his hands should he try to harm Bridget and her child.

Molly placed her hands over her still flat belly. Was there just a bit of roundness there, or was it her imagination? Her breasts were fuller, it seemed, and terribly sensitive. She was hungry all the time, but had not yet been subjected to the bouts of morning sickness Bridget and Stella had described to her with such clarity.

Wolf was going to get his redheaded child. Unless, of course, the baby had his black hair. If it were a boy, Molly wanted him to have his father's black hair and green eyes. It was such a striking combination.

She'd started several letters to her husband, to tell him the news. They'd all ended up as wadded balls in the wastebasket by the desk. He didn't care. Not for her, and certainly not for the child. He would find out eventually, and would no doubt be most pleased with himself. An heir, and so quickly.

That meant his use for her was over. He might visit Vanora Point once or twice a year, if it suited him, and while he was home he would seduce her with his touch and his smile, and then he'd leave her behind again.

If she were lucky some of those visits would leave her as she was now. Carrying his child. Then, at least, she wouldn't be all alone.

"Madam."

Molly's head snapped up. How did he do that? Mr. Larkin stood in the open doorway. She hadn't heard a sound, not his step or the opening of the door. "Yes?"

"Dinner will be on the table in half an hour."

"Thank you." She lowered her head. He was a spooky one, Wolf's Larkin. Always there, looking over the house and the people in it as if it were his only calling in life.

Molly hugged her arms to her chest. Summer was over. The nights were cold, and usually, after a warm supper, Molly retired for the evening with a book in her hands and a blazing fire in the stone fireplace in her bedroom. By morning it was always cold, but for most of the night she was quite warm.

Not as warm as if she'd had Wolf to hold in the night, of course, but warm enough.

Wolf tried to flatten the papers with his big hands, but the wrinkles refused to give. It made the smeared ink even harder to read.

"Dear Wolf,

I know you don't care, but you really should know . . ." There was a scribbled mess after that. Wolf looked for a legible note of some sort among the sheets of wrinkled paper, but there was nothing. The letters had arrived just that morning, postmarked in Kingsport but with no return address.

"Dear Mr. Trevelyan," the next letter began. The handwriting was the same, neat and with little flourish. The handwriting would have been quite legible if the ink weren't smeared in so many places. *"It is my great pleasure to inform you—"* Again, the message ended abruptly.

"Mr. Trevelyan."

His head snapped up as his assistant entered the room. "What is it, Horace?"

"We've just had a message from Mr. Young's office. They would like to move the meeting to four o'clock."

"Fine." Wolf dismissed Horace with a wave of his hand. The sooner he could meet with Clarence Young and be done with this deal, the better off he'd be. The steel mill had been a headache from the start. He'd be glad to be rid of it.

The Trevelyans had always made their money at sea. They'd gone from piracy to shipbuilding to a respectable shipping business.

"Wolf," the next letter began. *"If you were half a man you'd be—"* He smiled. Molly.

"My dear husband." Wolf held the last letter in his hands. *"It has always been your plan that I provide you with heirs, and I must tell you. . . ."*

He turned the letter over in his hands, looking for more, but there was nothing. She must tell him what? That he'd never get the chance to father her child? That she'd rather jump off Vanora Point just like the first Mrs. Wolf Trevelyan than allow him into her bed again?

Or was she trying to tell him that she was going to give him the heir he'd married her for?

In spite of the doubts the letters raised, Wolf found himself smiling. Good God, he missed her. More than he'd thought possible. His room at the club was no substitute for the suite he'd shared with Molly. His favorite brandy had no flavor, his cigars stank to high heaven, and there wasn't a game at Phil's to take the place of strip poker with his wife.

He spent more and more afternoons in the gymnasium at his club, taking out his frustrations with his fists until there was no one left who would spar with him, not even the hired boys who risked their jobs by refusing.

His life was just as he'd wanted it, just as he'd planned all along. A wife in Maine, to keep the vigilant matchmaking mamas away, an heir possibly on the way, and the freedom of a bachelor. Everything a man could possibly want.

And he was miserable without Molly.

He'd played a good game for the past month. No one knew he was miserable. He worked in his office all day, drank at Phil's half the night. As far as Foster or anyone else knew, all was forgiven. To allow otherwise was to admit that Molly meant more to him than he wanted anyone to know.

On the surface, Wolf's life was continuing as it always had, but there was one major difference.

Women. In spite of his reputation, Wolf had never lacked for a woman's company. Daring, bold women who laughed at convention. Women like Adele, or the adventurous ladies who frequented Phil's.

In the past month he had realized that not one of them excited him. To be honest, there wasn't even a flicker of interest when Adele offered herself to him, or when the tall blonde from Phil's draped herself over his shoulder.

But, dammit, he dreamed about Molly.

He had to know. Wolf smoothed the unfinished letters with the palms of his big hands. Maybe he couldn't be the husband Molly wanted, maybe he couldn't love her the way she wanted to be loved, but if she was having his child he had a right to know.

Wolf studied the smeared ink, trying to read something into the words that told him nothing. She hadn't been able to finish . . . had wadded the letters up and tossed them away.

So who had mailed the letters to him?

"Mr. Larkin," Molly called, pulling the wastebasket from under the library desk.

As she'd tossed another letter into the basket, she'd noticed that it landed in the bottom all alone. Those letters weren't meant for anyone's eyes but her own! She should have burned them!

"Yes, madam?"

As usual, Mr. Larkin had been close by. "I disposed of some trash here a few days ago, and it's gone."

He raised one superior eyebrow. "Yes, madam."

"Where is it?"

Of course he thought she was insane, asking after the trash. Mr. Larkin had a face as stony as Wolf's, but much more distant. He looked as if he were always thinking of something other than the conversation that was taking place, as if he were somewhere else entirely.

"Are you asking me to locate the rubbish I took from this room, madam?"

"Yes," Molly said impatiently. "Where is it?"

Wolf's infuriating butler hesitated, pinned those cold dark eyes on her, and lifted perfectly shaped eyebrows. "Madam, I assure you I disposed of the refuse in a proper manner."

"I just wouldn't want . . . anyone reading . . . what I threw away."

Was she imagining it, or did Mr. Larkin almost smile? "I give you my word, madam. After years in this household, I understand perfectly well how to properly dispose of such personal debris."

"Oh." She had no choice but to accept his answer.

It didn't matter if he or someone else had read those letters and deciphered them. Soon enough everyone would know about the baby.

She still had not been able to bring herself to share the news. Wolf should know first, of course; and since she couldn't bring herself to tell him she was keeping the child a secret. For now.

When Stella and Hannah had visited, arriving in the back of a wagon Wallace drove, she had been tempted to tell them the news.

But she hadn't, of course. If they knew it would be all over town before sundown. Besides, they'd

Big Bad Wolf

been so enthralled by the tour of the house they'd insisted on, including a thorough inspection of the third floor, that there had been no time.

Wally had toddled into Wolf's office, and had nearly knocked over a painted vase Molly had placed in the library. It had actually teetered on the edge of the table before she'd managed to right it, while Stella looked in awe at the collection of books, oblivious to the near disaster.

Mr. Larkin had kept a close eye on them all, until Molly had seen her guests to the door.

She was beginning to accept Mr. Larkin's uncanny ability to be wherever he was needed, to know instinctively what she wanted.

Once the baby was able to toddle about like Wally, it would be nice to have another pair of hands about.

And she'd said she wanted six!

Molly fished the most recent discarded letter out of the wastebasket, as Mr. Larkin disappeared into the hallway. Perhaps it would be best to burn this one.

Chapter Nineteen

Molly frowned down at the sampler as she finished another yellow flower in satin stitch. In spite of the fact that she found the sampler disturbing, it was certainly a waste of time to come so far on a project and then abandon it entirely. She'd spent hours on the piece, and she couldn't make herself lay it aside unfinished. Perhaps one day their child would like to have this as a remembrance of his parents.

She sat in her favorite library chair, where she read or stitched during most of her unstructured days. If only she were allowed in the kitchen, she'd be baking bread, but every time she poked her head into Harriet's domain, she was presented with a patient and despairing stare.

As the days passed, Molly didn't feel any more

at home than she had on her wedding day.

"Hello, Red."

Molly almost jumped from her chair as she lifted her head, knowing who she would see in the doorway. She stuffed the sampler into the basket at her side. "What are you doing here?"

Wolf stood casually in the open doorway of the library, leaning against the doorjamb and staring at her as if she didn't belong here. "It's my house."

With a deep breath, Molly calmed herself. Of course this was his house. She'd known he would come, but she hadn't expected to have to face him so soon.

"That's true. I'll be happy to stay in Kingsport with Mother until you go back to New York."

"I'm not going back."

"What!" Molly shot to her feet. "What do you mean you're not going back? You have to go back!"

"I don't, actually," he informed her blandly. "The business was getting tedious, so I sold the steel mill and the lumber mill, and the shipping business is so well organized that I'm rarely needed. I gave Horace an ungodly raise to administrate in my absence. Any business that I must have a hand in can be managed from here."

She wanted to believe that he had come back to Vanora Point for her, that he had realized in their weeks apart that he did love her . . . but she knew Wolf too well. He was bored with business. He'd be bored with her soon.

"Nothing to say?" he prompted.

When she realized that she was going to have his

child, would he be done with her? Would their baby be just another objective accomplished? "I didn't expect you," she said softly.

"Obviously," he growled.

"I don't know what to say to you."

There was a part of her that was overjoyed to see him, that wanted nothing more than to throw herself into his arms. He looked wonderful, not at all strained or disturbed by their weeks apart.

Pushing away from the door, Wolf finally entered the room and took long strides toward her. "I missed you, Red. Does that make you happy?"

"Not really."

He took her chin in his hand and forced her to look up at him. "It should. I've never missed anyone before."

She knew he would kiss her, that he would lay his mouth on hers and she would forget every hurt, every betrayal. It wasn't fair that he had that power over her.

When he did kiss her, softly, so gentle it made her heart flutter in spite of her resolve, Molly wanted to forgive everything.

Adele, his easy desertion on the night of the concert they'd never attended, the test.

She pulled her lips away from his, but he continued to hold her tight. "Let me go."

"Isn't this what you wanted, Red?" He pulled her close, so she could feel his arousal pressing against her. "I need you."

There had been a time when she'd thought it would be enough. That to have Wolf need her, in any way, was all she'd wanted. But not anymore.

She loved him too much, more than she'd ever thought possible.

Molly slipped one hand between their bodies, and pressed her palm against Wolf's heart. She could feel his heartbeat against her hand, the warmth of his body she craved at night. He grinned, no doubt thinking he'd won again.

"When you need me here, too, we'll have something to talk about." With that same hand she tried to push him gently away, but Wolf didn't budge.

His smile died. "You can't deny me, Molly. You're my wife."

"It's true, I am your wife," she whispered. "But don't try to scare me with threats or with that fierce stare of yours. In spite of everything you've done, I know you won't hurt me."

He released her and backed away. "You want an apology? All right. I'm sorry."

"I don't want an apology, and if I did those ungracious words would not have been sufficient." Molly felt braver with a few feet of space between them.

When Wolf was angry he seemed taller, wider, as menacing as his reputation. "What the hell do you want?"

Molly stood as tall as she could, which wasn't much compared to her husband. Did she dare to tell him? Would she scare him back to New York? Nothing could be worse than this limbo.

"I want you to love me."

He should have known. The simple words shouldn't hit him with such unexpected force, but he felt as if Molly had physically struck him. Of course that was what she wanted. What she'd wanted from the beginning.

"I never promised to love you."

"I know."

She was more beautiful than he remembered, her hair redder, her skin fairer, and he wanted her so much he hurt. He had every right to throw her over his shoulder and carry her to their bedroom, but he knew as well as Molly did that wouldn't happen.

"For a while, this marriage was fine. What we had was enough," he said.

"It's not enough any more," she whispered.

"Why the hell not?"

She looked as if she were on the verge of tears, but Molly never cried. Only when she had her face buried in a book did the tears flow. But right now her gray eyes were overly bright, and her face was flushed.

Had she hidden her tears from him, or was she as tough as she appeared to be? Arthur, that insolent bellboy, had accused Wolf of making Molly cry, but he hadn't really believed it was true.

"I loved you on the day we were married," she revealed in a soft voice. "And before. I came to your defense, and I gave of myself all that I could, and I loved you. My mother and my grandmother believed I only agreed to the marriage for the security that was promised them, and everyone else, including you, thought that I had married you for your money."

"Red, don't—"

"I hate your money," she interrupted. "Burn it all, and I'll still love you."

"Red." He took a step forward, and Molly stepped back.

"Let me finish. It doesn't seem to matter how much I love you. You don't even *trust* me. When I realized that, it hurt more than you'll ever know."

He knew. He'd seen the pain in her eyes. There was sorrow there now, and strength, so much strength.

"I said I was sorry—"

"It's not enough."

"I can't love you the way you want, Molly. And I won't lie to you and whisper pretty words to appease you and keep peace between us."

He stepped forward, alarming her, and so he stopped. "I can't give you any more than I already have."

She didn't falter. Did it mean nothing to her that he'd give up his life in New York just to be here? Did she not realize how much it cost him just to admit that he needed her?

There was no softening of her expression, no light of surrender in her eyes.

"You think you don't have any love in your heart, but I know you do. I've seen glimpses of it, when you let your guard down. Tell me you love me, Wolf."

He couldn't. It was like placing his head on a block and offering Molly an ax. Baring his soul to Molly was not as easy as baring his body.

"I need you," he conceded.

Molly shook her head. "I want it all."

"I don't have it in me to give you what you want."

"You do. Find it, Wolf. I can't live the rest of my life loving you like this, and wondering if there's an Adele waiting around the corner, or another test of my loyalty to be passed."

He wanted to ask Molly if she was carrying his child, but he couldn't. Not now.

"What we have is close to perfect, Red." He combed his fingers through his hair. Anything to keep from reaching out and grabbing her. "Passion, fun. Almost perfect."

"I want perfect," Molly whispered, and then she ran past him. He could have reached out and caught her, forced her to face him and tell him she'd discard what they had because it wasn't perfect.

But he let her go. Wearily, he sank down into the chair she'd been sitting in when he'd surprised her. It was still warm, still held her heat and the faint scent of the soap she preferred.

He'd expected her to be angry, had known he'd have to fight to regain what they'd had, but he hadn't expected her to be so adamant.

When he dropped his arms over the side of the chair, his hands brushed her basket and the wadded material within. She'd stuffed it in there awfully quickly when she'd seen him. Baby clothes, perhaps?

He lifted the linen, holding it carefully between two pinched fingers, and placed it on his lap.

With care, he unfolded the corners, knowing already that this was no baby gown. A silk tree grew in the middle of the sampler, stitched there by Molly's hand. How appropriate. It reminded him of their meeting in the forest, of the trees he'd spied her through that first day.

The flowers along the border were yellow and blue—just like the wildflowers he had tried to seduce her with. Wolf ran his fingers over the names she had stitched so perfectly. His on one side, hers on the other. In the middle, beneath the tree, she'd sewn the date of their wedding in tiny, perfect stitches.

"Welcome home, sir."

Wolf lifted his head slowly. Larkin never changed. He was an ageless, solid fixture at Vanora Point. The first words that came to Wolf's lips were caustic, but he bit them back. "Thank you, Larkin."

As if surprised by the lackluster and conventional greeting, the aging butler lifted his eyebrows, then began backing out of the room.

"Larkin," Wolf called sharply, and the butler stepped forward with a crisp snap of his head.

"What can I do for you, sir?"

Wolf folded the sampler neatly and returned it to the basket. "Have you ever been married?"

He obviously took the butler by surprise with the personal question. The old man's eyes widened, and he stiffened considerably. A feat in itself, since Larkin was unfailingly unbending.

"You've been here for years, since I was a child, but you've never said a word about your family."

Larkin took a deep breath. "I was married at a young age, sir."

"Kids?"

"Four."

"Good for you," Wolf said, surprising the old man again. "Tell me about your wife."

This conversation was making the staid Larkin very uncomfortable. "She was very pretty, and kind, and a good mother."

"Was?" Wolf's smile faded.

"She died giving birth to our youngest son."

"I'm sorry." He felt like a heel for reminding Larkin of his loss. "I didn't mean to pry."

Larkin made no attempt to leave the library, but stood at attention near the door. "It was very long ago, sir, when you were just a tot."

"Where are your children now?"

"Ann is married and has children of her own, sir. She lives near Boston. Harry and George moved out West several years ago, and Ross lives in Bangor. He has a business there." There was a touch of wistfulness in his voice.

"Why have I never met them?"

Larkin looked at Wolf as if he'd lost his mind. Not once in the seven years since his father's death had Wolf asked the butler, or any of the staff, a personal question. He hadn't even known their given names until Molly had told him.

"After my wife died, they went to live with my sister."

"When did you see them?"

Larkin looked absolutely confused, but Wolf had to know. "Your father was very generous with me, sir. I spent every Christmas and a week every summer with them, as the years passed."

306

Big Bad Wolf

A week and Christmas. It wasn't enough. Larkin had rarely seen his children as they'd grown up, just as Wolf would never see his if he stayed with his original plan.

"And now?"

"Sir?" Larkin lifted his eyebrows.

"When was the last time you went to Boston to see your grandchildren?"

The man turned pink, and he fastened his eyes above Wolf's head. "Three years ago, sir."

"Three years?" Wolf clucked and shook his head. "That won't do, Larkin," he said abruptly. "We will survive without you, you know."

"Yes, sir."

"You can leave next week," Wolf continued, his voice as businesslike and cold as it had been when he'd bargained with Clarence Young over the price of the steel mill. "Before true winter comes. Would two weeks be sufficient?"

"Yes, sir."

"And in the spring I think a month off is in order. Would you like to see the wild West, Larkin?"

"Yes, sir, but . . ." Uncharacteristically, Larkin stumbled over his words.

"You don't want to go?" Belatedly, it occurred to Wolf that Larkin might not be on good terms with his children, after all the distant years.

"It's not that, sir. It's just that I've seen to the running of this house for many years, and . . ."

Wolf noted the distress, and guessed at the problem.

"And you're afraid you'll find it in ruins when you return?"

"Yes, sir," Larkin sighed.

"With a little instruction Molly will be able to run this household well. She's a quick study."

"Thank you, sir."

Mentioning Molly's name brought all his own problems rushing back.

"How has Mrs. Trevelyan been since her return?" Wolf asked suddenly.

"Are you speaking of her state of mind or her physical well-being, sir?"

"Both."

"She's been rather quiet, though I can't say I know her well enough to know if that's unusual."

"It is," Wolf grumbled.

"She seems inordinately concerned with causing trouble in the household, with . . . getting in the way, as she puts it. She insists on calling me *Mr.* Larkin, when Larkin has suited for years." He took a deep breath. "Physically, I must say she seems quite healthy. I've never seen a woman eat quite as vigorously as Mrs. Trevelyan, and yet she is as small and quick as a hummingbird."

Wolf smiled at the apt description. Larkin had been doing his job as he had for years, watching out for the Trevelyans. One of the questions that had plagued him was suddenly answered. "Tell me, Larkin. Did you happen to send me an envelope a week or so ago? A few sheets of crumpled paper?"

The mask was back in place, and Larkin's eyebrows lifted in disdain. "I'm afraid I don't know what you're talking about, sir."

Wolf dismissed the butler with a wave of his

hand. As Larkin backed into the hallway, Wolf grinned.

"Thank you, Larkin."

He was almost certain he heard a faint "you're welcome, sir," as the door closed.

Molly paced, her eyes on the locked door that separated her room from Wolf's. She'd made herself perfectly clear, she thought. Until Wolf admitted that he loved her, they had no marriage.

But if he came to her, she wouldn't be able to resist him. He knew her body too well, could break down her defenses with a touch or two, with a gentle kiss . . .

But if he saw her unclothed, he'd know she carried the heir he demanded of her. The changes in her body were subtle, but she had no doubt Wolf would notice the slight bulge of her belly, the tenderness and swelling in her breasts.

There had been times, fleeting moments, when she'd believed that he did love her. She saw it in his eyes, felt it in his touch . . . but if it was true why wouldn't he admit to that love?

As she watched, the knob rattled slightly. She waited for Wolf to begin banging on the door, demanding entrance. For a moment there was nothing, and she could almost believe that Wolf had given up.

And then, with a loud crack and a crash, the door swung in—followed by a glimpse of Wolf's booted foot swinging to the floor.

Molly expected to see anger on his face, but he walked into her room with a wicked grin on his lips and a sparkle in his eyes.

"Don't ever lock me out, Red. It'll do you no good." There was no anger in his voice as he delivered his lighthearted warning.

Molly licked her suddenly dry lips, and backed up a step. A step which brought the backs of her thighs to the bed.

"You're my wife," he said in a low voice, and the grin faded quickly.

"I know," Molly whispered.

"You'll give me whatever I want," he demanded.

"I will not—"

"And what I want right now is a kiss goodnight."

Molly had no answer for that, and she held her breath as Wolf advanced slowly. When he stood before her he rubbed the back of his hand across her cheek.

"You broke down the door for a goodnight kiss?" Molly asked as he lowered his lips slowly to hers.

"Yes." He breathed the answer into her mouth as he closed his mouth over hers. It had been so long, and she'd missed this so much. Molly could feel herself giving in, yielding, as Wolf held her tightly, deepening the kiss, allowing her to feel his arousal against her belly.

Her knees were weak, her whole body glowed achingly, and all from a single kiss.

She couldn't stop the soft moan that caught in her throat, the way her body arched against his instinctively. Her hands crept around his waist, until she placed the palms against his hard and warm back. She needed to hold him.

She hadn't been able to tell him that afternoon, but she'd missed him, too.

When Wolf released her it was with obvious reluctance. His mouth left hers, and then was back for a quick kiss. His arms loosened, but slowly, and Molly dropped her hands from his back. When he had released her completely, he took her chin in his hand and lifted her face so she was forced to look into his eyes.

If he was trying to prove that she was defenseless against him, he'd done it well. She ached for him, and took little pleasure from the fact that she saw her pain mirrored in Wolf's green eyes.

"Tell me," he whispered. "That's not perfect."

With that he dropped his hand and spun away from her, to stride from the room without looking back. As he closed the broken door solidly, Molly sank onto the bed.

Wolf settled down for the night in his chair, cigar in one hand and brandy in the other. The nights were cold, now, so the blaze in the fireplace was necessary.

He no longer doubted that Molly was going to have a child. She was gently rounded, and her breasts were just a bit larger than he remembered.

His memory was not faulty in that area, he was certain.

It had taken every ounce of willpower he possessed to kiss her and then walk away. Particularly when he knew damn well she wanted him as much as he wanted her.

If he seduced Molly now, she'd never forgive

him. First, he had to prove to her that what they had was enough, that almost perfect was as good as anybody got in this life.

Wolf turned his head to the empty bed that was no doubt much more comfortable than his place by the fire, but he couldn't force himself to crawl into that bed alone. He wouldn't sleep there, anyway, not without Molly curled up against his side.

He hadn't had a decent night's sleep since she'd left him.

Wolf finished his cigar, sipped at the brandy, and listened to the crackle of the fire and the soft but constant movements from the room next door. Feet padding against the floor, a sigh, the sound of an uneasy body shifting again and again in the bed. Molly was restless, just as he was.

Wolf closed his eyes and pictured her, turning beneath the thick coverlet, sighing and attempting the impossible.

Comfort. He had to convince her that the only comfort she would ever have would come in his arms.

It wouldn't be easy, and it might take more time than he'd thought, but Molly would come to him.

Wolf fell asleep in his chair, with a blanket thrown over his legs and a small smile on his face.

Chapter Twenty

Molly rose and dressed quietly, after a disturbing and restless night. The sun was barely up, but she was wide awake and starving.

As she buttoned her pale blue gown, she kept her eyes on the door that separated her room from Wolf's, half expecting him to appear at any moment with a fierce grin on his face and a demand for a good morning kiss.

Tell me that's not perfect.

If Wolf would keep his distance, perhaps she could continue to insist on having it all. Deep in her heart she knew that if he continued to touch her, to kiss her, she would certainly lose this battle.

Mr. Larkin was waiting at the foot of the stairs, as if he'd known she'd arise early.

"Good morning, Mr. Larkin," Molly said as she descended.

"Good morning, madam." His greetings were always cool, distant. Perfunctory. "I'll have Cook prepare your breakfast immediately."

He was off, stiff in bearing and efficient to a fault. Since her return to Vanora Point, Molly had been eating ravenously, especially in the morning. It was the only effect, other than the slight rounding of her belly and the tenderness in her breasts, of her condition. She hadn't suffered from nausea in the morning, or from the terrible tiredness that had so bothered Stella.

But she did arise with a gnawing hunger.

She had tea and bread, and eggs and ham, and then more tea and bread. Mr. Larkin was there when her plate was empty, to take it away and replace it with more food. If he found her eating habits strange, he didn't give any indication. Not even the lifting of an eyebrow.

She couldn't face Wolf, not yet. She needed to strengthen her resolve, to remember why she was demanding more than her husband wanted to give.

Her life, their life together, depended on it.

"Mr. Larkin," she said, feeling much better once her mind was made up. "I'll be going into Kingsport today. Do we need anything from Mr. Mc-Cann?"

"I don't believe so, madam. Willie went into town for supplies just yesterday. If you'll let me know when you're ready to leave, I'll have him pull the carriage around."

"No," Molly said sharply. "I'm going to walk."

The only indication that Mr. Larkin was surprised was the very slight widening of his eyes. "It's quite a long hike, madam, might I suggest—"

"No," Molly said as she rose from her chair. "The walk will do me good."

Did Mr. Larkin sigh? She could almost believe he did as he turned his back on her.

The walk would do her good, and so would a visit with her mother, and with Stella and Hannah. If she planned this journey very carefully, she would return just before dark, eat quickly, and retire early pleading exhaustion.

All in all, it was a good plan.

Molly fetched her red cape from her bedchamber, moving slowly and silently so she wouldn't wake Wolf and have to face him as she left. She actually tiptoed down the stairs and into the hallway.

Shirley was just entering the library, a dust rag in her hand. Molly paused in the doorway and watched for a moment as Shirley polished the long desk where Molly had begun all those unmailed letters to Wolf.

When the maid lifted her head and saw Molly standing there, she actually jumped, she was so startled.

"Oh!" Shirley held the hand that still clutched her polishing rag to her chest. "For a moment I thought you were *him*."

"Him?" Molly repeated.

"Mr. Trevelyan."

Linda Jones

Shirley was shy and skittish, Molly had discovered, but she was truly horrified of Wolf.

"Shirley," Molly stepped into the room, "Has Mr. Trevelyan ever done or said anything to frighten you?" She knew what the answer would be, even before Shirley began to shake her head.

"No, madam." Shirley looked down at the desk, and started to dust with little enthusiasm.

"There's no reason for you to leap out of your skin every time he comes into the room." Molly held her tongue as further defense of her husband came to her lips.

"Are you . . . are you going to dismiss me, madam?" Shirley still refused to look up. Her voice was calm, as if she easily accepted losing her position.

"Of course not," Molly said, indignant at the very suggestion that she would take anyone's job away. "I just want to make one thing very clear."

Shirley lifted her face, at last, and Molly smiled in an attempt to put the bashful maid at ease. "There's no reason for you to be afraid of Mr. Trevelyan."

"But he looks so ferocious, and there are the stories," she said.

"We'll have no gossip in this house, Shirley." Molly's smile faded. "I won't allow it."

"Yes, madam." Shirley was staring at the desk again.

"But I will tell you a secret," Molly said softly as she approached the desk. "No gossip, but a fact."

Shirley lifted her pale face. The desk separated them, and Molly placed her hands on the surface and leaned forward, so she could whisper her secret.

"Beneath that ferocious scowl, behind that hairy chest . . ."

Shirley blushed, bright pink.

"There beats the heart of a spoiled, rotten little boy. A brat who never grew up. A great big ferocious baby."

"Oh," Shirley breathed.

"And he would never hurt anyone, in spite of what you've heard." Molly pushed herself away from the desk. "There's no reason to be afraid."

Molly didn't know if her explanations had helped Shirley at all, but if Wolf was to stay here at Vanora Point, at least for a while, it wouldn't do to have his staff jumping in fear every time he entered the room.

"I won't be back until late," Molly said as she left the library. As she left the house, closing the front door silently behind her, she felt as if she were accomplishing a great escape.

It was just a dream, Wolf reminded himself as he ran toward the cliff and the woman who was poised there. His limbs were heavy, leaden, and they would barely move, no matter how hard he tried to reach her.

She turned toward him, and as he watched in horror Jeanne's pale hair turned red. The child in her arms changed, too, from a faceless hairless infant into a child with red hair like Molly's and green eyes like the ones he saw in the mirror every morning.

Just a dream, he told himself, but his anxiety turned to dread as he tried to reach them in time.

The dream had changed, so maybe the outcome would be different. Maybe this time he would reach the cliff in time to save them.

He had to save them. This was Molly and their child, and she was poised at the edge of the cliff and staring at him with a serene expression on her face.

She smiled at him, and for a heartbeat he knew that everything would be all right. Molly wouldn't jump, the way Jeanne always did. Molly wouldn't jump because she loved him, and she loved their child.

She didn't jump. She fell. Molly's feet slipped out from under her and with the baby still clutched in her arms she disappeared over the edge.

Wolf woke with a start, practically coming out of the chair where he'd fallen asleep just a few hours earlier. His heart pounded against his chest, and the sweat that covered his body was not normal for such a cool morning.

Sunlight lit his room, but there remained a chill in the air.

He leapt from the chair, trying to escape the nightmare. The images in his mind wouldn't go away, not even when he closed his eyes and reminded himself logically that Molly was asleep in the next room.

Illogically, he had to see her. A glimpse would do it. Wolf quietly opened the door he'd broken in last night, hoping that Molly was still asleep and would never know of this implausible lapse.

The door opened just a few inches, enough for

Wolf to see the bed through the crack. Sunlight fell across an empty bed, and he pushed the door completely open to make absolutely certain she wasn't in the room.

The complete silence told him she wasn't there, but he crossed to the bath anyway. Just in case. He held his ear to the door, listening for a faint splash, a sigh, anything to tell him Molly was there.

Nothing. He opened the door anyway, just to be sure.

As Wolf dressed in the casual clothes he preferred while in Vanora Point, he told himself—silently and aloud—that what had disturbed him was just a dream. He was exhausted, and Molly was driving him to distraction, and he had substituted her face for Jeanne's in the old nightmare because he'd fallen asleep with Molly on his mind.

Larkin was not waiting at the foot of the stairs, a good sign. Perhaps he was serving Molly her breakfast, or watching after her in what Molly called his uncanny way.

The dining hall was empty. If she'd had breakfast all signs of the meal had been cleaned from the room. Wolf stood in the doorway and listened for a moment, trying to place Molly. Surely she was somewhere in this house.

Hearing nothing, he decided to check the library. Sitting in her chair and reading or working on her wedding sampler, she wouldn't make a sound.

There was nothing to worry about.

The maid was standing on a stool and dusting

books on the tall shelves, and Wolf expected, as she turned her head to face him, that she would fall from her unsteady perch as soon as she caught sight of him.

For once, though, the girl didn't squeal or twitch. In fact, she looked him square in the eye. "Good morning, Mr. Trevelyan," she said. Her voice was soft, but didn't tremble at all. "Do you need this room? I could finish here later."

She started to climb down, but Wolf stopped her with a raised hand. "I'm just looking for my wife."

"Oh." The maid—was it Shirley?—looked him square in the eye. "Mrs. Trevelyan's gone for the day, sir."

"Gone where?" He shouldn't feel such dread at the simple words.

"She didn't say, sir." Shirley stared at him with the oddest expression on her face, as if she were seeing him for the first time. "She did say she'd be quite late returning home. I suppose Larkin might know where she's gone."

"Well, where is he?" He hadn't meant to snap, and he fully expected Shirley to respond by withdrawing as she always did.

"I'm afraid I don't know, sir," she said stiffly.

No Molly, and no Larkin. Wolf knew, logically, that there was no reason to panic, but his long strides carried him from the house and to the cliff without hesitation.

Beyond the edge of the cliff, the ocean danced wildly. He'd always loved the power and the beauty of the sea, the magnificent vista that was spread before him. He'd grown up playing at the edge of the cliff, dreaming of following in the footsteps of his great-grandfather, the first Wolf Trevelyan, a fearless pirate.

How many days had he dreamed of escape from his father's structured life by way of the sea? How many nights had he watched the moon on the ocean, believing that there was nothing in the world more beautiful?

At one time he'd believed that, but he'd avoided the view for seven years.

As he reached the edge he looked down. He knew Molly wasn't there, that his fears were just the memories of a dream that wouldn't fade as it should, but he had to see for himself.

Waves crashed against the boulders and smaller rocks more than a hundred and fifty feet below, frenzied and forceful. White foam washed over the boulders, and at the sight Wolf exhaled the breath he hadn't realized he'd been holding.

Of course Molly wasn't there. He hadn't expected to see her body broken on the rocks below. A damned dream had sent him here, nothing more.

Wolf turned his back on the ocean, angry with himself for allowing his doubts to drive him to this insanity. For allowing Molly to become more important to him that he'd ever intended. For needing her.

Why did she insist that he declare his love? That he bare his soul to her? Molly was the only person in the world who had the power to destroy him, and if he had any pride at all he'd pack his bags and be gone before she returned to Vanora Point.

He didn't consider that alternative for more than the twinkling of an eye.

As Wolf rounded the house, he saw the oddest sight, Larkin walking quickly down the drive toward the house, winded and disheveled. His tie was askew, and his steel gray hair had been mussed by the wind so that it practically stood straight up.

As the butler came closer, Wolf saw further evidence of strenuous activity. Sweat and an incredibly red face. He'd never actually seen Larkin sweat before.

"Is everything all right?" Wolf called as Larkin approached the front door.

"I believe so, sir," Larkin answered breathlessly.

"I was looking for Molly. Have you seen her?"

Was that a curse just beneath Larkin's breath? Certainly not. "Mrs. Trevelyan has gone to Kingsport to visit with her mother and friends." Larkin held himself tall.

"And you walked with her?"

"In a manner of speaking, sir."

Wolf smiled, recognizing the truth at last. "You followed her?"

"Yes, sir." Larkin took a deep breath. "Just until she reached the edge of town." He straightened his tie and ran fingers through his hair, as if it would be profane to enter the house in his disorderly condition.

"Did she see you?"

Larkin shot him a look of pure disgust. "Of course not, sir."

Wolf glanced down the drive to the road that would lead him to Kingsport. He wanted to see Molly, needed to see her, but he wouldn't subject her or himself to the trials of facing the residents of that small and unforgiving town.

"Mrs. Trevelyan made it clear, before she left the house, that she would not be returning until late this afternoon." Larkin had already recovered most of his reserved composure, and he delivered this bit of information with a nonchalance he had perfected over the years.

"Thank you, Larkin."

"Just doing my job, sir," Larkin said as he entered the house, moving almost sideways so he did not present his back to Wolf. "And if I may be so presumptuous . . ." Larkin hesitated.

"Continue, Larkin," Wolf ordered.

The old man sighed, and cast a vaguely distressed glance Wolf's way. "You're making my job increasingly difficult, sir."

"Am I?" Wolf crossed his arms over his chest and shifted his feet. Larkin would not be intimidated.

"Yes, sir." For the first time that Wolf could remember, Larkin turned his back on him and walked away.

All in all, it had been a very unsuccessful trip, and Molly all but pouted as she walked down the road and away from Kingsport.

When it came right down to it, she hadn't been able to bring herself to tell anyone about the baby. Stella was feeling terrible, sick and exhausted and sniveling. Molly didn't want the first response to her news to be tears, and she knew that's what Stella would do if she knew about the baby. She still wasn't convinced that Molly was safe being Wolf Trevelyan's wife.

Telling Hannah was out of the question. Molly wasn't ready for the entire town of Kingsport to know. If Hannah, knew, it wouldn't be a secret for long.

She should have been able to tell her mother, but Mary had been so happy. Mr. Hanson hadn't left his bride's side during Molly's visit. They'd held hands and smiled at each other as if there were no one else in the room, during the entire visit.

Even if she had decided to tell them that she was going to have a baby, they probably wouldn't have heard her.

As she turned onto the road to Vanora Point, Molly had to admit that her perfectly good reasons for not telling anyone about the baby were just excuses. Wolf should know first. It was his right.

Molly was angry with herself for considering Wolf's rights. Had he thrown those rights away when he'd tested her? How much should his lack of faith cost him?

In truth, Molly had forgiven Wolf for the horrid test. It wasn't entirely his fault that he had no trust in those around him.

He was going to have to trust her enough to admit that he loved her before they could have the marriage Molly wanted, the marriage she and Wolf both needed.

Big Bad Wolf

Was she kidding herself completely when she looked into his eyes and saw love? Wolf had never gazed at her as lovingly and contentedly as Orville Hanson had looked at his bride. With passion, yes. With a love that seemed to pain him, yes.

Molly swung the basket her mother had forced into her hands as she'd left the house. It contained two loaves of bread, bread her mother had baked because she wanted to, not because she had to. She could thank Wolf for that, for her mother's happiness.

She gazed into the dark forest at her right. Whenever she saw the woods now, she thought of Wolf, of the way he had tempted her. She had fallen in love with him so easily and completely.

Unconsciously, she moved to the right side of the road. What a wonderful smell, pine and untended growth and a wild musky scent that belonged there in the forest. She would never again smell the wildness of the forest and not think of Wolf.

"What's in the basket, Red?"

Molly stopped, there at the side of the road, and looked into the shadow of the forest, past tall sheltering trees. Had she conjured up Wolf's voice, simply by thinking about him?

"Wolf?" Molly stepped off the road and poked her head cautiously past a pair of pines. "Is that you?"

She heard his footsteps first, heavy and slow and very close, and still she jumped when he appeared before her.

"Who else would it be?"

325

Molly straightened her spine and stepped backward.

"What's in the basket?"

Molly glanced down at the basket and bit her lower lip. This was her Wolf. No business suit, no gambling hall, no New York City. He was dressed as he had been when she'd first seen him, in a checked shirt and sturdy trousers. There was even an India rubber knapsack slung over one shoulder.

"Bread," she said softly. "My mother sent it. I hope Harriet is not insulted."

"All I have is hard bread and a bit of salted pork," he said casually.

Molly lifted her gaze from the basket. What was he doing? Was he trying to remind her of how quickly she'd fallen in love with him, or was he trying to begin again?

He leaned against a tall pine and stared into her eyes. There was a challenge there, and Molly realized this encounter was just another of Wolf's games, an amusement, an attempt to gain the upper hand in their battle, a battle she couldn't afford to lose.

Wolf stood several feet from her, in the gloom of the woods, and as Molly watched he raised his hand, palm upward, in a silent invitation.

"Come on, Red." His voice was husky, inviting. "Step into the woods."

Molly shook her head silently, but Wolf didn't drop his hand.

"Life's fun is off the path," he whispered. "And don't forget, I know all your weaknesses. All your vices. You need me, Red."

"I love you." Molly took another step back, until she was on solid footing on the road. "That's not a vice."

His hand dropped slowly. "It's a weakness." His patience was wearing thin, she could hear that in the sudden bite in his voice.

"Is that why you don't . . . why you can't . . ."

She couldn't ask. She didn't want Wolf to confess that he could never love her.

Wolf turned and disappeared, gone from her sight as suddenly as he'd entered it moments earlier. For several minutes, Molly stared into the woods. There was not a sound to indicate that Wolf was close by. No crush of his footsteps or crackle of displaced limbs.

No voice, either. No curse or invitation.

With a sigh, Molly turned back toward Vanora Point.

He couldn't miss the swirl of that red cloak through the thick growth of trees, even if he'd wanted to.

Wolf's silent path took him parallel to the road, and just behind Molly, so he watched her dancing cape and the back of her head as he followed.

Damn her, she was stubborn as a mule! If she'd just stepped into the woods, if he'd kissed her here and they'd made love on the ground, he could be certain that this ridiculous notion that he had to tell her he loved her would fade . . . eventually.

Why did Molly insist that he bare his soul to her? Why couldn't she simply accept what they had and be happy with it, as he was?

Any other man would have given her what she wanted. Three little words. They didn't have to mean anything.

When the house was in view, cold stone and the last light of day sparkling on the windows, Molly increased her pace. It was getting cold, Wolf realized as he stopped to watch her run away from him. She was anxious for a fire and a hot cup of tea, which Larkin would no doubt have waiting for her.

Why couldn't he just tell her what she wanted to hear? "I love you, Molly."

Wolf knew the answer. He couldn't give in because it was true. He did love her, more than he'd ever thought possible. Telling her would be like handing over his heart and asking her to stomp on it. Like offering his heart and his soul on a silver platter for Molly to play with as she wished.

In the back of his mind, there was always the fear that one day everything he had would be gone. His business, his home, Molly. One day she would realize what a mistake she'd made in marrying him, and if he had to watch her walk away he'd do it with a smile on his face and a sarcastic quip.

Christ, this wasn't the way it was supposed to be. His plan had been flawless, his execution without fault. Marry Molly, enjoy her for a while, and then *he* would be the one to walk away.

He'd never counted on coming to need her, as she'd planned, and he sure as hell had never planned to fall in love with her.

Chapter Twenty-one

Molly had extinguished all the lights so that her bedchamber was lit only by the radiance of the fire, and she burrowed under the covers.

Wolf had smiled at her and carried on an innocent conversation over dinner, never even mentioning their brief meeting on the road. Molly had tried not to look directly at him as she'd eaten her boiled beef and potatoes, but it was impossible not to glance at him on occasion.

He'd watched her through hooded eyes, as if he were afraid she'd see too much there.

Pleading exhaustion, she'd retired directly after dinner, leaving Wolf to his brandy and cigars. His whispered goodnight had been apathetic, but Molly found she was waiting anxiously for him to burst through her door with another demand.

Linda Jones

She missed what they'd had. The fun, the passion, the sharing. Her bed was cold, and she felt chilled deep down, inside, in her very soul. She needed Wolf to fill that void, to warm her body and soul.

She wasn't surprised at all when the broken door swung open with a loud creak.

"Wake up, Red," Wolf demanded as he entered her room.

Molly peeked from beneath her covers. He wasn't wearing anything but his trousers, and the firelight flickered on his bare chest and on the insolent face he turned to her.

"I'm not asleep," she whispered.

"Good," he said brightly. "I'm here for my goodnight kiss."

Was this to be a nightly ritual? Heavens, how would she bear it?

Before she could protest, Wolf was seated on the side of her bed. It sunk slightly and she couldn't help but roll toward him.

Molly tried to sit up, but Wolf placed his arms on either side of her and gently but effectively forced her back to the pillow.

She could see no emotion on his harsh face, no smile, no anger. The firelight danced across those hard features as if over immovable rock.

But his hands were soft, gentle. Wolf trailed his fingers down her cheek and neck, across her chest until they rested against one very sensitive breast.

Still, his face came no closer.

He teased her, and Molly was frozen. She couldn't make herself demand that he move away, that he stop touching her, any more than she could demand that he kiss her and be done with it.

"I've missed you," he whispered, trailing his hand lower. She felt the heat of his skin through her nightdress, and his light touch was as stimulating as if he'd caressed her bare skin.

"I've missed you, too," she admitted.

She was going to lose. Wolf was going to make love to her, and they would return to the kind of marriage they'd had, one where she could never be sure of her husband, where they had pleasure and fun and nothing else.

But when Wolf ran his hand over her hip, she forgot all that. She forgot why she'd insisted that he tell her he loved her, when he proved to her every day that he needed her.

It was enough, Molly decided as he finally lowered his lips to hers.

He didn't even try to be gentle, but thrust his tongue into her mouth and devoured her. He tasted of brandy, sweet and heady, and Molly parted her lips to savor him. The earlier chill in the air was gone, as Molly wrapped her arms around Wolf's neck and held him tight.

Every inch of her skin was glowing, it seemed. She was alive in a way that happened only when Wolf touched her.

She groaned. Wolf growled. She arched her back. Wolf slipped his hand between her legs and stroked her, the thin nightgown the only shield between his fingers and her throbbing flesh.

She wanted to protest when he took his hand

away to drag it upward and across her belly. Would he realize her secret before she ever had a chance to tell him?

When Wolf took his mouth from hers, the firelight illuminated a different, less composed face than the one he'd presented her with earlier. There was not enough light for her to see, as she would have liked, if there was love in his eyes.

She would make this be enough, if she had to.

He stroked her belly and frowned.

"Jesus, Red. Larkin said you'd been eating like a horse, but I didn't believe him. You're getting fat."

Molly sat up quickly as Wolf jumped from the bed and backed away.

"Fat?" she snapped.

He turned his back on her. "Goodnight, Red," he said lightly, not even turning to glance at her as he shut the door.

Wolf leaned against the door and closed his eyes. That had been close. Too damned close. In another minute he would have been inside her, he would have lost control and told her what she wanted to hear.

That would never do. Molly had to come to him.

His body didn't care, at the moment, about power and control and vulnerability. It hurt with wanting her.

He was a fool. His hand reached for the doorknob, even closed around it as his determination did battle with his desire, but he went no further.

Molly would come to him. Maybe even tonight.

And in his bed she would admit that almost perfect was enough.

She could be as stubborn and difficult as Wolf if she put her mind to it, Molly decided. It had taken her forever to get to sleep last night, after he'd stroked her and kissed her and left her there all alone, but she wouldn't let him know that.

He didn't need to know that she'd huddled there beneath the covers feeling empty and alone, that she'd twice left the bed and approached the door that separated them.

If he didn't love her, she would always wonder how long they had before he became bored with her. How long before he became enamored of another woman. He had love within him, if not for her, then for someone else.

She wanted it to be for her and for her alone.

For this to work, she had to be strong. Otherwise, Wolf would wear her down and make love to her, and they'd go back to almost perfect, and she'd never know, she'd never be certain.

After last night, Molly knew it would be impossible to face Wolf, hour after hour, day after day, and deny what they did have.

"Good morning," she stuck her head into Harriet's kitchen warily. "May I come in?"

Already the room smelled wonderful, with bread baking in the oven and fruit stewing on the stove. "Of course," Harriet nodded curtly and returned to her kneading.

"I'm going to see my grandmother today, and I wondered if there was any of that marvelous spice cake left. She'd love it, I'm sure."

Harriet smiled, just a little. "There's half a cake left. Of course you can take as much as you please, madam."

She still didn't feel like mistress of this house, in spite of the servants changing attitudes. They gave her respect she hadn't earned, and it made her feel guilty.

Molly wrapped a huge slice of cake in a linen napkin, and filled a jar with fresh lemonade. Carefully, she placed the goodies in her basket.

Grandma Kincaid didn't depend on her anymore. She had Larkin's sister Emily to care for her, and on her last visit Grandma had been quite well. This visit was as much for Molly's benefit as her grandmother's. She needed another woman to talk to, and though it hadn't quite worked out yesterday, if she didn't tell someone about the baby she was going to bust.

For her long walk, Molly had donned her own, old clothes, a linen blouse with wide sleeves and a heavy and serviceable brown skirt. There was a chill in the air, and so she grabbed her red cloak and placed it around her shoulders.

"Where are you going?" The question stopped her as she opened the front door, and Molly spun around to face her husband.

He had to have just awakened, but he appeared wide awake and calmly in control.

"I'm going to see my grandmother." Molly pulled her shoulders back and stood straight. Wolf could make her feel so small, when he scowled at her like that.

Big Bad Wolf

Wolf lowered his eyes slowly, taking in her outfit. Molly expected a word of disapproval. Her husband had never approved of her simple clothing, and what she wore was certainly not befitting a Trevelyan wife.

"Is Willie taking you?" Wolf asked, evidently chosing to ignore what she wore.

"No. I need to get out. The walk will do me good."

Wolf lifted his eyebrows in an irritatingly superior manner. "I'll take you in the carriage."

"I'd rather walk," she insisted.

"I'll follow you," he said quickly, "Just to be sure you're safe."

Molly lifted her chin, straightened her spine. "I forbid it," she said softly.

Wolf looked, for a moment, as if he were going to argue with her, but he didn't. For a long moment he just stared at her.

"Tell me, Red?" he finally asked softly. "How did you sleep last night?"

"Fine," she answered quickly, and she could feel the heat rising to her cheeks. She blushed so easily! Wolf would know she was lying.

"Me too," he said with a half smile.

Was she being too harsh, to insist that her husband love her? They did have something special. Something almost perfect.

Molly turned away from him, and Wolf stopped her with a softly spoken word. "Red?"

She turned in the open doorway. Wolf hadn't moved, and his hint of a smile had faded.

"Never mind," he said with a dismissive wave of his hand.

"You know what I want, Wolf," Molly whispered as she turned her back on him.

"Stay on the road," Wolf insisted as Molly pulled the door shut.

For a long time, Wolf stared at the heavy door.

No wonder Larkin and that bellboy had obeyed when Molly forbid them. She voiced her order accompanied by wide eyes and a slightly trembling mouth, and no man alive would dare to refuse her anything.

He couldn't give Molly what she wanted. Even if what he felt for her was love he could never admit it. In seven years, he hadn't allowed himself to be vulnerable, not to anyone. He was in control, dammit. To admit otherwise was to offer himself up like a sacrificial lamb.

He had never loved Jeanne, but losing her had changed his life. Men he had considered friends turned their backs on him, believing the worst. Strangers stared at him as if he were a monster. His own father . . . Wolf knew very well Penn Trevelyan had never fully believed that his only son was innocent of the crime of murder, that the old man had gone to his grave wondering if Wolf had killed his bride.

Wolf had never completely allowed anyone into his life since that night, until he'd met Molly. With her innocent smile and her wide eyes and her trust she'd broken down seven years worth of armament. With her love she threatened to destroy all he had left of his control.

Aimlessly, Wolf walked through the house. If he allowed it he did remember a time when he'd been happy here, before his mother's death. A time when the house had been filled with love and laughter, occasional parties and summer guests. Vanora Trevelyan's passing had all but destroyed her husband, he had loved her so much, and it had certainly destroyed the Trevelyan house.

Since then this house had been cold, a prison Wolf willingly subjected himself to on occasion. Penance, for his many sins. Punishment, for sins he'd never committed. Reparation, for never being quite good enough.

Not good enough to heal his father's broken heart, not good enough to be Jeanne's husband, not good enough to love Molly.

When he reached his study, Wolf frowned. Something was different. Wrong. There was too much light, and a vase of freshly cut flowers sat in the center of his desk. He turned his eyes to the sparkling windows, and saw that the heavy drapes had been pulled back and secured to a brass hook in the wall. A new addition to the room.

The pictures on the wall had been rearranged, so that when he sat at his desk he would be looking up into a soothing landscape, rather than the austere portrait of a long dead ancestor that had hung there for years.

Changes Molly had made.

Wolf walked through every room on the ground floor, and saw similar changes everywhere. Flowers, light, brightness.

Life.

Linda Jones

* * *

She stayed on the road for a while, and then Molly turned and slipped into the cool shade of the trees. Winter would soon be here, and there would be no more walks through the woods for a while. When spring came, she'd be too large and clumsy to walk to Grandma's house, but by summer she'd be able to wrap her baby up and carry it with her.

It was impossible to walk beneath the tall trees, through infrequent thin shafts of light that gave off no heat, without thinking of Wolf. Somewhere in these woods she'd first kissed him, first seen him smile, first known that she loved him.

Then, it had been enough. She hadn't expected Wolf to love her back, though she'd hoped for such a gift. Now, she loved him so much she couldn't bear to live with him if he didn't love her. Had she turned into the demanding wife he'd always feared?

It didn't seem demanding, especially when she was more certain every day that there was love in his heart. She wanted it for herself.

She remembered his words to Adele so clearly it was as if she'd just heard them. He'd married her for heirs, to keep matchmaking mamas off his back, and when that was accomplished he would return to New York and things would be as they'd always been.

Somehow he'd convinced her to forgive that, but she'd never forgotten. When she'd realized that he had tricked her, tested her by asking Foster to flirt shamelessly, it had hurt, and she'd been forced to face the certainty that she couldn't live that way—always waiting for Wolf to decide that he was finished with her, always wondering what doubts were in his mind. If he'd had no doubts, he wouldn't have found it necessary to test her.

A straight route through these woods should have taken her to the path, and saved her quite some time, but her mind wandered, and before she knew it, she was entering a section of the forest where the trees grew so thick, no sun shone through at all, and the growth at her feet was dense.

Molly stopped and looked back the way she'd come. A small twig beneath her foot was broken, but there was no other sign to indicate where her passage had taken her.

She couldn't be lost. Not now.

Molly tried to backtrack, but she soon discovered that it was impossible to walk in a straight line, for the thick growth, and so she had no way of knowing if she was returning to the road, headed for the path, or stepping deeper into the woods that covered miles inland of Kingsport and Vanora Point.

She stopped for a moment to try to get her bearings. She listened to the complete quiet, and wished that somewhere in this forest Wolf waited for her, but she knew he didn't. Knowing she had no choice, Molly plunged forward.

Wolf approached Grandma Kincaid's cottage with a second bout of uncertainty. This had seemed a good plan as he'd left the house, but right now it seemed no plan at all.

Linda Jones

Molly would be tired, and he would be doing his duty as a husband to give her a ride home. She couldn't very well avoid touching him if she were sitting in his lap atop his horse.

Of course, there was Grandma to consider. She'd attacked him once before with her cane. If Molly was crying, pouring out her heart to her grandmother, he'd likely be subjected to another beating.

He tied his horse's reins around the post not far from the cottage's door, and before he'd even had a chance to knock, the door swung open.

"Have you brought Molly to visit me?" Molly's grandmother asked with a wide smile that displayed none of her dislike for him.

Wolf's heart sank at the sight of the old woman's expectant face.

"She's not here?"

Grandma Kincaid's smile faded and mirrored his own concern. "No," Nelda Kincaid said weakly. "I haven't seen Molly in several days."

Another woman, shorter, stouter, and a bit younger, joined Molly's grandmother in the open doorway. Wolf knew this woman was Larkin's sister, but the only resemblance was in the stern eyes.

"Listen," Wolf said slowly. "I know you don't like me, but this isn't funny. If Molly doesn't want to see me right now, just tell me so, but for God's sake don't tell me she's not here."

He saw the undeniable concern in the old woman's eyes. "I haven't seen her. Saints preserve us, is she missing?"

340

Big Bad Wolf

A gust of wind could have knocked him over at that moment. Missing. Just like Jeanne. But Jeanne hadn't stayed missing for long. "She said she was coming here, should have been here hours ago. I told her to stay on the road."

"Molly never has listened to that sort of advice," Grandma said softly. "Do you think . . . do you think she's lost?" Her companion placed a comforting hand on her shoulder.

Hell, he knew she was lost. Wolf backed away from the door and faced the footpath where he'd first seen Molly. Lost. Hell, he couldn't take this again. "I'll find her," he said, heading for the forest.

"Wait!" Grandma cried, and Wolf came to an abrupt halt. He turned to watch the old woman venture into the yard cautiously, every step an effort. "You can't do this alone. There's too much distance to search, and not enough time."

Not enough time. The words chilled him, and he knew they were true. Already, the air was touched with frost, and after the sun set it would be downright cold. Too cold for a woman to survive in the woods.

And after dark the beasts would come out. The real wolves, the predators who would eat her alive.

"You must go to town and get help."

"What?" Wolf turned to the old woman. For the first time in his life, he didn't know what to do.

"Go into Kingsport, check with Mary just to be sure that Molly didn't change her mind about her destination after she left Vanora Point, and then round up a party to search these woods." Her words were strong, but there was a low tremble there. Fear. Wolf recognized it, because he felt it in his own heart.

"No one there will help me," Wolf said softly. "I'll just be wasting time I can't afford to waste."

He faced the woods and shouted her name at the top of his lungs, then held his breath as he listened to the echo and strained to hear a response.

There was no answer to his call. Nothing.

His heart told him to plunge forward, to enter the woods and not come out until he had his wife . . . until he'd held her and yelled at her for not staying on the road and told her what she wanted to hear. The truth.

That he loved her so much it scared him. That the thought of losing her sickened him.

But another part, his muddled brain, told him Grandma was right. There were miles of forest land out there, and by now Molly could be anywhere.

He couldn't do this alone.

He unhitched his horse and jumped into the saddle. "If she shows up here, tell her to stay," he snapped.

"I will." Grandma looked up at him with expectant eyes. All her hopes for Molly's safety were placed in his hands with that pleading look.

Dammit, he didn't want anyone to depend on him for anything but cold, hard cash. Molly had changed that, forever.

"If she shows up here before I find her, tell her I . . ." he swallowed his confession. The words still came hard. "Never mind. I'll tell her myself."

Chapter Twenty-two

She should have reached her grandmother's cottage hours ago. For the first time since she'd realized she was lost, Molly was scared. She hadn't passed anything that looked familiar, the footpath or a glimpse of the road, or Wolf's stream. Nothing.

With a sigh, Molly lowered herself to the ground and took what was left of the cake and the lemonade from her basket. Half of it was gone, consumed not long after she'd admitted that she had no idea where she was.

The lemonade was sweet and fresh, and the spice cake was wonderful. If she ever got the chance she'd have to remember to tell Harriet how they had seen her through the day.

Could it already be turning colder? Molly gathered her cape close, huddled with her knees to her chest and her back against the rough bark of a tall tree. Somehow, she had to find her way out of the woods before nightfall.

She shivered, more from fear than the cold. No one would look for her. Grandma Kincaid wasn't expecting her, and Wolf wouldn't miss her until it was late. Even then, he'd probably think she'd decided to stay with her grandmother.

Twice she'd needed him, and he hadn't been there either time. After Foster's outrageous behavior that she now knew Wolf was responsible for, all she'd wanted was for her husband to hold her, to keep her safe. She'd found him with Adele.

Even though he hadn't actually been unfaithful at that time, he had betrayed her in another way. She'd needed him to love her then, but of course, he hadn't.

Again, after Robert Hutton had made his proposal, Molly had gone immediately in search of her husband and found him gone. When she needed comfort, Wolf was nowhere to be seen, so why should she—even in her wildest fantasies—expect that he would be searching for her now?

Molly knew it was up to her to make her own way out of this mess.

"Well, little Wolf," she said, dropping her head and directing her voice to her belly and the child she carried. "What a mess your mama has gotten you into."

She'd already decided that if it was a boy she wanted to name him for his father. If it was a girl, she preferred Vanora, for the grandmother the child would never know.

This was all her own fault. If she'd told Wolf about the baby, he never would have allowed her to take off on foot. If she hadn't forbidden him to follow her she certainly wouldn't be lost right now.

In spite of Wolf's horrible timing when she really needed him, he could be so protective at times. Of course, he could be horribly distant a moment later, making her wonder if he cared for her at all.

She popped a piece of cake into her mouth, savored it, and then washed it down with a small swig of lemonade. Even though she was still hungry, she wrapped up a small piece of the cake and returned it to her basket. She didn't know how long she'd be out here.

It was too cold to be sitting still, so Molly jumped up and surveyed the woods around her. Pines and low growth and shadow, all around her. Everything looked the same.

"Which way, little Wolf?" she asked softly, and then she began walking.

Mary Hanson's face was as transparent as Molly's always was. Wolf saw the surprised expression as she opened the door, the moment of fear that came and went quickly, the suspicion she couldn't hide.

"Is Molly here?" he asked gruffly, wishing he didn't sound so damn scared and uncertain.

"No." Mary stepped back and invited Wolf to enter, and he did.

"I think . . ." Wolf began, "I know Molly's lost. In the woods somewhere between Vanora Point and her grandmother's house."

Mary lifted her eyebrows in apparent dismay, but she didn't seem terribly worried. "Well, perhaps this will teach her to stay on the road."

Wolf wanted to shake the woman, but he clenched his fists and forced himself to remain calm. "Don't you understand? She's lost!" He hadn't meant to shout, but the little house reverberated and Mary Hanson backed up a single step.

"You'll just have to find her," Mary said softly.

This was where Molly had come by her serenity, her sense that everything would always work out for the best. Wolf knew that was a nonsensical quirk. Life rarely worked out for the best.

He didn't want to stand here and list all the horrible dangers that could face Molly if she were still lost when the sun set. He'd gone over them again and again in his mind, and he couldn't stand to torture himself anymore.

Wolf wasn't surprised to find that Molly was not at her mother's house. He knew she wasn't safe, knew it deep down, on an instinctive level that scared the hell out of him. That undeniable connection frightening him almost as much as knowing that Molly was lost.

To his astonishment, Mary Hanson smiled at him. "You'll find her."

"How can you be so sure?" Against all reason, Wolf wanted her to give him something to hold onto, something tangible.

"Molly has great faith in you," Mary revealed softly. "I didn't understand that until recently. Perhaps I still don't understand it completely."

"Why?" Wolf faced the woman who had wailed as if her heart were being torn from her chest as she'd watched her daughter marry him.

"I can't answer that, any more than I can tell you why she loves you."

Wolf shook his head. This was all wrong. Molly should be safe, happy, and she should have fallen in love with someone who could tell her he loved her without feeling so damn scared.

Good God, was that all it was? Fear?

"Mrs. Hanson," Wolf looked into the woman's eyes, saw a bit of Molly there in the gray depths. "Did Molly say anything to you . . . anything about a baby?"

"No. Is she in the family way?"

Wolf shook his head again. "I don't know. I thought, maybe—"

"And you're worried about the baby, too?"

Mary Hanson laid her hand on Wolf's arm, as if to comfort him. "She would have told me, I'm sure. Don't worry."

Don't worry. What a ridiculous suggestion.

Mary's new husband, Orville Hanson, grabbed his coat and accompanied Wolf to the tavern, where many of the townsmen would be gathered for the afternoon.

It had been years since Wolf had set foot in Kingsport; nothing had changed. Passersby stared openly, and when he stepped into the tavern an abrupt and complete hush fell over the room.

These people hated him, and with good reason. Wolf half expected one of the men to throw a stone, like the last time he'd made the mistake of coming to Kingsport.

This wasn't for him, it was for Molly.

"I need your help," Wolf said, closing the door behind Hanson. One man, an unseen patron sitting in the back corner, laughed out loud.

Wolf didn't have time to allow his anger to propel him, not now. "Molly's lost, somewhere in the woods out past Nelda Kincaid's house, and I . . . I don't have time to search for her by myself. I need help," he repeated.

The faces that were turned to him were uncaring, distant, the rough faces of men who worked hard for very little, and had no sympathy for a man in Wolf's position. Even without the scandal of his past, he'd be unlikely to find a friend in this room.

"Well, well." The voice that piped up probably belonged to the man who had laughed. The man, dressed in a red flannel shirt and sporting an untended beard, stood. "What do you know? Wolf Trevelyan's lost another wife."

He didn't even remember crossing the room, but he had the man by the collar, and pressed him against the wall with a choking grip. "Molly's not dead," he seethed. The man's face turned red, and then purple, before Wolf felt Hanson's restraining hand on his arm.

"Let him go," Hanson urged softly. "We'll find her without their help."

Wolf dropped the man, whose only response was to gasp loudly and clutch at his throat.

Men stared as Wolf passed, but no one challenged him as he headed for the door with a singular purpose.

He threw the door open, bemoaning the time he'd lost by coming here, knowing that with only the two of them it would be difficult, maybe impossible, to find Molly in those woods.

In the open doorway, he turned. "If any of you were lost, Molly would look for you. She wouldn't hesitate, wouldn't think twice, no matter what."

Blank faces stared back at him. "She's the best person any of you have ever known." Something in him broke, but he couldn't afford to feel it. Not now. "And she's the best part of me," he muttered as he turned his back on the tavern patrons.

Before the door swung closed, Wolf heard chairs scraping across the floor, but he didn't look back.

His horse took him to the edge of the wood, there where, months ago, he'd seen Molly enter to take the footpath to her grandmother's house. Hanson assured him that at least a dozen men followed them, but Wolf wasn't about to wait for them. Who knew how long it would take those fools to band together and begin the search?

Hanson promised to organize the party, making certain that the searchers fanned out so they wouldn't miss Molly, and he also promised to send someone to inform Larkin of the situation.

Larkin would want to look for Molly himself, so Wolf sent strict instructions that he was to wait at the house, in case Molly returned.

She'd be scared, and he wanted someone to be there for her.

They decided on a signal, two shots fired into the air, to alert Wolf if Molly was found by someone else.

Once he'd entered the woods, Wolf didn't stay on the path for long. If Molly had found her way to the path she would have made her way to Nelda Kincaid's house. No, she was lost in here somewhere, turned about and confused and scared. In a couple of hours it would be dark and cold, and she would be almost impossible to find.

He wasn't coming out without her.

Wolf passed the stream where he'd tried unsuccessfully to seduce Molly. The wildflowers were all gone, now, and wouldn't reappear until spring. He followed the stream for a while, and when he veered off into the deepest part of the woods, he called her name.

Even though he'd been unable to admit the fact aloud, he knew he loved Molly. More than he'd thought possible. If he didn't find her, if he didn't have her with him, he was nothing. That realization came with a knot in his throat and a sick heave in his stomach.

He called her name again, bellowing into an empty forest that gave up nothing but a sickening echo.

Mary Hanson had said that Molly had *faith* in him. It was a difficult concept for Wolf to accept. He hadn't had faith in anything since early in his childhood, since his mother had died.

He didn't have faith in Molly, in the repeated assertion that she loved him, and he sure as hell didn't have any faith in himself.

It was instinct that guided him, as he walked deeper into the growth of old trees. She could be anywhere, miles away or just beyond his reach. At regular intervals he called out to her, only to be answered by the reverberation of his own voice.

"Come on, Red," he whispered hoarsely as he plunged forward. "Don't do this to me." No more than a minute had passed, when he called out to her again. This time he was rewarded with the sound of his own name, a faint cry that seemed to come from directly ahead.

He ran, pushing aside a low branch and yelling again, louder this time, and when Molly answered he was sure it was no delusion.

Relief washed over him when he saw a glimpse of red through the brown and gray tree trunks, that bright red cape a beacon for him to follow.

Molly ran, as he did, weaving past young and ancient growth that stood between them, but just when they were about to meet, they both stopped. Simultaneously.

Molly's hood was thrown back, and her hair was tangled and embellished with a couple of small dead leaves. Her face was flushed, but she appeared to be rather calm.

"You found me," she said softly.

Wolf had never been at a loss for words, until now. "I told you to stay on the road," he said lamely.

"Yes, you did." Molly looked down at the basket

351

she clutched with both hands, properly contrite.

Wolf took the basket from her and dropped it to the ground, and he forced her to look up at him, taking her chin in his hand and tilting her head back. He'd never lied to Molly, not really, and he'd always prided himself on being a somewhat honest man, but this kind of honesty hurt.

"You took ten years off of my life," he said.

"I'm sorry." Her lower lip trembled a little.

"There's a search party looking for you, all the men I could round up."

Her eyes widened, gray eyes so honest he could glance at her and know every emotion she felt. "You went to town for me?"

"I thought it was the only way, Red. Good God," he gave in and gathered her into his arms. He needed to hold her, just for a moment. "When I thought of you lost in these woods, of how cold and dark it would be tonight, I knew I never should have let you leave the house alone."

"You found me," she said soothingly against his chest, trying to calm him. "Everything's going to be fine."

She'd been lost all day, and *she* was comforting *him*.

"I love you, Red," Wolf said quickly, before he lost his nerve.

"Don't say that just because you know it's what I want to hear," Molly whispered against his chest.

Wolf forced her to look up at him again. "Have I ever told you what you wanted to hear?" he snapped.

"No," she said with a smile. "You've always been

brutally truthful with me."

She sighed and fell against him.

"Always," Wolf whispered.

For a long moment he just held her, wondering how he could have ever thought to let her go.

"I've been a little less than truthful with you, lately," Molly whispered hesitantly. "It's not a lie, exactly, just . . . not all of the truth."

Molly took his hand, and placed it over her belly. He pressed his fingers against the slight swell of her stomach and a smile spread across his face.

"I'm not getting fat," she said petulantly. "This is our little Wolf," she whispered.

"My first redheaded child." Wolf kissed Molly gently, then lifted her and spun her around.

Molly was giggling when he finally set her on her feet, but her laughter died quickly when he kissed her.

She was enjoying the kiss so much, he was surprised when she pulled her mouth from his.

"Wolf, darling," she said breathlessly, "would you think me terribly wicked if I asked you to make love to me?"

"Here?" he asked, glancing to the hard ground and dried pine straw at their feet.

"Here," she whispered. "Now. In the forest where I found you."

"I always thought I found you," he said as he lowered Molly to the ground.

He pushed her skirt out of the way, released his swollen manhood, and with a gentle push he was inside her. With her red cape as a mattress, he made love to her as she'd asked.

This was no vice. It was sacred, beautiful, heaven sent. Molly didn't own him, body and soul and heart, she was a part of him, body and soul and heart.

The best part of him.

Smiling and covered with dead leaves and pine straw, they headed back the way Wolf had come. They walked hand in hand, Molly's basket swinging easily beside her. At times Molly had to follow him, through a narrow space between two trees, but he never released her hand.

When they heard the calls of another searcher, Wolf answered quickly. A moment later a huge man appeared, wielding an axe in one hand and carrying a rifle in the other.

The man looked briefly at Wolf, not bothering to disguise his hate, and then turned his narrowed eyes to Molly. "Are you all right?"

"I'm fine."

The man pointed his rifle barrel into the air and fired two shots.

Wolf didn't like the way the man hefted his axe and glowered, as they continued toward the road.

"Are you sure, Miss Molly, that you're all right?" the burly man asked as they hurried forward, trying to reach the road before dark.

"Very sure," she said brightly.

"It's just that, well, you *are* married to Wolf Trevelyan."

Wolf held his tongue. He'd probably have to deal with this all his life. People would always wonder why someone like Molly had married a man like him. He didn't understand why he continued to smile.

Molly squeezed his hand as she answered. "I appreciate your efforts, Wallace, your attempt to save me from the forest. But if you think I need saving from Wolf, you're wrong."

"Or late," Wolf muttered.

Molly laughed. "Much too late."

Epilogue

"Vanora Trevelyan, stay on the path."

Molly tried not to smile at Wolf's barely restrained instruction to their oldest daughter, but she couldn't help herself.

At seven, Vanora was the eldest and the most adventurous of their four daughters, and she led the way to Great-grandmother Kincaid's house along the path Wolf had forged years earlier. Wolf always accompanied them, and he was a stickler about keeping his four redheaded daughters on the path.

Bridget tossed back the hood of her red cape, and unruly curls sprang free as she skipped after her sister. Mary Jane followed, her little legs not able to move quite as fast as those of her older sisters. Her boundless energy made up for her shorter legs.

Little Ariana, who was not yet three, didn't have a chance. They hadn't gone far before Wolf swung her into his arms to carry her effortlessly along the path.

All four of the girls had curling red hair, matching red capes made by Great-grandmother Kincaid, and little baskets in which they carried gifts to the cottage. Bread, an embroidered hankie, a drawing, and, in Ariana's basket, a pretty rock.

"Vanora, you wait right there," Wolf ordered as they watched their oldest disappear around a bend in the footpath.

The girls loved their father, but they did test him constantly. They had the upper hand, because no matter how he threatened, no matter how fiercely he growled, they knew Papa wouldn't spank them.

The three girls waited patiently until they were joined by their parents and the youngest girl they still called "the baby." Not for long, Molly mused. Perhaps this time it would be a boy who would carry on the Trevelyan name, though Wolf didn't seem to care.

"We stay together," Wolf ordered, "and we all stay on the path."

Reluctantly, Vanora led the way at a sedate pace. "Tell us the story about the time Great-grandma Kincaid beat you up with her cane."

"She didn't beat me up," Wolf protested, as he always did when the girls asked for this story.

"Actually, she did," Molly confided.

"She beat you up because you wanted to marry Mama, isn't that right?"

"Yes, it is," Wolf agreed with a smile.

"But she didn't scare you away," Bridget added adamantly, looking over her shoulder and up with wide green eyes. "Did she?"

"No."

Mary Jane lagged behind, until Wolf almost tripped over her. "Because you wanted to marry Mama."

Wolf grinned. He hadn't actually had to tell this story for years. The girls always told it for him. "That's right."

Ariana placed her chubby arms around Wolf's neck. "Because if you didn't have Mama you couldn't have redheaded girls like us."

"Exactly."

Ariana squirmed, and Wolf set her on her feet. Vanora had already picked up her pace, and the other girls were right behind her. They danced down the footpath, red capes swirling behind them.

Wolf slid his arm around Molly's waist. "They're so much like you," he said softly.

"But not entirely." Molly leaned against Wolf as they followed the girls. "Bridget and Mary Jane have your eyes, and Ariana is much taller than the others were at three. She has your height. And Vanora . . ."

About that time Vanora poked her head around a tree, just to see what was on the other side.

"You told me more than once that all life's fun lay off the path."

Big Bad Wolf

Wolf winced. "Don't remind me."

Without caution, Vanora stepped into the woods.

"Vanora!" Wolf shouted, and she stepped quickly back onto the path. "Hold Ariana's hand, until we get to the cottage."

Vanora sulked, but did as she was told. Who would have thought that Wolf Trevelyan would turn out to be such a strict and loving father?

Of course, Wolf hadn't really changed all that much. He'd be tired at the end of a day like this one, after herding the girls and facing Grandma, but when the rest of the house was sleeping, a rousing game of strip poker would liven him up.

It always did.

The Snow Queen

Anne Avery

When Boston-bred Hetty Malone arrives at the Colorado Springs train station, she is full of hope that she will soon marry her childhood sweetheart and live happily ever after. Yet life amid the ice-capped Rockies has changed Michael Ryan. No longer the hot-blooded suitor Hetty remembers, the young doctor has grown as cold and distant as the snowy mountain peaks. Determined to revive Michael's passionate longing, Hetty quickly realizes that no modern medicine can cure what ails him. But in the enchanted splendor of her new home, she dares to administer the only remedy that might melt his frozen heart: a dose of good old-fashioned loving.

_52151-2 $5.99 US/$6.99 CAN

Dorchester Publishing Co., Inc.
65 Commerce Road
Stamford, CT 06902

Please add $1.75 for shipping and handling for the first book and $.50 for each book thereafter. NY, NYC, PA and CT residents, please add appropriate sales tax. No cash, stamps, or C.O.D.s. All orders shipped within 6 weeks via postal service book rate. Canadian orders require $2.00 extra postage and must be paid in U.S. dollars through a U.S. banking facility.

Name _____

Address _____

City _____ State _____ Zip _____

I have enclosed $_____in payment for the checked book(s).
Payment <u>must</u> accompany all orders.☐ Please send a free catalog.

A FAERIE TALE ROMANCE

VICTORIA ALEXANDER

Ophelia Kendrake has barely finished conning the coat off a cardsharp's back when she stumbles into Dead End, Wyoming. Mistaken for the Countess of Bridgewater, Ophelia sees no reason to reveal herself until she has stripped the hamlet of its fortunes and escaped into the sunset. But the free-spirited beauty almost swallows her script when she meets Tyler, the town's virile young mayor. When Tyler Matthews returns from an Ivy League college, he simply wants to settle down and enjoy the simplicity of ranching. But his aunt and uncle are set on making a silk purse out of Dead End, and Tyler is going to be the new mayor. It's a job he takes with little relish—until he catches a glimpse of the village's newest visitor.

_52159-8 $5.50 US/$6.50 CAN

A Faerie Tale Romance · **The Mirror & The Magic**

CORAL SMITH SAXE

Bestselling Author Of *A Stolen Rose*

Sensible Julia Addison doesn't believe in fairy tales. Nor does she think she'll ever stumble from the modern world into an enchanted wood. Yet now she is in a Highland forest, held captive by seven lairds and their quick-tempered chief. Hardened by years of war with rival clans, Darach MacStruan acts more like Grumpy than Prince Charming. Still, Julia is convinced that behind the dark-eyed Scotsman's gruff demeanor beats the heart of a kind and gentle lover. But in a land full of cunning clansmen, furious feuds, and poisonous potions, she can only wonder if her kiss has magic enough to waken Darach to sweet ecstasy.

_52086-9 $5.99 US/$7.99 CAN

Enchantment

Coral Smith Saxe

Bestselling Author Of *Silver and Sapphire*

They call her the Hag of Cold Springs Hollow, yet Bryony Talcott can't even cast a spell to curdle milk. Then she chants an incantation to bring change into her life and, to her surprise, conjures up dashing Adam Hawthorne. Beneath his cool demeanor, she senses a wellspring of passion that frightens her innocent heart even as it sets her soul afire.

Out to discredit all so-called witches, Adam is prepared to unmask the Hag as a fraud—until one peek at Bryony rising from her bath convinces him that she is not the wretched old bat he expected. Shaken by temptation, Adam struggles to resist her charms. But he is no match for Bryony or a love that can only be magic.

_51968-2 $4.99 US/$5.99 CAN

The Gentle Beast
COLLEEN SHANNON

GIVE YOUR HEART TO THE GENTLE BEAST AND FOREVER SHARE LOVE'S SWEET FEAST

Raised amid a milieu of bountiful wealth and enlightened ideas, Callista Raleigh is more than a match for the radicals, rakes, and reprobates who rail against England's King George III. Then a sudden reversal of fortune brings into her life a veritable brute who craves revenge against her family almost as much as he hungers for her kiss. And even though her passionate foe conceals his face behind a hideous mask, Callista believes that he is merely a man, with a man's strengths and appetites. But when the love-starved stranger sweeps her away to his secret lair, Callista realizes that wits and reason aren't enough to conquer him—she'll need a desire both satisfying and true if beauty is to tame the beast.

_52143-1 $5.99 US/$6.99 CAN

Flora Speer
Rose Red
A Faerie Tale Romance

Once upon a time...they lived happily ever after.

"I HAVE TWO DAUGHTERS, ONE A FLOWER AS PURE AND WHITE AS THE NEW-FALLEN SNOW AND THE OTHER A ROSE AS RED AND SWEET AS THE FIRES OF PASSION."

Bianca and Rosalinda are the only treasures left to their mother after her husband, the Duke of Monteferro, is murdered. Fleeing a remote villa in the shadows of the Alps of Northern Italy, she raises her daughters in hiding and swears revenge on the enemy who has brought her low.

The years pass until one stormy night a stranger appears from out of the swirling snow, half-frozen and wild, wrapped only in a bearskin. To gentle Bianca he appears a gallant suitor. To their mother he is the son of an assassin. But to Rosalinda he is the one man who can light the fires of passion and make them burn as sweet and red as her namesake.

_52139-3 $5.99 US/$6.99 CAN

Dorchester Publishing Co., Inc.
65 Commerce Road
Stamford, CT 06902

Please add $1.75 for shipping and handling for the first book and $.50 for each book thereafter. NY, NYC, PA and CT residents, please add appropriate sales tax. No cash, stamps, or C.O.D.s. All orders shipped within 6 weeks via postal service book rate. Canadian orders require $2.00 extra postage and must be paid in U.S. dollars through a U.S. banking facility.

Name _____

Address _____

City _____ State _____ Zip _____

I have enclosed $_____ in payment for the checked book(s).
Payment <u>must</u> accompany all orders. ☐ Please send a free catalog.